Also by Nicola Cornick

THE PHANTOM TREE
HOUSE OF SHADOWS

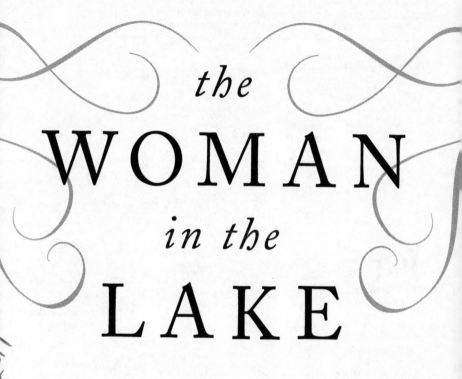

the

WOMAN

in the

LAKE

NICOLA CORNICK

GRAYDON
HOUSE

**GRAYDON
HOUSE**

Recycling programs
for this product may
not exist in your area.

ISBN-13: 978-1-525-82355-8

The Woman in the Lake

GraydonHouseBooks.com
BookClubbish.com

Printed in U.S.A.

For Julia, a Swindon girl.

the
WOMAN
in the
LAKE

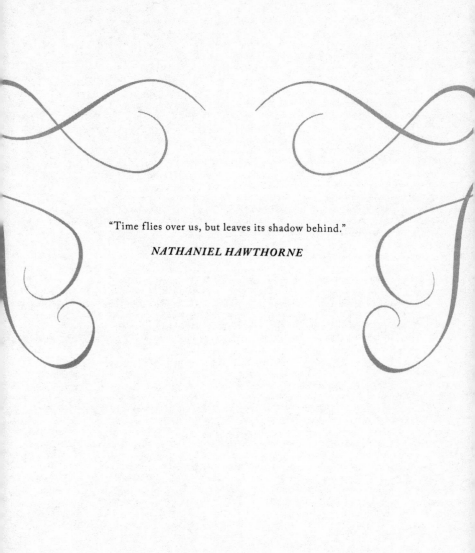

"Time flies over us, but leaves its shadow behind."

NATHANIEL HAWTHORNE

Prologue

Eustace

April 1765

I KNOW WHAT THEY WILL SAY OF ME WHEN I AM dead. I will be cast as a madman and a fool. They will blame the divorce, so scandalous for a peer of the realm, and claim that it drove me to misery and delusion, that it turned my mind. They will rake up all the old gossip and call my wife a whore.

It pleases me that society will slander Isabella over again. I will gladly tolerate being painted a cuckold and a weakling if it hurts her. I wish I could hurt her more, but she is beyond my reach now, more is the pity.

There are those who call me a wicked man. They are wrong. True evil requires intent, and I never had the will or the cunning to be truly wicked. Only once was I tempted to commit murder and even then it was not my fault, for I swear I was possessed. It was the golden gown that moved me to evil and the gown that led to that most terrible mistake.

I remember the horror of it to this day. I still see the scene so clear before my eyes. She was walking ahead of me, through the dappled moonlight, and I recognized the gown and hastened my step. I swear I had no fixed intention, no thought of murder, not at that moment. I wanted to talk, to reason with her. Then, on the path by the mill, she seemed to stumble and fall, and all of a sudden I was seized by the thought that this was my chance to be rid of the threat forever. I could not bring myself to touch her directly so I nudged her body with my boot and she rolled gently, so gently, over the edge and into the pool.

I see it all again: the silver moon swimming beneath the water and the golden gown billowing out about her like a shroud slowly unfurling. I needed to claim that gown but my fear made me clumsy, and I ripped it from her body when it would not yield to my hands. And then...

I break out into a cold sweat whenever I remember. Everything is so vivid. The sweet scent of lime blossom mingled with the stink of dank weed from the millpond, the endless roar of the water over the sluice like the rush to bedlam.

And then... The body rolled over in the water and I saw her properly for the first time in the moon's reflected glow. It was not the face of my nemesis. I stood there with the gown dripping in my hands and then I was sick—sick with revulsion, sick with fear, sick with disappointment.

Binks came upon me as I knelt there, retching up my guts.

"I will attend to this, Lord Gerard," he said, as though he were my butler tidying away a glass of spilt wine. "You should have left it with me, as we agreed."

Binks was a damned impertinent fellow but a useful one, and I was not going to argue with him. I took my carriage back to Lydiard House and I sat here in my study and I drank more than I had ever taken before. I was out cold for three days.

When I came to my senses, the first thing I saw was the golden gown draped across the end of my bed like a reproachful ghost. I wanted to be rid of it, to burn it, rip it to shreds or give it to the first beggar woman I saw, but at the same time I was too afraid, afraid that somehow, some day, it would return to haunt me. My only safety lay in keeping it close to me. Wherever I went the gown came with me, wrapped up tightly, hidden away to contain its poison, but with me all the same. And that is how it haunted me forever after. That is how it has possessed me, in mind and body.

I have no notion what happened after I left Binks to do the work that I dared not do. I heard reports of the tragedy, of course, for the servants were full of the story and it was in all the local newspapers. It was a famous scandal that respected Swindon banker and businessman Samuel Lawrence had drowned his wife in the millpond and then apparently taken his own life, following her down into those dark waters.

In time I almost came to believe those stories myself.

Except that for as long as the gown is with me, I will remember the truth. I will remember Binks, who disappeared like a will-o'-the-wisp once the deed was done, and I will remember Binks's men, the Moonrakers—hard men, smugglers, criminals. I have lived in fear of them these past twenty years for I know they hate me for killing one of their own. My life is so much more precious, infinitely more important than theirs, and yet I live in fear of a gang of felons.

From the drawing room window I can see the lake here at Lydiard Park glittering in the morning sun. On the days when I am too drink-sodden and addled to walk, the steward places me here, telling me that it will raise my spirits to see the world outside. Little does he know that nothing could cause me more pain than to look upon the shining water. Or perhaps he does know it, and places me here to torment me. Perhaps he hates me too.

The Moonrakers will come for me soon. This morning I received a token from their leader. It was such a beautiful gift, an inlaid box. I unwrapped it with greedy excitement until I saw the drawing on the lid: a hanged man, the word "remember," and the initials CL. Then I dropped it, and it went skittering away across the floor, propelled by my sick revulsion.

She need have no fear. I shall never forget that day. The gown will remind me. It will possess me to my last breath.

The sun swims under the rippling water and the day turns dark. The Moonrakers are ready. Ready to fish for their fortunes again, ready for time to repeat itself, ready for the secrets to be told.

1

Fenella

2004

SHE COULD NEVER FORGET THE DAY SHE STOLE
the gown.

Twenty-three of them visited Lydiard Park that day. It
should have been twenty-five, but Emily Dunn had chicken
pox and Lauren Featherstone's parents had taken her on hol-
iday to Greece despite the fact that it was still term time and
Mrs. Holmes, the headmistress, disapproved. Mr. Featherstone
paid the fees, though, so Mrs. Holmes kept quiet.

There were three teachers as well, not that many to keep
them all under control. Two of them looked harassed—Miss
Littlejohn always looked harassed, and Mr. Cash didn't really like children much—they all knew it even though he
never said so—but Miss French was all relaxed and smiley.
Miss French was cool, more like a big sister than a teacher.

"Just one more room to visit, girls," she coaxed, when they
all started to drag their heels through heat and tiredness and

endless stately home corridors, "and then we can go to the tea room and the shop."

Fen didn't have any money to spend in the shop because her grandmother had forgotten again. She wasn't sure if anyone remembered to pay her school fees either, but until someone said something she was stuck at St. Hilda's and that was fine. She'd been to worse schools, plenty of them, some of them boarding, some not. She made friends quickly and easily because she'd learned how. It was either that or forever be the loner, the outsider, the one who came and went without leaving a trace.

"Fen." Jessie, her best friend, all brown curls and bossiness, was pulling on her sleeve. "Come on."

But Fen lingered in the state bedroom as the gaggle of schoolgirls in their red-and-white summer dresses and red blazers went chattering through the doorway into the drawing room. As soon as they were gone, the silence swept back in like a tide, cutting her off. It was odd, as though a thick door had slammed somewhere separating her from the rest of the world. She could hear her own breathing, feel the sun on her face as it fell through the high windows to speckle the wooden floor.

It wasn't a room that appealed to her at all. Her bedroom in her grandmother Sarah's house in West Swindon was quite small, painted pale green and had an accumulation of vintage bits of china and glass and other small pieces that Sarah had encouraged her to buy on their trips to the flea markets and car boot sales. This huge space with its flock wallpaper, soaring white pillars and four-poster bed with its embroidered hangings seemed completely lifeless. It was no one's room, merely a museum. The whole place felt empty to her and a bit creepy; the other rooms held waxwork type figures in period dress that had made her shudder. The other girls had giggled over them but Fen had imagined them as zombies or automatons come to life, stalking the corridors of the old house.

There was a door in the corner and beyond it a room that looked to be full of light. It beckoned to her. Fen peeped inside. It was small, oval-shaped, painted in blue and white like the Wedgwood vases that her grandmother collected. What caught her eye, though, was the stained-glass window with its tiny little painted panels depicting colorful pictures of fruit, flowers, animals—was that an elephant?—something that looked like half man, half goat, a ship to sail away in, a mermaid… Fen could not draw very well, which frustrated her because she like pretty things and wanted to capture them. The window enchanted her.

She stretched out a hand towards the light, wanting to touch those bright panes and experience that vivid world, but before her fingers touched the glass there was the sound of running footsteps behind her.

"Fen! Fenella! Where are you?"

It was Jessie's voice, anxious and breathless now. Fen dropped her hand and turned quickly, hurrying back through the door of the closet into the bedroom beyond. Jessie was not there. Everything looked the same, as empty and lifeless as before. And yet on second glance, it did not. It took Fen a moment to realize what was different. The shutters at the windows were closed and the lamps were lit. They smelled unpleasantly of oil and heat. Perhaps one of the curators had come in whilst she was in the blue closet and had decided to block out the bright sun in case it damaged the furnishings.

That was not the only difference, though. The bed was rumpled, covers thrown back, and the wardrobe door was half-open, revealing shelves of clothes within that looked as though they had been tossed aside by an impatient hand. All of a sudden the place looked lived-in rather than frozen in time. It was an unsettling feeling; instead of making the house seem more real to her, it gave Fen the creeps. Looking straight ahead, aware that her heart was suddenly beating hard but not quite sure why, she walked quickly through into the drawing room to find the rest of the school trip.

In the drawing room the differences were even more marked. There was a fire burning fiercely in the grate even though here the shutters were thrown back and the room was in full sunlight. It was so hot and airless that Fen felt the sweat spring on the back of her neck and trickle uncomfortably beneath her collar. The whole house was as quiet as a sepulcher. It was uncanny.

Over the high back of one chair, shimmering in the light with a soft, golden glow was the most beautiful dress Fen had ever seen. She stared at it. It felt almost impossible to tear her gaze away. She did not even realize that she had started to move towards it; her hand was on the material and it felt soft as clouds, lighter than air, a trail of silver and gold spangled with stars.

"Pound? Where the hell are you, man?"

Fen had not seen the figure sitting before the window, almost hidden by the high curved back of a wing chair. She jumped at the crack of his voice and spun around. He was fair, florid, dressed in a wig and badly fitting jacket with some sort of scarf wound carelessly about his neck and a waistcoat flapping open. He looked bad-tempered and drunk. Fen was only thirteen, but she knew an alcoholic when she saw one. She could smell the fumes on him from where she was standing. Nevertheless she opened her mouth to apologize. He was probably a reenactor or some sort of room steward, although really it didn't seem appropriate to have drunks in costume wandering about the place.

"I got lost—" Quick, facile lies came easily to Fen; they were her survival tactics. But the drunk wasn't looking at her, more over her shoulder towards the doorway.

"Pound!" the man roared. "Damn you, get in here now and pour me more wine!"

There was a bottle on the table, Fen saw, cruelly placed either by accident or design just out of his reach. He lurched forward and almost fell from the chair, clutching at the sides to steady himself. She saw his face clearly then, the vicious lines drawn deep about the mouth, the pain and frustration and anger in the eyes. Panic seized her. She wondered if she had unwittingly stumbled into some sort of performance put on for the visitors. Yet that didn't feel right. There was no audience apart from her and the intensity of the man's fury and desolation seemed all too visceral. She needed to get out of there.

"Take me…"

The golden gown seemed to call to her. She felt the allure of it and was helpless to resist. The impulse was so strong and so sudden that she reacted instinctively. She grabbed the gown and ran, fumbling to push it into her rucksack, her feet slipping and sliding on the wooden floor. She was panting, her heart thumping, and she stopped only when she burst through the doorway into the hall and saw the startled faces of staff and visitors turned in her direction.

"Fenella Brightwell?"

A woman with iron gray hair and an iron demeanor, a museum piece herself, marched up to her.

"Yes," Fen said. Her mind was still grappling with what she

had seen, with the violence and the anger. Were they making a film? How embarrassing if she had accidentally wandered on to the set mid-performance. She would never live that down. Everyone would be laughing at her. No doubt the iron woman was about to tell her off.

"We've been looking for you everywhere," the woman said. Her gray eyes snapped with irritation. "The rest of your group have gone back to the coach. If you run, you might catch them."

"What? Oh, thank you." Fen dragged her mind from the scene in the drawing room and the old man. There had been something pathetic about his impotent desperation.

"Excuse me," she said, very politely, "but is there some sort of film being made in the drawing room? Only there was an old man sitting in a chair by the window and I thought—"

"It's forbidden to sit on the furniture," the woman said. "How many times do I have to tell people?" And she stalked off towards the drawing room.

Fen hoisted her rucksack on to her shoulder and went outside. It was a relief to be out in the fresh air. There had been something smothering about the room and its occupant, brimful of his anger and misery.

She started to walk up the wide gravel path through the woods. She had no intention of running all the way back to the car park. The coach wouldn't go without her. The teachers would get into too much trouble if they did.

She looked back at the house. There were visitors milling around in the drawing room. She could see them through the glass of the sash windows. The chair looking out over the gardens was empty. It was odd that the drunk had disappeared, but perhaps the iron gray woman had thrown him out already. He was probably homeless or something. She had more pressing things to think about anyway, such as the need for a plausible excuse for where she had been so that the teachers didn't get cross with her.

"You got locked in the lavatory!" Miss French said, eyes lighting up with amusement, as Fen clambered aboard the coach and made her apologies. "Oh, Fenella! Only you!"

Even harassed Miss Littlejohn relaxed into a smile. Mr. Cash didn't; he looked hot and annoyed and had been searching the gardens for her. He didn't look as though he believed her either, but Fen didn't care.

"I looked for you everywhere," Jessie whispered, as Fen slid into the seat next to her. "How did you get out?"

"They had to break the door in," Fen said. "The lock had jammed. They sent for a carpenter." She smiled. "He was cute."

"Fen was rescued by a cute carpenter," Jessie said, giggling, to Kesia, who was sitting across the aisle. Word went around the coach. Soon everyone was hanging over the back of the seats or crowding the aisle, wanting to know what her rescuer had looked like.

"Sit down, girls," Mr. Cash snapped. "You're a health and safety hazard."

There was more giggling at that.

The coach dropped Fen off at the end of her grandmother's road. No one else from school lived in The Planks, although the houses were very nice. Most of the girls lived in the picture-postcard villages outside of Swindon rather than in the town itself. There was always a slight drawing back, eyebrows raised in surprise, when Fen mentioned that she lived in town, so she never told anyone.

When she pushed open the back door, she could hear the sound of the television, very loud. It was four-thirty. Her grandmother would already be halfway down her second bottle of wine by now, watching the afternoon soaps with her spaniel, Scampi, sleeping next to her. Fen didn't interrupt her. Her grandmother was a happy drunk but not if someone disturbed her when she was watching TV. Anyway, she had homework to do, an essay on the visit to Lydiard Park, but that could wait. She rummaged in her coat pocket and took out a battered copy of *Bliss* magazine that she had found under Kesia's seat in the coach and lay back on her bed with a contented sigh. She thought that Kes had probably dropped the magazine accidentally rather than finished with it, but her loss was Fen's gain. She'd give it back when she had read it since Kes was her friend.

At five o'clock the living room door banged and there were footsteps on the stair.

"Fenella!"

Her grandmother never called her Fen. She thought it was common to shorten people's names.

"Darling!" her grandmother rushed in and wrapped her in a wine and patchouli scented hug. "How was the trip? Did you have fun?"

"It was great, thanks." Fen never told her grandmother anything significant. She had learned long ago only to give adults information on a need-to-know basis. Perhaps the lesson had been learned when she had first tried to explain to her mother about her grandmother's drinking.

"We all like a glass of sweet sherry now and then, Fenella," her mother had said on a crackly telephone line from Patagonia, where she had been leading an archaeological dig. "Don't worry about it. Your gran is fine."

It was then that Fen had realized she was on her own. Her father had run off with one of his PhD students when she was only seven; they didn't talk anymore. In fact she had no idea where he was, or even if he was dead or alive. One of her brothers was at boarding school, the other on a gap year in Malawi. Her elder sister, Pepper, was with their mother in Argentina, working as an unpaid assistant on the archaeological dig. Fen couldn't tell either Jessie or Kesia about her gran even though they were her closest friends at school. They might laugh at her or tell other people. It was too much of a risk.

"I must show you the bracelet I bought in a charity shop this afternoon," Fen's grandmother was saying. "I'm sure they're real rubies, and nineteenth century too!"

"Well, you never know," Fen said, squeezing her hand. She felt a rush of affection for Sarah. Her grandmother had been there for her when everyone else had buggered off and left her, and that counted for a lot even if it meant that Fen was looking after Sarah most of the time rather than vice versa. Besides, she knew that Sarah was sad. Fen didn't remember her grandfather, who had died when she was only three, but by all accounts he had been a wonderful man as well as a rich one. Once widowed, Sarah had had plenty of suitors, as she quaintly called the men who were after Granddad's money, but none of them held a candle to him.

"What's for tea?" her grandmother asked now. With a sigh, Fen put aside the magazine and stood up. She knew she had better find something or it would be a tin of baked beans again.

It was only later that she opened her rucksack. The golden dress from Lydiard Park was bundled up inside. Fen had known it was there, of course, but she had deliberately ignored it because to think about it was too difficult. She didn't know why she had stolen it. She wished she hadn't. Sometimes she took small things: sweets from the post office, a pair of tights or some lipstick or face cream. She didn't do it for the excitement. It was weird really. It scared her but at the same time she needed to do it. The impulse was uncontrollable. She had no idea why. It wasn't as though she needed to steal. Her grandmother was generous with pocket money when she remembered. It wasn't even as though Fen wanted the things she took. She usually threw them away.

The golden gown, though… That had felt different. The impulse to take it had been more powerful than anything she had ever previously known. It had been totally instinctive and irresistible. Which was very frightening.

She wondered if anyone had noticed that it had disappeared. Surely they must and tomorrow there would be a message waiting for her to go to Mrs. Holmes's office and she would be arrested for theft, and then she would need to make up another story and convince them that she had taken it by accident. She screwed her eyes tight shut. She wasn't a bad person. She did her best. But sometimes she just could not help herself.

She should give the gown back. She should own up before anyone asked her.

Fen stood irresolute for a moment in the middle of the bedroom floor, clutching the gown to her chest. She did not want to let it go. Already it felt too precious, too secret and too special. It wasn't the sort of dress she would ever wear, but even so, she knew how important it was. She just knew it.

Her palms itched. Was it guilt? Greed? She was not sure. She only knew that it was essential she should keep the gown. It was hers now.

She laid it flat on the desk and looked at it in the light from the Anglepoise lamp. The material felt as soft as feathers, as light as clouds, just as it had when she had touched it first.

It was so fine. She had never seen anything so pretty. The gold glowed richly, and in the weave there was a bright silver thread creating elaborate patterns. Lace adorned the neck and dripped from the sleeves.

Then she noticed the tears, two of them, ugly rips in the material, one at the waist, one on the bodice. She felt a sense of fury that anyone would damage the gown. She would have to sew it up and make it whole again. She felt compelled to repair it at once.

The sensation was quite uncomfortable. It was urgent, fierce, as though the dress possessed her as much as she possessed it. She did not like the way it seemed to control her and tell her what to do. It felt as though she should go and find the needlework box right now and start work on the repairs at once.

Fen didn't like anyone telling her what to do. She fought hard against the need to do as the dress demanded and folded it up again, very carefully, and placed it in the bottom drawer of the battered chest in the corner of the room. She didn't like the chest much, but Sarah had bought it at an antique fair in Hungerford and had sworn it was Chippendale. There was nowhere in the house for it to go, so it had ended up in Fen's room, the home of homeless objects.

She pushed the drawer closed and the golden radiance of the gown disappeared. Immediately she felt a little easier, safer in some odd way. Out of sight, out of mind. She could forget now that she had stolen it, forget the drunken man and his fury, the overheated room, the smothering blanket of silence. She wanted to forget and yet at the same time the gown would not allow it...

The phone rang downstairs, snapping the intense quiet, freeing her. Fen waited for Sarah to answer it, but there was no sound, no movement above the noise of the television. The bell rang on and on. It would be her mother, Vanessa, Fen thought, checking the time. It was early evening in Patagonia. She could tell her all about the visit to Lydiard House and how she had got locked in the lavatory even though she hadn't. At the end her mother would say, "only you, Fenella," like Miss French had, and laugh, and they would both be happy because everything seemed normal even if it wasn't really. Vanessa never wanted to know if there was anything wrong. She certainly would never want to know that her daughter had stolen a gown from a stately home, a gown that even now Fen itched to take from its hiding place and hug close to her. It felt like a battle of wills, as though she was possessed. Which was weird because at the end of the day it was only a dress.

She went to answer the phone and when she had finished chatting to her mother and had roused Sarah, grumbling, from the ten o'clock news, she went to bed. She half expected to dream about the gown since it was preying on her mind, but in the end she didn't dream about anything at all, and in the morning she got up and went to school and she wasn't called into Mrs. Holmes's office, and no one talked about the visit to Lydiard at all.

On the way home she went into town with Jessie and Kesia and Laura and a few others, and when they weren't watching she pocketed a silver necklace from the stand on the counter in the chemist shop. It was only a cheap little thing and when she got back and put it on the desk it looked dull in the light. One of the links was already broken. She knew she wouldn't wear it, so it didn't matter. That wasn't why she had taken it. There wasn't a good reason for her actions. The dress, the necklace… She just had to take things. It made her feel better for about five minutes, but then afterwards she felt worse.

"Fenella!" Her grandmother was calling her. Fen wondered if they had run out of milk. She hadn't had a chance to do the shopping yet.

"Jessie's mother's here," Sarah said when Fen came downstairs. "She wonders if you would like to go over for tea?"

"That would be lovely," Fen said. At least that way she would get a meal she hadn't had to cook herself. Through the window she could see Jessie in the back of the Volvo and Jessie's older brother in the front, a thin, intense boy with a lock of dark hair falling across his forehead. He looked impatient.

She grabbed her bag and ignored the coat Sarah was holding out to her. Old people always thought you had to wear a coat or you'd catch a chill, but she never felt the cold. For a moment she wondered what sort of state Sarah would be in when she got home, but she pushed the thought away. It would be good to be part of a proper family even if it was only for one evening. Perhaps Jessie's mum would make shepherd's pie and they could all sit around the telly and maybe she might even be asked to stay over.

She sat in the back of the car beside Jessie and looked at the little silver charm in the shape of a padlock that was attached to Jessie's mum's handbag. It was a pretty little thing, and Fen wanted badly to take it, so badly it felt as though her fingers were itching. In the end she never got the chance, but when she went to the cloakroom later she found another silver charm just lying on the windowsill, this one shaped like a letter A. She took that instead. She didn't like taking things from Jessie's house, but the urge was just too strong and in the end there was nothing she could do to resist. By the time Mrs. Ross took her home, she had also taken a little

leather notebook and a nerdy-looking digital watch that probably belonged to Jessie's brother. She didn't like the watch; it
was ugly, so she threw it in the bin as soon as she got home.

2

Isabella

London, 1763

"DR. BAIRD IS HERE, M'LADY."

Constance, my maid, held the bedchamber door wide for the physician to come in. Her gaze was averted. I knew she did not care for doctors, viewing them as akin to magicians. She would not meet Dr. Baird's gaze in case he cast a spell on her. Nor could she look at me that morning. She could not bear to see the effects of Eustace's beatings. I did not mind for I had no desire to see pity in the eyes of a maidservant.

"Good morning, Lady Gerard." Dr. Baird, in contrast, had no difficulty in greeting me as though everything was quite normal. Perhaps this was his normality, tending to the battered wives of violent and syphilitic peers across London. I had no notion. It was not a matter I discussed with my acquaintance.

Only once had my cousin Maria confided that her husband had beaten her, and then she had looked so mortified to be so indiscreet that she begged me to forget she had spoken.

"Dr. Baird." I did not try to smile. It hurt my face too much.

"I was sorry to hear of your indisposition." He was sympathetic but brisk, placing his bag on the upright chair, crossing the room to my side. Dr. Baird and I shared many secrets, but he was not a man with whom I felt comfortable. He was too urbane, too accommodating. Often when he had been to visit me, he took a glass of wine with Eustace in the library. Eustace was the one who paid his bills. I often wondered what they talked about, the viscount and the doctor. They were of an age, but their lives were so very different. Dr. Baird was from a good family, I seemed to recollect, but they were poor.

He turned my face gently to the light that streamed in through the window so that he could see my injuries more clearly. His hand was warm against my cheek. It was quite pleasant and I forgot for a moment why he was there. Then I saw Constance flinch at the sight of my face and immediately I felt ashamed, of how I looked, of people knowing.

"Another fall?" Dr. Baird asked.

"As you see."

This was the fourth time he had been called to see me. On one occasion I had severe bruising to my arms, necessitating the wearing of unseasonably warm clothing all through a very hot June. On another I had been pregnant but thankfully had not lost the child.

"Do you have any other injuries?" His tone was bland, revealing no emotion. I studied his face, so close to mine, wanting to see a hint of something. Shock, perhaps. But Dr. Baird had, I imagined, seen far worse sights than the one I presented and there was nothing to see there but professional concern.

"Fortunately not this time," I said.

He nodded, opening his bag to take out a jar of ointment.

"This should help you heal. It will take a few weeks."

I did not reply. The scent of beeswax reached me, not quite strong enough to conceal the smell of something more rancid beneath. Dr. Baird approached me, pot in one hand. As he leaned over me I could smell the scent of his body beneath the elegant clothes. It was not unpleasant, but it felt too intimate to be so close to him. It seemed my senses were too sharp today, as though my skin was too thin, my body vulnerable to a bombardment of sensation as a result of Eustace's assault. The call of the birds outside was too loud, as was the rustle of cloth as Constance moved over to the window so that she did not have to watch the doctor ministering to me.

"Lady Gerard. I feel you should…" Dr. Baird hesitated. In the waiting silence I thought: *Do not let him say that I should be more careful, or I may have to break my teapot over his head, thereby requiring the physician to treat himself.* But perhaps he was right. Perhaps I should tread more quietly, turn a softer answer to Eustace's fury, placate him. Yet if I did he would probably hit all the harder. He was perpetually angry and everything I did only served to feed his fury.

"You should, perhaps, spend some time in the country." Dr. Baird was not looking at me but was concentrating on delicately applying the ointment to the bruises and abrasions. I forced myself to keep quite still though it stung horribly. "It would be good for you, the fresh air, the change of scene." He stopped, his hand upraised for the next dab. It reminded me unpleasantly of Eustace. I recoiled instinctively.

"Your pardon." Dr. Baird resumed the dabbing. "Your husband…" He paused again. "Is he away?"

"Lord Gerard left for Paris this morning." *With his latest mistress.* Last night he beat me and forced himself on me, and today he takes his doxy abroad. I wondered about her sometimes, who she was, whether he treated her as he did me. I hoped he did, for it would be intolerable to think there were women he cherished.

"Then this is an ideal time in which to take some rest." Dr. Baird smiled at me encouragingly. "Perhaps a family visit—"

"No." I did not want to go to Moresby Hall, with its huge dark rooms cluttered with the spoils of war. I had hated Moresby as a child, and even now, as an adult, that dislike persisted. It was a vast, echoing barn of a house that was no home, only a mausoleum to my grandfather, a dead war hero. My brother lived there now, but he had changed nothing and the house offered no comfort.

"Perhaps not." Dr. Baird had misunderstood me. "I appreciate that you might not wish to see anyone at the moment. But some time in the country might be restorative after the bustle of London."

I glanced towards the window. Constance had pulled back the drapes and was looking out over the gardens now in order to avoid having to look at me. The window was open, and a light summer breeze stirred the air. It was very quiet. I could hear no carriage wheels, nor voices, nothing to connect me to the world outside. London was light of company in the summer, of course, when most people were at their estates, and what company there was I could not be seen in, not with a face like this. Dr. Baird was correct. The heaviest veil would not conceal Eustace's handiwork, and the most convincing story could not account for it.

I felt so tired all of a sudden. To go anywhere, to do anything, would be the most monstrous effort. Merely to think of it made me want to close my eyes and sleep.

"Lady Gerard." Dr. Baird's voice prompted me. I wished he would cease nagging.

"I will consider it."

There was a crease of concern between his eyes. They were hazel in color with very thick, dark lashes. I had not noticed before but now I did, and a moment later I realized that he was a good-looking man.

"I do feel," he said slowly, "that for the sake of your health you should consider speaking to your brother."

I knew at once what he meant. When my sister Betty had left her husband, it was George who had given her shelter and helped to effect a reconciliation between her and Lord Pembroke. I knew George would be prepared to do the same for me, but my situation was very different. Eustace and Jack Pembroke were both philanderers, but Jack had never raised a hand against my sister. If I left Eustace I would not want to go back.

"I will consider speaking to the duke," I said. Then, with an effort: "Thank you for your concern, Dr. Baird."

The frown remained in his eyes. He knew I would not approach George for help.

"Is there anything else I can assist you with, Lady Gerard?" His tone was bland again, but his gaze dropped lower, making his meaning precise. It was all I could do not to squirm in my chair with the power of suggestion.

"No, thank you," I said. "I am well at present."

"You have no need for a further dose of mercury?"

I repressed a shudder. "No, I do not." Regrettably, that had been the other occasion on which Dr. Baird had had to treat me: when Eustace gave me a dose of the pox passed on from some whore he had bedded.

"I'm glad to hear it." Dr. Baird snapped his case shut. It was his custom to leave at that point, and briskly, his task accomplished. This time, though, he lingered.

"Please consider my advice," he said. His tone had changed. He sounded almost diffident. "For the sake of your health— for your safety, Lady Gerard—I do counsel you to leave."

I looked up, startled. This was too close to plain-speaking. If he continued in this vein we could no longer pretend.

"Dr. Baird—"

He swept my words aside, reaching for my hand. "I have watched for too long in silence. Now I must speak. If you need assistance, Lady Gerard, if I can help you in any way, you need only ask. It would be an honor. I appreciate that you might not have financial means of your own and so may need money or some other support—"

I heard Constance gasp. So did Dr. Baird; he looked over at her quickly, nervously, as though he had forgotten she was in the room. It was too late for concealment now. His words, his touch, had given him away. In my preoccupation I had been very slow to realize how he felt about me. Dr. Baird liked to save people. I suppose it was laudable in a man of his profession. Unfortunately he wanted to save me from my husband and that was impossible.

"You are very kind." I moved to extricate him from his mistake, releasing myself gently from his grasp and releasing him from his unspoken pledge. "I am grateful to you for your advice and I will consider it." Then, as he opened his mouth to speak again: "Good day to you, Dr. Baird. Pray send your bill to my husband as usual."

I saw the withdrawal come into his eyes. He bowed stiffly. "Lady Gerard." The door closed behind him with a reproach-ful click. Constance turned towards me.

"Oh, ma'am!" she said. "That poor man. He is smitten by you."

"You have too soft a heart," I said. "What would you have

me do? Accept his attentions?" I could just imagine my great-grandmother, the duchess: "A physician? My dear, if you must dally, at the very least you should choose a gentleman."

"He only wanted to help you." Her chin had set obstinately. Constance, so well named, saw the world in very simple terms.

"There is always a price." I picked up my cup. The tea was cold.

"I'll call for more." With a practical task to perform, Constance was restored to good spirits. I watched her busy about my chambers. I could not have moved if I had tried. My body felt weighted with lead.

She rang the bell, then started folding and tidying away my clothes. Over the back of a chair I saw the golden gown that Eustace had given me the previous night. It was exceedingly pretty, with silver thread woven through the silk and a soft, shimmering appearance. I had seen it as a peace offering, which had been foolish of me. It was not peace Eustace wanted, except perhaps from the torment of both hating and desiring me.

He had presented the gown to me with a great flourish, just as Constance had been dressing me for dinner. It had been an odd business, for Eustace never normally gave me clothes, having a very masculine inability to judge my size. I could see at once, simply looking at it, that the gown was too large for me. Not only that, but the silk weave was of too thick and heavy a style for the summer.

"How beautiful it is, my dear," I said. "But tonight is so very hot, don't you think? I would rather save such an elegant gown for the winter balls—"

I got no further for Eustace swept every item from the surface of my dressing table. Powder clouded the air, brushes and combs flew, my pearls clattered to the floor. Constance hurried forward to try to pick them up and he turned on her.

"Get out, girl!"

She ran.

But not I. Eustace never let me run. He smiled at me, that madman's smile, and then he struck me. I had learned not to try to defend myself. It only made him more determined. I stood and waited; I absented myself from my body.

"Ungrateful jade," my husband said. My petticoats were flimsy and they ripped all too easily beneath his grasp. One careless swipe of his hand and I fell like a broken marionette.

I watched with detachment as he raped me. It was over very quickly. Small mercies.

Eustace heaved himself up and stood panting over me. I thought he might kick me as I lay there; I wanted to close my eyes against the threat but I did not and, after a moment he walked away, weaving across the room like a drunkard, leaving the door swinging wide so the entire household might see the fate of an unappreciative wife.

"My lady?"

Constance was watching me. She had seen me staring at the gown, reliving the memory.

"I'll take it away, milady." She seemed eager. "You won't be wanting to look at it again, I daresay, after what happened."

I disliked her imagining that she knew how I felt, but for all that she was right. I did not want to look on it and be reminded of Eustace's cruelty.

"By all means," I said. Then, reminding her that it was my decision alone: "Wrap it up and put it away. I may want to have it altered some day."

Constance looked taken aback. "You wouldn't wear it, surely? Not now!"

I wondered if she had thought I would give it to her. I had given her small items before: gloves, shawls, articles for which I had no further use, and even an old cloak once and a worn-out spencer. It was the prerogative of a lady's maid, after all, to take her mistress's castoffs. A gown was a different matter, however, especially one as costly as this. I had seen the look in her eyes as she had watched me unwrap it. There had been envy there and wistfulness. Well, she would not gain by my injuries.

"Who knows?" I said. "Perhaps I may, one day."

"Very well, milady." Her lips pursed and she looked censorious. It amused me, little Constance Lawrence disapproving of me. She waited for me to give her direction on whether I would get dressed, take breakfast in my room or call for paper and ink to write to my brother as Dr. Baird had suggested. I could not decide. The shades were down in my mind, shuttering me in, trapping me. I was too tired to move, too tired to think.

"Cover the mirrors," I said abruptly. I did not want to see my reflection and the devastation that Eustace had wrought on me.

She opened a drawer and took out the drapes, moving from one gilt mirror to the next, arranging them over the glass as though the house had suffered a bereavement. I stood up, moving stiffly, and crossed to the chair where the golden gown lay. Like me it looked crumpled and disjointed.

I took it up in my hands. The silk felt very soft. I wanted to hold it close to me.

The strangest thing happened then. It felt as though a spark had been lit deep inside me and started to burn. I clutched the gown tightly, and it fostered the light, feeding it, stoking it to a blaze. It gave me strength and cleared my mind. I knew then that there was nothing to be gained from writing to George or seeking reconciliation with Eustace, nothing but further grief and pain.

"Eustace must die…"

The words rippled through my mind like a gentle wave over sand. My fingers tightened on the golden cloth and the idea took root immovably in my mind. It happened so quickly, so easily. One moment I was standing there broken, at a loss, and the next I was fired with determination.

A widow had by far a better deal than a wife. Therefore Eustace must die. It was as simple as that. I might wait for providence to assist me, I supposed, but that was an uncertain business. It might take years. Eustace might drink himself to death or be trampled by one of his racehorses, but I could not wait. I needed to take action.

I had no idea how my husband's murder might be achieved, but I knew I would think of something.

3

Constance

I HAD NEVER LIKED LADY GERARD. OVER TIME, I grew to hate her.

It began the day she would not give me the golden gown. I had not anticipated that she would wish to keep it, not when it had provoked so vile a scene between her and his lordship. Perhaps that had been naïve of me for she was never generous. While other maids were well rewarded by their grateful mistresses, I received very little but complaint. Many were the times that I sat late into the night, mending her clothes so meticulously until the candle smoke stung my eyes and my vision blurred, only for her to decide the following day that the stitches were too large and I must unpick them and start again. She was an ingrate.

Lord and Lady Gerard had no money. The household lived on promise alone. Lord G was always in debt, or drunk, or both, lurching from one unhappy scandal to the next, from one syphilitic-ridden mistress to another. He and Lady Gerard could not bear one another. It only astonished me that they had thought to marry in the first place.

Don't misunderstand me. I hated him too. He was forever angry, violent and unhappy as though driven by devils. It was Lord G who had appointed me her ladyship's maid two years before, and she had accepted without a demur. No doubt she was pleased that I was small and dark and plain beside her fair, glowing prettiness. Lord G might hate her, but there were many men about Town who did not. Not one of them looked at me when she was by, and that flattered her vanity.

What she did not know was that I might be her maid, but I was Lord Gerard's spy, as well. In that sense I was as contemptible as a whore, bought and paid for. I had to please him. My life depended on it.

Early that morning, before he left for Paris, Lord G called me to his study. He was dressed for traveling, pacing the room as though he were anxious to be off which, given the violent row he had had with his wife the previous night, hardly surprised me.

"Lawrence," he said, on seeing me. "I have a task for you."

It was not the first time.

"Yes, my lord?" I cast my gaze meekly on the floor the way he liked me to do.

"The golden gown I gave my wife last night." He was standing directly in front of me. I could see his boots, highly polished, against the colorful pattern of the carpet. "I want you to destroy it."

I knew better than to question Lord G no matter what it was he demanded of me. I knew better than to speculate on why he acted as he did. I kept my mind blank and my voice quiet.

"Yes, my lord."

"You *must* do as I say. It is imperative." He took my chin in his hand and forced my face up so that I met his eyes. They were fierce, as was the frown between his brows. He looked very angry, but then I had never known him otherwise.

"Yes, my lord," I repeated.

His hand tightened about my jaw. "And no one must know. Do you understand?" He gave me a little shake. My teeth chattered.

I could not have spoken had I wished, but he must have read my acquiescence in my eyes for he nodded and released me. My chin felt bruised, registering the imprint of his fingers. "Good girl." He moved away from me, turned back. "Your family are all well, I hope?"

I felt a chill. Here was the reminder, the threat, to ram home the need for me to obey. "They are all very well, thank you, my lord."

"Good." His look was sharp, matching his tone. "Make sure you keep it that way. We would not wish the authorities to enquire too closely into your father's business, would we?"

I felt a flash of hatred. "No, my lord."

He nodded. "Off you go then, Lawrence. Oh—" His voice stopped me at the door. "Be sure to write to me with the details of how Lady Gerard progresses."

You would think he was concerned for her welfare, but I knew better. He wanted to know who she saw, where she went, what she did. As I said, I was his spy.

A half hour later the door banged behind him as he left for Paris, and a gloomy quiet settled on the house. I crept upstairs to the dressing room, anxious not to disturb my lady, since she was always in a bad mood early in the morning.

The door to her bedroom was ajar. I could hear her snoring and was relieved that she slept. I had imagined that she would lie awake all night in pain, tormented by the terrible argument and the violence that had followed. But perhaps she was sick and exhausted. I should feel more sympathy for her. Yet I did not. Many men enforced their will through their fists. It was a fact of life. Besides, her ladyship provoked her husband with her flirtations. I was her maid, so I knew all about the late night trysts and the whispered promises, the dallying-in-the-dark walks at Vauxhall. What did she expect in return? Not many men happily accepted that what was sauce for the goose was also sauce for the gander. It was a matter of pride to them, a matter of reputation.

Pale light from a crack between the curtains glimmered on the material of the golden gown. It lay across the back of one of the chairs where Lord G had thrown it when her ladyship had declined to wear it. All I had to do was creep into the room and take it before she woke. I could destroy it as Lord G had demanded, and when—if—she asked me, I would pretend I knew nothing of it.

"Constance?"

Too late. She had woken. It was her "pity me" voice.

I pushed open the door and went in.

"Madam?"

"Call Dr. Baird. I need him. At once."

My heart beat a little faster. I could not help myself. At one time I had imagined myself marrying Dr. Baird. Why should I not? He was handsome and clever, and I was an educated woman, suitable to be the wife of a professional man even if I was only a lady's maid. He would smile on me sometimes. We would exchange a few words. That was all it took for me to fall in love with him, and I allowed myself to dream that we might be together.

One night I did more than merely dream. I called by his lodgings to collect some medicine for my lady. I should have sent the footman, of course, but she insisted on discretion and that I should be her messenger. So I went.

He seemed quite different that night. He was in his shirt-sleeves, his neck cloth undone, a bottle of red wine on the table by his chair and a fire in the grate. I joined him in a glass and sat with him in the warmth and we talked, and when he kissed me and drew me down to lie with him before the fire I had no thought of resisting. I was full of joy.

But I soon saw that what was for me infinitely precious was to him... Well, I know not what: nothing out of the ordinary, perhaps, a diversion, or even a mistake.

It did not take me long to realize that Dr. Baird was even more ambitious than I. He would never again look my way, other than to ask me to pass him a bowl of water with which to tend to Lady Gerard. Knowing that did not stop me loving him, of course, but it did curdle that loving into bitterness.

"Constance. You're dreaming." Her voice snapped sharp enough for a sick woman. And I automatically dropped a curtsey.

"Your pardon, my lady." I was so adept at being meek.

I went to find a footman to run the errand. When I returned, my lady was reclining on her pillows so that the light accentuated her pallor and the bruising to her eye and cheek. She was a talented artist and could never resist a pose. I turned away in disgust.

"Constance, fetch me my yellow peignoir." She was looking around, fussing. "And tidy the room. Not that—" She spoke sharply as I reached over to grab the golden gown from the back of the chair. "Leave it. Fetch me tea. I don't want toast. I cannot eat."

"My lady." My mother would have been proud of my obedience. She had told me from the first what an honor it was to have been chosen to wait upon Lady Gerard. Poor mother. She understood nothing: nothing of the role Lord G had selected for me, nothing of his hold over our family and nothing of the world she inhabited or the price at which it had been bought.

Dr. Baird came, hasty as you like. He had eyes for no one but my lady, of course. Even when she had been treated so cruelly she was like a rose, all pink and amber, delicate, precious. He was dazzled. She was helpless. I was so sick with jealousy I could not look at either of them.

I showed the good doctor out after he had made his foolish suggestion to elope with her and she had turned him down. "He is smitten with you," I said. I wanted to know her feelings even though I knew I should leave well alone.

"You have too soft a heart," she said. "What would you have me do? Accept his attentions?"

She was so callous. It mattered nothing to her that she had enchanted him. She took it as her due and she felt nothing in return.

"He only wanted to help you," I said.

"There is always a price." She sounded weary. She took a sip of tea, but the pot was cold by now.

"I'll call for more." I was glad of the distraction, glad to be able to subdue my unruly feelings with practical matters. I rang the bell, then noticed that she was looking at the golden gown. I remembered again Lord Gerard's instructions, and my heart leapt with anxiety.

"I'll take it away, milady." I said. "You won't be wanting to look at it again, I daresay, after what happened."

She gave me a look. "By all means," she said haughtily.

Then, just as I thought the deed was so easily accomplished: "Wrap it up and put it away. I may want to have it altered some day."

I spoke before I thought. "You wouldn't wear it, surely? Not now!"

She raised her brows and looked down her aristocratic nose at me. "Who knows?" she said. "Perhaps I may, one day."

"Very well, milady," I said. In truth I was vexed almost beyond bearing. There was no knowing when she might want to see it again. She might choose to have it altered tomorrow or she might never ask for it again. It would be typical of her contrariness that if I destroyed it as Lord Gerard had ordered, she would demand to wear it the very next day, and then how would I explain myself?

I was about to take the gown and fold it away whilst I thought about what to do, but she snatched it up and clutched it to her bosom as though it had suddenly become very precious to her. She closed her eyes for a moment and drew in a deep breath. When she opened them again her face was flushed and animated and her eyes bright as stars. It was quite a transformation.

"Pack my bags, Constance," she said. "Tomorrow we go to Lydiard."

I caught my breath. Lydiard Park, one of Lord Gerard's many estates, was close by my family home in Swindon. In the two years that I had been serving my lady we had never gone there.

I must have been gaping like a simpleton for she gave me a smile. "You will be pleased to see your parents again, I imagine."

Pleased? Pleased to return to Swindon, where my father had sold me into Lord Gerard's service, pleased to enter once more into that web of deception and criminality? It was not the word that I would have chosen. What pleased me was to be as far from Swindon and the smuggling gangs as I could possibly be.

When I did not reply, Lady Gerard turned away. She was not particularly interested in my emotions, being far more concerned with her own.

"Dr. Baird was correct," she said. "Fresh country air and a change of scene will be most restorative."

"Yes, madam." I started to run through in my mind all the things that we would need to take. Suddenly there was so much to do. My lady was at her querulous worst, sending me running hither and thither on endless errands, demanding that I pack a dozen gowns and then removing them immediately from the portmanteaux in favor of a different style, dispatching me to the *perfumier,* the haberdasher and the bookseller. By evening I was hot and sweaty and exhausted whilst my lady turned the house on its head in her haste to be gone.

"You will bring the golden gown with us," she ordered at one point, thrusting it into my hands. I could not see that she would have opportunity to wear the wretched thing, but I had more pressing matters to think of so I folded it small and forced it into an empty corner of the last box. Perhaps when we were in the country she might forget about it and I could destroy it as Lord G had demanded.

Eventually, when her ladyship had driven us all, coachman, maids, footmen and the cook to utter distraction with her orders for the following day, I had the idea of giving her some of the dose Dr. Baird had left to alleviate the pain. She had not asked for it, but it was laudanum and it made her sleep.

I dragged myself wearily up the wooden stairs to my room under the eaves. It was stifling hot in there as evening fell over the city, and though I opened the tiny window that was too high up to give me a view, no air stirred. First I packed my own small portmanteaux and then I sat down at the bare wooden table and drew from the drawer paper, quill and ink.

"My lord," I wrote, "I write to acquaint you with Lady Gerard's business." The letter would not reach him for ten days or more, I knew, but he expected me to provide a regular report. "This morning she sent for Dr. Baird who recommended that she spend some time in the country." I paused, biting the end of the quill, trying to decide whether to mention the doctor's indiscretion, tantamount to a declaration. It would be malicious of me to write of it when Lady Gerard had very properly declined his offer, but the sour resentment I felt towards them both had my pen scurrying across the page.

"The doctor offered Lady Gerard his personal assistance." I underlined the last two words. That would be sufficient to have Dr. Baird dismissed, which gave me great satisfaction.

"We travel to Lydiard House in the morning," I finished.

I paused again, looking at the candle flame as it burned low. Should I lie or should I omit?

"I have completed the other commission you required of me," I wrote. "The gown has been destroyed."

4

Fenella

FEN CAUGHT THE LAST TRAIN FROM LONDON Paddington to Hungerford. Swindon station would have been much closer, but there was a bus replacement service yet again for part of the journey and she did not relish walking through the center of Reading at midnight for the privilege of being stuck on a coach for another hour.

She took a window seat in the first of the two carriages, only realizing when a businessman in a striped shirt wheezed into the seat beside her that she was trapped. She felt a moment of panic, the old feeling of sickness in the pit of her stomach, her pulse racing. Then the man settled back on to the seat with a waft of stale sweat and a contented sigh, and she almost laughed aloud. The train was packed, and she was safer with this bulwark between her and the crowds.

She could feel the tide of friendship and laughter starting to wear off now, like champagne left open. Perhaps it was because she hadn't actually had any champagne—knowing she was driving later had been her excuse, but the truth was she did not trust herself after a few glasses. It was very easy to lose what small shreds of self she had left.

These days she didn't often go up to London. She had lived there with Jake for eight years, but oddly her old life felt, at the same time, both distant and dangerously near. Her old friends seemed such a long way away that even when she was sitting in the club with them it was as though they were on a far shore and she was an observer not a participant. She had tried so hard: laughed, danced and chatted as much as she could above the pounding beat of the music. They had all known that something had changed. She had seen it in the puzzled smiles and the slight awkwardness. No one understood why they could not go back to how it had been before. No one mentioned it, though, not even Kesia, who had been the person who had invited her in the first place.

"We'll go somewhere new," she had said when she had called Fen. "Somewhere you never went with Jake. Don't worry—" she had added, taking Fen's silence for impending refusal "—I know you're still a bit iffy about going out, but we'll all look after you."

"I know you will," Fen said. She had injected some warmth into her voice. "Thanks. You have all been fabulous."

"So you'll come?" Kesia sounded eager. "Please do, Fen. We miss you. Jessie's gutted she can't be there too, but Dev is whisking her away somewhere for their anniversary."

"She told me," Fen said. Jessie was still her best friend, the one constant in a life that had changed almost out of recognition. Her schoolgirl friendship with Kesia had survived too, although Kes had been abroad traveling a lot. She was back in London now and keen to meet up with everyone, hence the invitation.

"You can't keep hiding away," Kesia said now. "It's two years, Fen. Show that loser he can't ruin your life."

Fen appreciated the sentiment even if it was expressed somewhat insensitively. She no longer wanted to scream when people gave their opinion about her relationship with Jake. They had absolutely no idea what she had been through, but she had accepted that now. She simply closed her ears to the words and accepted the clumsy kindness in the spirit it was meant.

"Well…" she said cautiously.

"You'll come!" Kesia said instantly. "Fantastic!"

Of course Fen had agreed. She acknowledged now that refusal had been impossible. Kesia and Laura and the others were amongst her oldest friends, and they loved her. They had all stuck together through thick and thin, through college and awful first jobs and slightly less awful second ones. There had been marriages, children, divorces, affairs, all the successes and disasters of life. They had celebrated and commiserated, fixed the problems with wine and conversation like old friends did.

Murder was different, though.

Murder was unfixable.

It had been an accident. Everyone said so, even the police. They had not pressed charges. Only she knew different.

"Don't leave me," Jake had pleaded. He had been very white. "I love you. Why would you walk out on me when we've been through so much together?"

She had withstood his emotional blackmail that final time and she had gone, as she should have done years before, changed her name back, changed her appearance, changed her job, her home, her life. Yet the old one dogged her foot-steps like a nagging shadow. She understood now that no one ever escaped their past, no matter how hard or fast they ran. You took it with you; it was a part of you.

The train trundled into another station. It was stopping at every town and village between London and Newbury, or so it seemed. Fen glanced over her shoulder through habit, but it was so dark outside and so brightly lit in the carriage that she could see nothing. It made her feel unpleasantly vulnerable, a sitting duck, even if there was no one out there, watching for her.

The businessman got off at Reading. Fen watched him heave himself out of the seat and take his briefcase down from the rack overhead. There were dark sweat patches under his arms. She wondered if she was stereotyping him; city worker, a banker perhaps, expense account dinners, high blood pressure. She wondered what people thought when they saw her. Normally she dressed to be invisible. Tonight she had tried to dress the way she had done in the old days, in her favorite sequin skirt and white crop top, nude heels. She had straightened her hair so that the haphazard blond waves were tamed into a shiny fall. She had even worn makeup. It felt as though she was in disguise. She had changed her appearance so many times over the past two years that she did not really know what she looked like anymore: glasses or lenses, brunette or buttermilk blonde, heels or flats, smart or vintage, real or a total fake.

The train started to move again. She reached into her bag for the book that Laura had given her, *Black Sheep* by Georgette Heyer, an old favorite from their college days.

Someone sat down beside her and she glanced up.

"Evening." He nodded, smiled. It felt odd, courteous but

ridiculously old-fashioned to be greeted formally by a complete stranger who had randomly chosen to sit next to her on a train. She almost smiled because it was so sweet.

"Hi." She looked back down at her book. Then she looked up again. She couldn't help herself. She might be single by choice, but she wasn't immune. Thirties, dark hair falling across his brow, deep brown eyes, good-looking without being devastating... There was something about him that drew her gaze. The hard line of his cheekbones and jaw made him look uncompromising in a way that might have intimidated her had it not been for his smile, which was dangerously disarming.

He yanked his tie off as though it constricted his breathing and undid his top button, resting his head against the seat back, closing his eyes. Fen realized that she was staring.

She went back to her book. The train was picking up speed. Brief flashes of street lighting, car headlights, isolated houses, punctured the darkness outside. The interior of the train was so bright in contrast that it made her head ache. The familiar words on the page blurred before her eyes.

"Haven't we met before?" The man had turned towards her and opened his eyes. They were a very dark hazel rather than brown. Nice.

Fen sighed. As a pickup line it was extremely lame.

"No, I don't think we have," she said.

"Sorry." He sounded crestfallen. "I know it's a cliché."

"Yes, it is." Fen could feel herself warming to him against her will. It was disconcerting. That easy smile was too charming. She felt a surprise tug of attraction and thought that at another time, in another life, she might have liked him very much.

"I'm too old to indulge in wretchedly poor chat-up lines,"

he said. "I really did think that there was a connection between us."

"If you say so." Fen buried her nose back in her book. Time
passed. She realized she had not read a line, nor turned a page.

"Is it a good book?"

She wasn't expecting further conversation. It startled her.
"Sorry?"

"I asked if it was a good book."

"Um… It's okay." She felt a little off balance and answered
at random. "I used to love it when I was younger. But it was
written a while ago and it feels a bit dated to me now."

He tilted his head to read the title and author. "Georgette
Heyer," he said. "I've never heard of her."

"Wow," Fen said blankly. She had never met anyone who
hadn't heard of Heyer.

He laughed. "Thanks for making me feel illiterate," he
said dryly.

Fen realized she had been rude. She blushed with embarrassment. Then she met his eyes, saw the amusement there,
and came to the conclusion that probably very little, least of
all her bluntness, could dent this man's confidence. There
was a core of steel beneath that easy manner.

"Is she famous, Georgette Heyer?" he said. "Have any of
her books been made into films?"

Fen made an effort. "Uh… No, I don't think so," she said.
"She's dead. Maybe they did a while ago." She smiled despite herself. "Though I don't expect you would have come
across them if they had. You don't look like a fan of 1940s'
and '50s' costume dramas."

"Don't judge," the man said mildly. "You never know."
He looked cramped in the train seat, folded in, his legs too
long for a comfortable fit. She could not look at him properly

without turning sideways, and that felt too blatant. She did not want to give the impression that she was interested. She wanted to go back to the book for the protection it gave her, but the archaic language seemed unappealing all of a sudden.

"You're right, as it happens," he said. "Thrillers, action films… That's my sort of thing. Very conventional."

Fen never read crime or thrillers. There was enough darkness in real life.

"Why pick it up if you don't enjoy it?" the man asked.

Fen gave up, putting the book away in her bag. "It was a present," she said.

"Birthday?"

"No, just…" She let the sentence fade. What had it been? An attempt to re-create the past? An apology?

"Just a gift from a friend," she said. "We hadn't met up for a while. A few of us had dinner together."

"In London?" Like her, he must know this was the last train.

"Yes." She made an effort and wondered why she was bothering. "You?"

"I've been at work." He closed his eyes, massaging the back of his neck. "Nothing exciting. I'm hoping to be made redundant."

"Then you're going about it the wrong way," Fen said, "working late."

He opened his eyes and smiled at her. Wow again. She blinked.

"I suppose so," he said. "Hadn't thought of that."

"What would you do if you *were* made redundant?" Fen asked.

He thought about it for a moment. There was nothing

rushed about him, nothing that wasn't thoughtful and considered.

"I'd go traveling," he said, after a moment, "and write about it."

"Nice."

"Nothing exotic," he continued. "Just local. It's beautiful around here, you know?" He waved a hand towards the blank train windows. "The river and the landscape, the water meadows, the hills…"

"I'm not familiar with the countryside around here," Fen said. She remembered the view from the window earlier as she had traveled up; fields of honey-colored corn in the sunlight, pale green hills, the curl of the river in the lazy haze. "I can see it can be beautiful," she said, "but what about all the bits in between—the railway sidings and industrial units and shopping parks?"

"There's always bits in between," he said. "Anyway—" he settled his shoulders back against the seat "—it's just a dream."

There was silence again, the rattle of the train, the hum of the wheels on the line. They were slowing down into another station.

"What about you?" he asked.

She wanted to tell him that she didn't want to talk about herself, but it seemed too much effort. What about her? What was she now? Who was she? Fenella Brightwell, twenty-seven years old and starting her life over again…

"I'm a writer." She chose a job at random, perhaps because she could still see the corner of the book sticking out of her bag. It didn't matter what she said when she wasn't going to see him again. Licensed to lie was how she thought if it. Her past, her new beginning, gave her the right to pretend.

His eyes gleamed. She wasn't sure whether he believed her, but it didn't matter.

"That's exciting. What sort of books do you write?"

"Science fiction."

"Are you published?"

"Yes."

"Does anyone beyond your family and friends actually buy your books?"

Fen smothered a laugh. Suddenly she was enjoying this.

"Yes. Quite a few people."

"Are you a bestseller, then?"

This time she laughed aloud. "No. Of course not."

He raised his brows. "Lots of authors are."

"Proportionally few." She knew that; the world was flooded with books. Very few of them were by people anyone had heard of.

She noticed for the first time his crumpled but elegant suit and the expensive watch on his wrist. How awkward if *he* were a rich and successful author. He'd said something about writing about his travels. But he had also said he was hoping to be made redundant, so he couldn't be self-employed. He probably worked in IT. A lot of big companies were based in Reading. IT, or insurance or banking. Something boring. Something normal.

"I'll look out for your books," he said. "Do you write under your own name?"

"No," Fen said. She hesitated, enough to give herself away. "My pen name is Julie Butler." Where the hell had that come from?

"And your latest book?" The gleam was back in his eyes. He knew she was making this up. "What's that called?"

"It's called…" They passed a billboard with an advertisement for moisturizer. *"The Dove Flies Out."*

"Intriguing." He smiled at her. "What's it about?"

"It's set on a spaceship," Fen said. "A spaceship like an ark. They send the dove out when they get near a new planet, to see if it's suitable for landing."

"Imaginative."

More like imaginary, Fen thought. "Thanks," she said. "People usually say that when they think something sounds awful."

"I'll look out for it when I'm next in town." He stood up, and for one moment she thought he was going to shake hands, but he didn't. "This is my stop," he said. "It was nice to meet you, Julie Butler."

"You too," Fen said. She thought of the old days, the days before Jake. She would have asked for his number, or given him hers. They might have met up and had a drink. It would have been good to see him again. There was a connection there, a spark. But perhaps she had imagined it. She wasn't good at relationships.

The signs for Newbury slid past the train window. She watched him stroll down the carriage to the door, waiting with the cyclists and the late shoppers and the suits, standing back to let an elderly couple get to their feet. He turned and looked at her. Her gaze met his, and she felt the connection between them again like a physical jolt. He walked back to where she sat.

"In case we meet again," he said, "or in case we don't, my name's Hamish. Hamish Ross."

"Hamish," she repeated. "Well, it was good to talk to you."

He smiled, a last smile, and raised a hand, and in that minute Fen realized where she had seen him before. He had been right when he had said that he thought he knew her. It hadn't been a line.

He was Jessie's older brother.

She opened her mouth to tell him, but it was too late. The doors hissed shut behind him. She did not see him on the platform. There weren't many people left in the carriage now, and the night air from the open windows was making her feel cold. Ten minutes to Hungerford, then she had a half hour's drive on empty country roads and then home. Not that the flat in Swindon Old Town was home yet. It was too recent and too impersonal.

The car park was deserted. She'd deliberately parked right under one of the huge, bright lights. She walked straight over to the car looking neither left nor right, feeling the cold night air on her face and blinking in the harsh light. Her keys were already in her hand; she slid into the driver's seat, slammed the door, locked it and took a deep steadying breath. Safe.

She thought about Hamish Ross whilst she drove home. On reflection, she realized it was lucky she hadn't told him about the link between them since she had also told him a tissue of lies. She hadn't seen him since she and Jessie had been about fifteen and Hamish had been eighteen and about to go to university. He hadn't taken any notice of her back in the days when she would go round to Jessie's for tea. From a purely selfish point of view it was nice to know that she warranted more of his attention now. She hadn't had a crush on him back then, not really. When you were stuck at an all-girls' school, people's brothers tended to be alien and exotic creatures, especially if they were older. Hamish had been… She searched her memory. Nice, she thought, kind to Jessie in an absentminded sort of a way. Patient. He had helped them with their homework sometimes. He had not been so good-looking in those days, or at least she didn't think so.

She wondered whether he was married. He hadn't been wearing a ring, but that meant nothing. Perhaps he was a player, like Jake had been, a man who hit on a different woman each night on the train home from work. She didn't know. Although she'd seen Jessie quite a bit since she had come back to Swindon, her friend hadn't mentioned her brother much. And since Jessie was called Jessie Madan now rather than Jessie Ross, it had taken a moment for the penny to drop.

Fen bit her lip. Damn. She had to hope that Jessie wouldn't invite her to a party or something that Hamish would also attend. It would be awkward to try to explain how Fen Brightwell had morphed into the novelist Julie Butler. In fact it would be excruciatingly embarrassing. Still, it was unlikely to happen. Whilst Jessie had moved back to a village near Swindon and Hamish evidently lived in Newbury, they weren't a family who were in each other's pockets. They seemed fond enough of each other in a nice, mutually supportive way. They were so normal.

Fen sighed, narrowing her eyes against the glare of oncoming headlights, fighting the tiredness that snapped at her heels. She didn't really know "normal" that well. Her own family background was too fractured, and as for her relationship with Jake, that had been so far from normal that there wasn't a word for it.

She pulled on to the motorway. It was still busy with late night weekend traffic heading for the West Country. She only had one junction to go though. She stifled a yawn and turned on the radio to help her focus. A group of earnest people were talking about literary criticism. She turned it off. That was more likely to lull her to sleep than wake her up. Her sister Pepper was the bookish one with a first-class degree in archaeology. Her eldest brother Jim was a high-achieving lawyer in Sydney and the younger one, Denzel, was a drifter last heard of surfing in San Diego. They were scattered in character and interests as much as in location, perhaps because they had all had such dislocated childhoods. It had not drawn them back together as adults.

Suddenly the orange haze of streetlights punctured the darkness up ahead, and she took the exit, turning right towards Swindon, past the hospital and into upmarket suburbia, the big 1930s' houses, the wide open spaces of the country park. After she had left Jake she had relocated to Manchester and then to the Midlands but she had felt rootless and lost, so after eighteen months she had gone back to Swindon, where she had grown up. It felt safe enough; she had not lived there for twelve years and had never told Jake anything about her childhood anyway. Besides, he was living abroad now and probably didn't give a thought to where she was living or what she was doing. She had to try not to be paranoid. She didn't want to spend all her life feeling hunted. If she thought about Jake constantly he would still dictate her life; he would have won. She was not going to allow that. Even so she knew it was not that easy. So often he trod the edges of her mind like a ghost.

She slid the car down the narrow alleyway between the flats and the row of houses next door, a line of old cottages that tumbled down the hill towards the new town. As she turned into the entry, the arc of the headlights caught a man's figure, stepping sideways into the shadows. She caught only the briefest flash of his features, but it was enough.

Jake.

She slammed on the brakes, and the car stalled, stranded half in, half out of the alley. Without conscious thought she threw open the door, so hard it scraped along the wall, and jumped out, running round the back of the car and out into the street. A horn blared, lights swerved. Someone swore at her but she barely noticed.

The street in both directions was empty. Only the faintest echo of receding footsteps came to her ears. Fen stood there irresolute for a moment, then shook her head sharply. It could only have been her imagination. She had been thinking about Jake, and so she thought she had seen him when she had not.

She restarted the car and drove around into the parking lot behind the flats, locked it, double-checked and walked swiftly, head down, across to the entrance where she buzzed herself in. Only when she was in the bright passage, with the door firmly shut behind her, did she allow herself to draw a breath. It had been her mind playing tricks. She told herself that, very firmly, and ignored the slight shaking of her hands.

5

Isabella

Lydiard Park, Summer 1763

THE CLOCK ON THE STABLES WAS STRIKING A quarter past the hour of one as my carriage rattled into the coach yard at Lydiard Park. After so many miles the sudden cessation of noise and movement was shocking. The silence was loud, the stillness made me feel sick.

There was no light outside and no welcome. Not that I was expecting one. I had not sent ahead to warn the servants of our arrival. There had been no time.

The carriage swayed as the coachman jumped down. I wondered if he were as stiff as I, tired, filthy and bad-tempered from traveling through the night. He had certainly driven like a man in a rage, sparing us nothing, which had made the journey all the more uncomfortable.

Constance stirred in her seat, but she did not wake. Poor child, at the last change of horses she had looked so pale and hollow-eyed from exhaustion that I thought she might faint with the effort of carrying a cup of broth for me and I made her drink it herself.

I pushed the window down. "Farrant! Drive around to the front. Do you expect me to walk?"

I heard him swear. I had suffered the coachman's and groom's snide disrespect all the way from London. How quickly the servants picked up on the mood of their master and acted accordingly. They all knew about Eustace's treatment of me, and so they thought that gave them license to behave with insolence. But I was a duke's daughter; I knew how to deal with impertinent servants.

"Ma'am—" Tarrant's surly response was interrupted as a wavering light appeared, a lantern held in the hand of a very young ostler who scuffed his way across the cobbles, yawning and rubbing his eyes. Behind him I saw the shadow of a cat slink away.

"What's to do?" His Wiltshire burr was so thick I could scarcely make out the words. "Who calls at this time of night?"

"It is my Lady Gerard." The coachman was peremptory, using my authority to bolster his own now it suited him. "Look sharp, lad, and send someone to wake the house, and fetch more men to help with the horses."

"There's no one here but me." The poor lad sounded panicked, as though he did not know what to do first. I took pity on him, leaning from the window.

"Farrant, open this door. I can announce myself at the house." Turning, I shook Constance awake gently. Her shoulder felt brittle beneath my hand, and she turned her head against the velvet cushions of the seat as though for comfort.

"Come, Constance," I said. "You are home."

She opened sleep-dazed dark eyes and looked at me, waking suddenly, despite the care I had taken not to startle her.

"Home? Lydiard? Oh, madam!"

She scrambled up and thrust the door wide, jumping down before the groom had stirred to come and help us. I smiled wryly to think that one of us at least was pleased to be here.

I had not been to Lydiard since the first year of my marriage. I had been happy enough then, although perhaps not as happy as I should have been as a new bride. Marriage had not been at all as I had imagined.

"What on earth were you thinking, Bella?" My sister Betty had asked bluntly when my betrothal was announced. "Were you drunk? Everyone says you must have been to accept Eustace Gerard."

It was true that Eustace had proposed to me at Vauxhall Gardens, but I had been quite sober that night. It had been a whim, an impulse, I suppose. He had offered escape, or so I had thought, and I had been bored with my pattern-card life as a young lady of the ton and had grasped after something different. In those days Eustace had made me laugh. He made no such efforts to amuse a wife. I drew my cloak a little closer about me. For all that this was July, the air was chill and fresh out here in the country. It had a different quality from London.

The lad from the stables had run on ahead to raise the house whilst the groom and coachman dealt with the horses. By the time Constance and I reached the door, there was a lantern flaring in the hall, and Pound, the steward, was shrugging on his jacket and hurrying towards us, cross and flustered. His shirt flapped loose and his hair stood up at the back.

"My lady! We did not expect you! If you had told us—"

I raised a hand to stem the flow of reproach. I was too

weary to hear him out. "It is of no consequence. All I require is my usual room made up and some hot water and a little food..."

He looked appalled. Such simple matters seemed impossible to achieve. For the first time I looked about the hall and saw what the darkness and lamplight had concealed, the cobwebs and dust, the filthy drapes. There was a smell of stale air and old candle wax. It was cold. Probably there were rats.

"Surely," I said, my voice sharpening, "my lord pays you to maintain his house in an appropriate style even when he is not present?"

Pound's face pursed up like a prune. "Had we known to expect you—" he repeated.

"You should always expect me. I do not have to give you notice of my whereabouts."

"No, my lady." His expression smoothed away into blandness, but I knew that for all the outward show, he was annoyed. That, however, was not my concern.

Constance, looking from one of us to the other, stepped forward. "I can go to find some food and some hot water, ma'am," she said, "if Mr. Pound can raise the housekeeper and see to your room."

Constance was always the peacemaker. Probably Pound was some distant cousin of hers; she came from a village only a few miles distant, and everyone in those parts was related to one another.

"I'll wait in the drawing room," I said. "Thank you, Constance."

Pound's gaze flickered between us, hard to read. He seemed surprised that I addressed Constance by her first name. It was not the custom, but with a personal maid I always felt the need to be less formal. We were friends of a kind, after all. She dropped a curtsey and sped off towards the kitchen passage. Pound followed more slowly, adjusting his jacket and smoothing his hair for the housekeeper's benefit if not for mine.

The drawing room was as unwelcoming as the hall. There was no light, so I went back to the hall and took a branch of candles from the table by the door. From upstairs came the sound of voices raised in altercation. I had not met the Lydiard housekeeper and did not know her name, but it seemed she had a fine pair of lungs even if she did not know how to keep house.

Pulling one of the covers off a chair I sat down and waited. Even with the candlelight the room looked sad and dark. Shrouded pictures of Eustace's ancestors looked down their Gerard noses at me as though I, the daughter of a duke, was not good enough to marry a mere viscount. No light or warmth had penetrated here during the day, and I thought I smelled damp plaster. The grand marble fireplace yawned cold and empty, full of the winter's ashes. I wondered for a moment why I had come here, to the end of the world, and then I remembered. I remembered the golden gown, I remembered Eustace's violence and I remembered that I planned to be revenged on him. Here, at Lydiard, I would settle the score.

Constance was the perfect accomplice. I knew she was Eustace's spy. She had been from the moment he appointed her as my maid. They both thought I was unaware of it, but I had known all along. It did not matter to me; she was useful in passing on the information I wished Eustace to receive, and now I would use her to lure Eustace to Lydiard so that I could deal with him.

I think I must have fallen asleep where I sat, for when I woke the candles had gone out and the room was full of darkness and silence. I felt cold, stiff and confused, my mind fogged with dreams. I stumbled to my feet, clumsily bumping into the corner of a table, reaching out to steady myself but touching nothing but thin air. Why had everyone left me alone in the dark? I felt both forlorn and furious at the same time.

A sliver of light showed in the corner of the room. I groped my way towards it. My fingers met the smooth panels of a door and the hard edge of the doorknob. I turned it and realized that I was in the little dressing room that lay in the northeast corner of the house, facing the church. Faint light fell through the window with its intricate painted diamond panes, suggesting that dawn was coming. I stood for a moment watching the strengthening light deepening the colors in the glass. I had loved that window from the first moment I had seen it. It had given me so many ideas for my drawing and painting; Eustace had laughingly said the room must become my studio.

But this was odd. If I was in the little dressing room, then I could only have come through the door in the corner of the grand bedroom and not from the drawing room, where I had sat down and apparently fallen asleep... And now I looked about it, the room was much changed, painted in blue with a strange-looking desk all gold and black in the alcove, and on the walls were drawings, pastels and sketches in a hand I immediately recognized as my own.

Except that the pictures were unfamiliar, and their subjects and settings were completely unknown to me.

A long, cold shiver ran along my skin. I walked up to them to stare more closely. The room was as bright as day now, but I had not noticed the change at once because I was too intent on the images on the wall. There was a charming pastel of a woman and a child holding hands and dancing, a drawing of three little rounded cupids sporting together and, there in the corner of the room, a pencil sketch of an elegant lady seated on a terrace with a little dog curled up on a cushion beside her.

There could be no mistake. I knew my own style and design as one does a hand so familiar that it is instinctive. I turned slowly to take them all in and saw a watercolor of a spray of flowers I had seen in a hedgerow in spring. I had taken a rough copy of them in my notebook, and here they were in a painted panel, pale pink and white on blue, entwined with leaves, just as I had envisaged drawing them. There was china and porcelain adorned with the same sorts of patterns. And there, on the shiny black top of the desk was a portrait framed in wood of a very pretty girl. It was signed with the initials IACB. I leaned closer to read the square piece of card beneath: "A stipple engraving published by John Boydell in 1782 after Lady Isabella's 1779 painting of her friend and cousin Lady Georgiana Cavendish."

I sat down very abruptly in the little wicker chair by the desk.

We were in the year 1763.

I knew nothing of a John Boydell who published stipple engravings.

As for the china and porcelain, a lady might draw and paint but she did not produce designs for commercial use.

And my cousin was Lady Georgiana Spencer, not Lady Georgiana Cavendish, and she was a sweet child of six years.

Then there was IACB, the artist who had drawn the portrait... I wrapped my arms about myself to drive away the cold that possessed me. Isabella, Ann and Charlotte were my names, and suddenly I knew with the insight of a soothsayer, a witch, that I was the artist. The Isabella whose work was displayed here inhabited my future...

"My lady? Madam?" It was Constance's voice from beyond the doorway. I jumped like a startled cat. The light was fading again, and the pale blue walls seemed to shimmer. I gripped the arm of the chair so that the wood scored my fingers. I needed the reassurance of the pain to convince me I was not in a dream.

Light wavered across the floor, and then there was Constance, a branch of candles in her hand. "There you are," she said, sounding so surprised that the deference had gone from her voice. "Why would you sit in here in the dark?"

The room, revealed in the soft golden light, was the one that I knew. The window was the same and the beautiful plaster of the ceiling, but here too the furniture was now covered in cloth and there was nothing on the walls other than an oil of a rather angry-looking dog standing over the prone body of a dead hare. I remembered Eustace telling me that it was a favorite of his father's.

Constance was still looking at me curiously, but she had remembered her manners now. "There is food in the drawing room, ma'am," she said, "if you would care to come through. The water is heating and your chamber is almost ready. Mrs. Lunt apologizes for the delay and will present herself to you directly."

"Thank you," I said. I followed her out into the grand bedchamber, glancing back over my shoulder at the little dressing room. It had fallen into darkness.

IACB... If this really were me, then by the time the portrait was published I would have a different surname. I would be remarried. Eustace would be dead.

The thought gave me enormous pleasure. It warmed me,

nurturing the flame of revenge that burned deep inside. I felt new life and energy course through my veins again, just as I had when I had held the golden gown. I decided that whilst I planned Eustace's demise I would start to draw again.

"I shall set up my easel in that room tomorrow," I said to Constance. "The light is perfect for my art. Please talk to Mrs. Lunt to make sure it is clean and ready for me in the morning. There is much I need to do."

6

Fenella

THERE WAS A PARCEL WAITING FOR FEN ON THE walnut table in the hall when she came back from work on Monday. It was unexpected, and she felt her heart contract with a little lurch of fear just as it always did when something unforeseen happened. It felt as though these days she had no protective layer. Everything had been stripped away when she had walked out on her past life, and as yet she had not been able to reconstruct herself.

Since Friday night she had felt on edge anyway, jumping at shadows. She knew she must have imagined seeing Jake. He lived in Berlin these days, or so she had been told. Yet just the thought that she could summon up his ghost so easily chilled her. She had spent the day trying to forget, immersed in work, the seminars and tutorials with her students, discussions on design ideas with colleagues, her research. The routine and familiarity had restored some of her equilibrium, but term was ending and soon the college corridors would be echoing and empty through the long weeks of summer. She already felt lonely and vulnerable.

"There's a special delivery for you," her landlord said. He had come out of his own flat when he heard the main door open. He had a mop in his hand, but Fen knew he had no intention of cleaning the tiled hall. For a start it was spotless, and secondly, he employed a whole team of cleaners to service the flats. It was part of the rental agreement.

"It was lucky I was here to sign for it," he said. "Otherwise they would have taken it away again."

"Thanks," Fen said. She hadn't talked to him much in the six months she had been back in Swindon. She knew he was called Dave and that he shared his flat with a male partner and that he ran a small property empire from within the elegant Georgian building. That was about all, other than that he used the mop as an excuse to engage the tenants in conversation whenever he heard the door open.

"It's postmarked Norfolk," Dave said. He waited, clearly hoping for some information in return.

Fen glanced at the scrawled address which looked as though it had been written in a hurry by someone who couldn't give a toss whether the parcel arrived at its destination or not. She thought it odd to send it special delivery if they couldn't even be bothered with a proper postcode. Then she realized that it was Pepper's writing, which explained everything. Pepper's life was one whole long impatient scrawl.

"It's from my sister," she said.

"Lives there, does she?" Dave's eyebrows waggled with excitement.

"No," Fen said. "She's clearing out my grandmother's cottage in Hunstanton. Gran died a couple of months ago."

"Condolences." Dave rubbed vigorously at an imaginary spot on the colored tiles. "I hope she had a good innings?"

"She did, thanks," Fen said. It was hard to speak about Sarah without feeling a multitude of emotions, of which grief and regret were very close to the top of the list. Everything had gone wrong with their relationship. When Fen had reached sixteen she had headed out into the world like a bird freed from a cage. She had only wanted a bit of breathing space after the claustrophobic years of caring for Sarah, but no one had understood. Her family had thought she was an ingrate. Sarah wrote her vitriolic letters accusing her of willful cruelty. Even Pepper had called her selfish.

"Really, darling," her mother had said plaintively, from an archaeological dig in Greece, "you're throwing away all your future chances without a decent education. No one who leaves school at sixteen has a hope in hell of making anything of themselves. And what about your grandmother? Who's supposed to care for her now you've gone? I've had to call in an army of carers, and that is so expensive!"

Fen had felt bad about that, abandoning Sarah to flea markets and the bottle, but it had felt as though something might snap in her head if she didn't get out. Jessie, knowing something was wrong even though Fen hadn't spilled the details, had tried to persuade her to go to stay with them so that she could carry on at school, but Fen had needed to get out right away, put some distance between her and Swindon for a while. Kesia had a cousin in London and Fen had gone to stay with her, found work as a waitress and moved from job to job, rented flat to rented flat, until she had met Jake, an importer of luxury goods, and he had helped her get work as a secretary. It wasn't what she wanted to do forever, but she had only been twenty and she had thought there would be plenty of time to decide on a proper future, and whatever her mother thought, there were plenty of opportunities...

She picked up the parcel, which was much lighter than she had expected from its size, and carried it up the stair at the rear of the hall. Muted summer sunshine fell on her from the fanlight high above her head, mingling with drifting shadow. She had never lived in an old house before but found it pleasantly cool in the heat of these July days. She had been surprised to find how much she liked the Georgian style of Villet House, with its paneled hall and carved oak stair. Her flat was on the first floor, two bedrooms, a spacious living area with a big bow window to the street at the front, a tiny kitchen and bathroom and a view out across the car parks and rooftops behind. It wasn't the most attractive view in the world, but if she craned her neck she could see the green haze of the trees in the park, the spire of Christ Church and the rows of houses leading down the hill into Swindon New Town.

She put the parcel down on her dining table and went into the kitchen to pour a glass of water. She felt hot and sticky from the walk home even though the college was only five minutes away. Her hair smelled of diesel fumes from the buses, and it felt as though there was a layer of summer dust overlaying her skin. She needed a shower.

Halfway down the hall she realized that she had forgotten to put the chain on the door. It shocked her to be so careless. Vigilance was a habit with her. She fumbled for the links with fingers that shook and slid it into place.

The cold shower restored some of her calm. She knew she had changed since leaving Jake; she was much more wary, less open with people, and no matter how she tried, the lurking sense of unease was never far away. People spoke of starting a new life as though it were fresh and exciting. What they didn't realize was that you could not shake off the past. It was in your head, sometimes, even in the marks on your body.

It was too hot to eat. She was meeting some colleagues from work in the wine bar on Wood Street at eight and knew she should at least have a salad or something small before she had anything to drink. Not that she was likely to say something she shouldn't, but there was always a chance she might forget which story she was telling today, who she was... She never talked about her real past, not with those people who had not known her before. She did not know any of them well enough to trust them and she didn't want to talk about it anyway; why rake it all up, dissect it again, see the shock and pity in people's eyes? It had been hard enough with family and friends at the time:

"But we all thought Jake was so charming," they had wailed as a chorus, and the look in their eyes had so often suggested that she must have been at fault and that it was her judgment that in some way was suspect...

As she tossed some basil, mozzarella, sliced tomatoes and avocado into a bowl and sloshed in some olive oil, Fen caught sight of the parcel, still sitting on the table, waiting. She realized she didn't want to open it. She had no idea what her sister could have sent her since Sarah had cut Fen out of her will and left most of her money to charity. Pepper had been furious at having the burden of sorting through all of Sarah's accumulated stuff—trash, she had called it—when she wasn't even getting much of a legacy for her trouble.

"It's all right for you," Pepper had said crossly. "If Gran hadn't moved nearer to us, I wouldn't have got lumbered with all of this."

"Hunstanton isn't near Lincoln," Fen said.

"Mother thinks it is," Pepper said bitterly. "She told me I

was the one who was closest, and I should do the house clearance. And I can't just throw it all away, Fen. You know what Gran was like. There might actually be something valuable in amongst all the rubbish."

"Well, God forbid you should miss that and give it to charity by accident," Fen had said and Pepper had put the phone down on her. Happy families, Fen thought. With a sigh, she put the salad bowl down carefully on the counter, wiped her hands down her jeans, and went through the arch into the living room.

She needed scissors to open the parcel. Pepper had sealed it up so thoroughly that there seemed no way in. She inserted the blade beneath the brown sticky tape and cut into the cardboard. She felt a whisper of something soft and light against the blade and stopped immediately, sensing a flash of some emotion that felt oddly like panic.

The lid of the box lifted away to reveal layers of tissue paper with a neat cut sliced through them. On top was a piece of thick, cream-colored writing paper, folded in half, covered with Sarah's imperious handwriting. It felt very odd to see it now, her grandmother speaking to her from beyond the grave when she had barely spoken to her at all in the last twelve years of her life.

Fenella.
This is yours. Do with it what you think best but be aware of the danger.

The note was unsigned.

Fen's heart started to race. She knew at once what *this* was. Carefully and with hands that shook, she unfolded the rustling layers of tissue paper. A faint smell came from the box—

lavender, conjuring up the memory of her grandmother's garden in the summer and the sun on hot stone, and mothballs, a pungent smell she had always hated. Her fingers brushed something soft and smooth, silk, aged and pale yet still retaining the shimmer of gold.

A sensation shot through her, recognition and dread and a strange sort of excitement.

The golden gown came free of its wrappings with a whisper of sound that was like the past stirring. It felt as though it sighed, shivering in Fen's hands. Unconsciously, she held it close to her heart in exactly the same way she had done in her bedroom fourteen years before.

She had had no idea that her grandmother had known about the golden gown. When she had left Swindon she had abandoned it in the bottom of her wardrobe underneath her sports kit and her hockey stick. It felt like something she had outgrown along with her childhood. She needed to leave it behind and move on.

She wondered if Sarah had found the gown when she had packed up to move back to her native Norfolk. It was odd that she had said nothing at the time, but then they had not really been on speaking terms.

Fen picked up her grandmother's note again, frowning a little.

This is yours. Do with it what you think best but be aware of the danger.

What on earth had Sarah meant by that?

Fen knew all about danger. She had an intimate, atavistic relationship with it that raised the hairs on the back of her neck. The memory of terror stalked her. She only needed to close her eyes to see each episode unfurl like a film reel. She would be running, tripping in her haste to escape, her heart pounding. Then Jake would catch her. She could feel his grip on her arm, the wrench of her bones as he hauled her back against him and held her close.

"I love you," he had kept repeating, as though that were a charm that warded off all evil. "I love you so much. I will always love you."

She never wanted to hear those words again.

She gave a violent shudder and came back to the room and the bright sunshine and the golden gown. How could it be dangerous? It was just a piece of old silk and lace.

Pepper had not bothered to enclose a covering note, so there was no explanation. Nor was there anything else from Sarah, no words of endearment, no mention of any regrets her grandmother might have had about their estrangement. The initial breach between them had never healed, and when Fen had divorced Jake the year before it had worsened.

"You always were selfish," her grandmother had snapped. "That poor boy. After all he's been through! He stood by you. He didn't press charges when he could have done. How could you do this to him, Fenella?"

"You don't understand," Fen had said. "It wasn't like that." She had repeated the words so often, but no one was listening. No one wanted to hear. Sarah had always liked Jake. Everyone did.

"Darling," Fen's mother had said vaguely from a research conference in Tanzania, "you know what Sarah's like. She'll fall out with someone else in the family soon and you'll be reinstated." But it had never happened. The estrangement had frozen into a permanent separation, and now Sarah was dead and the only word from her was the gown and a warning. Fen felt the familiar mixture of misery and frustration possess her. She had loved Sarah. She had wanted them to be reconciled. This gesture only made her feel worse, and she wondered whether Sarah had done it deliberately to upset and challenge her.

Her phone rang, and Fen reached automatically to answer it.

"Hey." It was Jessie's voice, warm, happy and all loved up. Fen felt a stirring of envy. Jessie and Dev were the proof that not all relationships were waking nightmares.

"Hi," she said. "How was Paris? Did you have a good time?"

"Lovely," Jessie said. "Crepes and croissants in Montmartre, silhouettes down by the Seine, theaters, museums…" She sounded dreamy. "What about you? How did it go in London?"

"We missed you," Fen said truthfully, "but it was a nice evening." *And I met your brother on the train home.* She felt a pang of regret mingled with awkwardness. She had already decided not to tell Jessie about her encounter with Hamish. Least said soonest mended had been one of Sarah's maxims, although in this particular instance, it was more a case of say nothing and hope for the best.

"I heard you had fun," Jessie said. "Kes said it was just like the old days and that you looked amazing."

"I do still scrub up all right," Fen said lightly.

"Come round for a cup of tea on Sunday and tell me all about it," Jessie said. "Dev's away." Fen heard the tiny ripple of hesitation in her voice. All her closest friends were always ridiculously careful not to talk too much about their partners in front of her, not after what had happened with Jake. Fen loved them for their thoughtfulness but wished they would treat her like a normal person.

"I'd like that," she said. "You can tell me about Paris. I've never been. So where's Dev working this week?"

"Sydney," Jessie said, "stopping off in Singapore on the way back."

"Tough job," Fen said. "Couldn't you have gone there for your anniversary instead of Paris?"

"I do have work of my own to do," Jessie said primly. "Never mind the cup of tea—come for lunch on Sunday. That'll give us a chance for a proper catch up."

"Thanks," Fen said. "That will be lovely. I'll see you then." She pressed the button to end the call, and her phone pinged again with an incoming text. It was Lucie from work; they were already in the bar and thinking of moving out of town to a country pub as it was such a hot evening. Where was she?

Fen ate the tomato and mozzarella salad slowly, knowing they would wait for her. She made friends easily, always had. She'd only been back in Swindon for six months, and yet already she was at the core of this particular group. She knew how to integrate. It was a talent she had learned young: to be all things to all people. Her work colleagues weren't true friends in the sense that Jessie and Kesia were, but they were good enough company.

She folded the golden gown up with the tissue paper and put it back in the box. The material felt a little stiff, as though movement were unfamiliar to it after so many years locked away.

Do with it what you think is best...

The best thing to do would be to take the gown back to Lydiard Park. Fen hadn't been to Lydiard for years, but she assumed the museum was still there, and she could stroll in and hand it over, explaining vaguely that she had found it amongst her grandmother's effects and understood that it had some connection to the house. She didn't need to tell anyone what had really happened all those years ago and that she had stolen it when she was a teenager.

Until she had the chance to do that, though, the cupboard in the second bedroom was the best place to store it. She carried the box through to the vestibule, holding it carefully, as though it contained china rather than material. The spare room had a closed-up smell to it made up of heat and stale air. This was where Fen kept the vintage stock she resold in her little booth at the Hungerford Antiques Arcade. Dealing in vintage items was something she loved and had done on and off for years, even during the time she had been with Jake. It was a passion that was all hers, something she really cared about, springing from Sarah's influence, perhaps, from the time of her childhood. Jake had professed an interest in vintage too when they had first met at an auction at Bonhams, but Fen soon realized he was only interested in items that might turn the greatest profit. That wasn't why she did it; she loved the quirky pieces and the insight they gave into people's lives.

She locked the box away on a shelf with her Victorian glass vases, some retro china and a couple of ornaments. She was just starting to build up her stock and her business. It fitted neatly with the part-time art and design teaching she did at the local college. That paid the bills at present. Just.

She gathered up her keys, her phone and her bag, and let herself out of the flat. She could hear the hum of Dave's television behind his door but no other noise in the building. Sometimes it felt as though the two of them were the only occupants of Villet House, although she knew that wasn't the case. It just seemed so private, so quiet. She reminded herself that that was why she had chosen it.

It was still fiercely hot and humid out on the street even though it was past eight o'clock. Fen had forgotten her sunglasses and squinted against the glare, hurrying across the main road and into the shadows of the buildings on the other side. She didn't particularly want to go out for a drink tonight, but it was something to do. It helped the time to pass. Besides, she had to fight the insidious desire to hide behind closed doors. If she allowed herself to weaken, the fear would win and she would hide away in the dark until it became her new normal. Each day was a fight and some days more than others.

Fen found herself thinking about the golden gown later that evening in the noisy confines of the wine bar. The conversation had been fitful between them all, stopping and starting because everyone was hot and tired, and when it came to it, no one could be bothered to drive out of town. The room with its low ceiling felt stifling, and the turning fan only displaced the hot air from one place to another. Fen wished they could sit out on the pavement at a table beneath one of the stripy umbrellas, but when she suggested it, Lucie complained that it was too noisy and the air was polluted. Instead Fen sweltered in a window seat and looked out as the heat lifted and the darkness crept in. Now, as the shadows lengthened, it was almost possible to see the old Swindon beneath the veneer of the new, the Swindon Fen remembered her grandmother telling her about when she had been a child. Sarah had loved the town's history and had told her so many stories. Their road, The Planks, was very old, Sarah had said, originally boarded over to provide a dry pathway for people to walk to church. Their house had been opposite the ruins of Holy Rood church and the site where the old Swindon Manor had once stood, now a park called The Lawns. In the old days there had been springs and a big pond and a mill with an enormous wheel, Sarah said. She had seen pictures of it. She had wanted to take Fen to a talk about Old Town history but frankly Fen hadn't cared. What mattered to her at fourteen was that there was nothing for teenagers to do and it was a mile away down the hill to any proper shops in the town center.

Here in Wood Street she was in the heart of the old town, and in twelve years it had changed. There was a deli, an expensive fishmonger's, smart bars and restaurants. The old buildings were being renovated and their beamed frontages repaired so that it was easier to see how they must once have appeared in the past overlooking the muddy lanes and the street market, to imagine the fine ladies holding their skirts as they picked their way along The Planks to church in their Sunday best. Fen, her senses dulled by wine and heat, imagined wandering those lanes in the golden gown.

"You're half asleep," Lucie chided her when someone asked her a question and she looked vacant. "Penny for your thoughts?"

"I was just thinking about work tomorrow," Fen lied.

Everyone groaned. "Thanks for bringing us down, Fen," Max said with a smile. He lectured in ceramics and was Lucie's ex but the breakup had been amicable, so they both said, and now he had his eye on Fen instead. He was a hipster, not Fen's type at all, though he seemed to think she should be grateful for his interest in her.

"It's all right for you, Fen." For a moment Lucie looked baleful. "You actually enjoy your work whereas most of us only do it for the money."

"I do like it," Fen agreed. She and Lucie had started at the college around the same time and had met on the induction course, but whereas Fen worked in the art faculty, Lucie was stuck in the finance office and made no bones about hating it.

"I enjoy my job," Max objected. He glanced around the table. "Most of us here do."

Lucie ignored his comment. "You were lucky," she said to Fen. She speared an olive discontentedly. "Not many people turn up for an interview for an admin job and end up teaching instead."

Fen knew this was true. She had originally applied to be an admin assistant in the estates department but had mentioned on her CV that she had done a teaching qualification at night school and had subsequently taken some classes in vintage design. The college had snapped her up.

There was an awkward silence. Lucie looked round the table as though challenging anyone to defend Fen against this accusation of benevolent fate. No one did. Lucie's mouth turned down at the corners, and she played with her empty wineglass, glancing under her lashes at Max to see if he might take the hint to suggest another round, but he turned his shoulder to her and leaned towards Fen.

"How is your vintage business going?" he asked her. He liked to pretend he was heavily into vintage fashions, but Fen thought his clothes were pure high street hipster.

"Pretty well," she said. "I'm actively looking to acquire new stock. Sales are usually good in the summer, and the beauty of being a part of the arcade is that I don't need to be there all the time. The people staffing the front desk take all the payments for the stallholders plus any messages and commissions. It's a good arrangement."

"I must drop by your booth sometime," Lucie said. She stifled a yawn. "I've never been in the arcade, but Claudia says you have all kinds of cute little knickknacks for sale."

"They're vintage items," Fen corrected. She squashed down the prickle of annoyance she felt and smiled at Lucie. "A few clothes, some old china and glass, that sort of thing."

"I thought vintage was just a term people used to describe rubbish," Lucie said. There was no mistaking the unfriendly glint in her eye now.

"Some people call it rubbish and others call it cute little knickknacks," Fen agreed pleasantly. "I like to think it has some merit even if it isn't antique as such."

She wasn't sure what she had done to upset Lucie other than attract the unwanted attentions of Max. Perhaps that was enough, coupled with the fact that Lucie probably envied her the teaching contract. She had been picky with Fen from the start of the evening, pulling her up on keeping them all waiting, sniping at her a couple of times, refusing to sit outside. It had made Fen realize how shallow the roots were of their friendship and how little she knew these people.

"I need another drink." Lucie stood up abruptly. "Max?" She looked round the table at the others. "Eddie? Another pint? Caro, what will you have?" She didn't offer to buy for Fen.

"I'll come with you." Eddie squeezed out of his seat and followed her to the bar. Max was talking to Caro, Eddie's girlfriend, leaning in close to her in the way that Fen hated. Caro didn't seem to mind it.

Fen noticed that Lucie's bag was still on the seat next to her and that she had left it unzipped when she had taken out her purse. She stared at it for several seconds. A feeling took her that she barely recognized for it had been so long, a sensation that was part excitement, part terror. There was a beat in her ears over and above the pulse of the music. It seemed to fill her head until she was aware of nothing else. She dug a hand into Lucie's bag and grabbed the first item she found, a pen by the shape of it, and then, burrowing deeper, something that felt hard and round. In one quick move she slid them into her pocket without even looking at them.

The buzz in her head eased a little, like a headache fading. She looked up, glancing round the bar. No one was looking at her. Everything seemed to be exactly the same as it had been a few moments before, the frenetic chatter, the dim lights. Max was draining his pint whilst Caro talked animatedly about something that clearly bored him since his gaze had wandered from her. Lucie and Eddie were heading back from the bar with their hands full of glasses.

Fen got to her feet.

"I'm off," she said. "Thanks for a great evening."

Max stood up too. "I'll walk you back," he said. He sounded eager.

"No need," Fen said. "But thank you for the offer."

Max looked crestfallen. "Do you have time for lunch tomorrow? Just the two of us?"

"Sorry, I can't do lunch at the moment," Fen said, deliberately vague. "You know how it is at the end of term... So much to do." She gave him a peck on the cheek.

"See you, Caro..." She waved at Eddie across the room. Lucie ignored her, looking the other way.

It was only a five-minute walk back to the flat down Wood Street and Cricklade Road. Fen strode quickly without looking over her shoulder. She felt different, lighter, more powerful and in control. It was easy to think like that, though, buoyed up by a few glasses of wine. Or perhaps it was something else...

She crossed the road at the traffic lights by the bank and walked briskly past the ivy-clad walls of the Goddard Arms.

She wished she could remember more of those stories of Swindon history that Sarah had told her. She thought that the Goddards had been the lords of the manor and that they were the ones who had lived at the lost house by the ruined church. Most people seemed to think that Swindon had no history before the coming of the railway. And yet here she was, surrounded by it.

She reached Villet House and stopped to look up at the carved gargoyles on the elaborate frontage as they leered down at her in the orange glow of the streetlights. She had to wonder at the mindset of a man—she assumed it was a man—who had built an elegant Georgian house and then adorned it with such weird carvings. There was something grotesque and slightly menacing about them.

The hall was in darkness, but the lights sprang automatically into life when she stepped inside. It was so bright it made her wince. She glanced up automatically at the eye of the CCTV camera. Dave said that it gave the residents a sense of security and reassurance, but it was also a spy, recording deliveries and visitors, noting the movements of the residents with an impersonal eye. The presence of a camera should have reassured her, but tonight it made Fen feel uneasy.

Her footsteps echoed on the stairs. Up in the flat she took out the stuff she had stolen from Lucie's handbag and looked at it for the first time. The pen was a cheap ballpoint with some sort of company logo on it. The hard, round object proved to be a silver bracelet in a lovely, old-fashioned style with a safety chain and Lucie's initials engraved on the inside.

Fen felt nothing as she looked at them; there was emptiness under her heart and an odd absence of emotion in her mind, as well. She had expected to feel something: shock or guilt at the way she had behaved, puzzlement as to why, after all this time, she had started to steal again, but there was nothing at all. It was as though some sort of trapdoor had closed in her mind, locking the thoughts out so that she was utterly emotionless.

Strange.

She waited. Nothing. Then at the back of her mind was the glitter of a gown of silver and gold. It seemed to speak to her and remind her that this was the way things used to be.

She left the pen on the table and took the bracelet to the cupboard where she had stored the gown. Immediately she felt an impulse to take the box out and open it. She wanted to see the gown again. The instinct was so strong that she found her hand was halfway towards reaching for it before she consciously realized what she was doing.

Danger...

What had Sarah meant by that?

A shadow flitted behind her and Fen spun round, her heart in her mouth. No one was there. The overhead light glowed as brightly and impersonally as ever, making the room's emptiness look harsh. Fen hadn't bothered to do anything to the space since she only used it as storage, and the window looked out onto an alleyway at the back of the building. No one had been to stay in the six months she had lived there because she had not invited anyone. It was a hollow shell.

As her heartbeat slowed again Fen closed the door of the cupboard and walked slowly back into the living room.

Something felt different. She could not place the cause of her disquiet, but she felt it immediately. It was a ripple along the skin, a warning that had her heart pounding again. Very slowly she looked around the room. Everything appeared exactly the same, and yet there was a disconnect between what she was seeing and how she felt. She knew that something had changed.

The pen she had stolen from Lucie's bag had gone from the table. Fen blinked and looked again. It was not there. She got down on her hands and knees to see if it had rolled off the edge, but there was no sign of it lying on the floor. She scrabbled around under the table with increasing desperation as she tried to find it. There was nothing but dust under the sofa and an old ticket for a play at the Wyvern Theatre tucked into the skirting board.

Fen sat back on her heels. She was panting. She told herself that this was stupid, she must have moved it somewhere and forgotten about it. It was only a cheap pen anyway. It didn't matter.

And yet it did. Doubt worried at her, flowering into panic. The shadow across the window, the missing pen... Had someone broken into her flat? Was it Jake? Had she really seen him on Friday night and not imagined the whole episode? Was he here now, hiding, waiting? The dread built in her mind, brick upon brick, until she was almost taken over by it, left shaking and immobile. Silence pressed down on her, alive and menacing.

With one hand she grasped the leg of the chair and pulled herself to her feet, resting her palms on the table, closing her eyes, breathing hard. Everything was fine. She was safe. There was no one here. Nothing was going to hurt her.

She went into the kitchen and gulped down a glass of tepid water from the tap. It helped to steady her and bring her back to the present, to the sound of rain on the roof and cars in the street outside, and raised voices as people went home from the pub. Exhaustion dragged at her all of a sudden. She needed to go to bed but she thought it unlikely her mind would rest. She had learned how to train herself in ways to calm her thoughts, but tonight the clamor felt too fierce.

She checked all the rooms, in the cupboards, under the beds, everywhere someone might hide and plenty of places they could not. Only when she had assured herself that there was no one else in the flat did she fall into bed, but she didn't sleep.

7

Constance

SO MANY TIMES I ASKED MYSELF WHY I HAD LIED
to Lord Gerard about the golden gown. The question obsessed
me, troubling my thoughts as I went about my work each day,
creeping like a dark stain across my mind. So many times I
wished I could recall the letter and cross out the words and
yet surely it scarcely mattered. I would get my chance; my
lady would tire of the gown as she did all of her possessions
and cast it aside. Then I would take it and destroy it.

I found living at Lydiard more difficult than I had anticipated. London was alive with company. There were places
to visit, errands to run, shops and entertainments. The city
overflowed with people. In contrast the country estate had
its own routine, and I had no part in it. Lady Gerard and I
existed in a separate world, touching the other only when we
required food or clean linens. The housemaids envied me,
I knew—the position of lady's maid was much coveted, and

yet of all the household roles it was to me the least interesting. I felt bored and confined.

Lady Gerard did not pay visits or receive calls. Early on any number of local gentry left their cards, hoping to be able to boast of acquaintanceship with her. Mr. Goddard called three times. On each occasion she sent her regrets, explaining that she was indisposed, in the country for her health, not for pleasure. It was not true. Every day she would venture out across the fields like a milkmaid, though with her artist's easel rather than a pail. She was consumed by the need to paint.

In contrast I had no interests. The beauty of the countryside, the warmth of the sun, the golden days of summer counted for nothing to me. I had grown up in a country village and left it behind. It was no pleasure to return. Yes, there was a discontentment in me during those long, hot days, an unhappiness that seemed to seep into every corner of my life and feed on the dissatisfaction it found. I hated the sensation, yet I could not escape it.

One evening I was tidying my lady's closet for want of anything better to do when she returned from her latest ramble demanding hot water to wash and dinner on the table.

"I am sharp set," she said, smiling. She looked browned from the sun, and though it was not considered ladylike to be other than pale of complexion, I had to admit that it did become her. She glowed, pink and pretty. I felt a stab of furious jealousy.

"I have worked so hard! I do not notice the time when I am painting," she said.

"Yes, madam," I said. Her idea of hard work and mine were far apart, and anyway I knew for a fact she had taken and consumed a vast picnic. I had seen cook assembling it that morning: bread and cheese and a chicken pie, apples and pears, enough for a family of four.

I sent the footman to notify the kitchens that my lady required another meal and asked him to fetch the water for her. In the meantime I finished tidying the shelves, selecting a clean dress for her and a shawl. The cupboard was huge and capacious, dark wood in an old-fashioned style. At least it was large enough to hold madam's extensive wardrobe. On the shelf opposite her silk petticoats lay the golden gown. Even in the shadows it looked ethereal and radiant, glowing just as my lady did. The jealousy in my gut twisted another notch.

Then I saw it. A cat was lying on the gown, stretched out, asleep. The sight made me jump. I swatted at it.

"Out!"

There were plenty of feral cats in the stables. They kept the mice and rats at bay. I had never seen one in the house, though. Lady Gerard disliked all animals. They made her sneeze, and she would be incensed to know that one had penetrated as far as her boudoir.

The cat did not move. I grabbed it by the tail and dragged it out of the cupboard, fully expecting it to run off in a flurry of teeth and claws. Instead it hung rigid from my grasp, its body swinging gently.

Several things happened at once. The door opened and a housemaid came in with the pitcher of water. Lady Gerard screamed, striking out with her hands, sending the ewer flying. Water splashed everywhere, slopping over the housemaid's feet. She screamed in turn.

I dropped the dead cat in the grate. I could not slap sense into Lady Gerard of course, but I took great delight in doing so to the maid, who was running around shrieking with her apron over her head.

"Be quiet, you fool!" I hissed. "It cannot hurt you. It's dead!"

Her screams quieted to sobs. Lady Gerard had started to sneeze.

"Get rid of it," she gasped, doubling up, snatching for breath. "Now!"

I had sometimes wondered whether a person might die from such an affliction. Certainly Lady Gerard looked most unwell, her eyes distended, her face reddened as she coughed and wheezed. The cat also did not look its best, for it had not had a peaceful death. Its small body was contorted and stiff, and its lips drawn back in a vicious snarl.

"Who could have done such a thing?" her ladyship enquired tearfully, later, when the cat had been thrown on the rubbish heap, her sneezes had subsided and, pale and shaking, she was sitting in bed with a dose to steady her nerves. "Who would be so cruel as to place a dead cat in my closet?" She grabbed my hands, a pitiful expression in her blue eyes. "You would not be so unkind to me, would you, Constance? I could never believe it."

"Of course not, my lady," I said, mentally counting up the number of people who bore her a grudge. Lord Gerard hated her. Perhaps he had asked Pound to introduce the cat into her rooms in the knowledge it would cause her such sickness and misery. All the servants despised her because she made no bones about criticizing their lack of London polish. As for me... Well, she was fair and far out if she thought we were friends.

"Perhaps," I said, "it was pure mischance. Very likely the cat was hale and hearty when it crawled in there and was taken sick later."

This did not console her. "I will not have a cat dying in

my closet," she said. "Whoever heard of such a thing? It is quite unacceptable."

"I am sure it will not happen again," I said. I stood up, freeing myself from her grasp. "You should rest, madam. You have had a nasty shock."

"In a little while." She lay back against the pillows and gave a pretty little sigh. "First I need you to bring me the gown."

"The gown?" I looked at her blankly.

"The special one." She sat upright, irritable now. Her moods were as variable as a weathervane. "The golden one. The one the cat *died* on, Constance."

I rubbed my forehead, not quite believing that the golden gown could be in any way special to her. However, it was no jest. She was looking at me expectantly so I walked over to the cupboard and brought it out, placing it in her outstretched hands.

"I knew it!" She ran her fingers over the silk of the weave. "His claws have pulled the threads."

"Do not hold it so close, my lady," I said. I was fearful she would start sneezing again, and then the whole wretched business would start afresh. "I will take it away," I said, adding: "Now it has fur upon it, you cannot wear it again for fear it will infect you."

Her jaw set stubbornly. "You will mend it and clean it for me. I have in mind to wear it soon."

I bit my lip hard to prevent the retort that there would be no occasion to wear it. Was she to go to the Swindon assembly and make a grand entrance amongst the provincial flock in their summer muslins? I thought not. But she did not want to hear my opinions.

"Of course, madam," I said.

Once that was assured she took the remaining dose of

laudanum I had left beside the bed and was soon sleeping. I thought I might go to Swindon in a day or so and visit the chemist. My stocks of the draught were low; I had used almost all that Dr. Baird had given me. I might visit my family whilst I was in the town, though the idea held very little appeal.

I took the gown with me to my room. Here at Lydiard I did at least have a chamber close by my mistress, unlike in London where I had been up in the attics. The corridor was quiet. A sepulcher had more life than this house. I shuddered.

Once in my chamber I was sorely tempted to destroy the thing there and then and have done with it. I could withstand my lady's wrath. But how was I to accomplish it? It was too hot to build a fire, and my tiny grate could not accommodate so rich a funeral pyre. I supposed I could cut it to pieces, but I was tired and resented the effort. It would be easiest to give it away to one of the women who scavenged in the streets for cast-off rags. If I took it with me to town I would be sure to find a beggar to take it off my hands.

Except… I felt the material, soft as gossamer against my fingers, and watched the golden sheen of it shift in the candle's light. It was too fine to end its days in a tavern or bawdy house, adorning some trull, or be dragged filthy through the gutters. It should light up a ballroom. My hatred of Lady Gerard returned then in a rush of feeling that was almost ungovernable. I shook with fury. The fierceness of it scared me. For there was no doubt that she and the gown belonged together, both so delicate and fine.

I could not destroy the gown. It felt impossible. Carefully I folded it up again and hunted in my little wooden chest for a bag in which I could wrap it. It was late and I had no intention of starting work on mending it tonight, particularly as I could not see any of the pulled threads that Lady Gerard had been so insistent were there.

I found the bag my mother had given me when I left Swindon two years previously to serve Lady Gerard. It was a simple calico pocket with blue embroidery. I had wondered at the time what I might use it for. It was perfect to keep the gown protected.

There was a tiny dusting of powder on my hands, white like flour. I brushed it off and pulled the drawstring of the bag tight. Another few specks of white were sprinkled across the black of my gown. I stared at them, then dabbed carefully, raising my fingers to my mouth. They tasted of nothing...yet a faint echo of bitterness, of metal, seemed to linger on my tongue for a moment. It brought to mind the mill at home and the rats scuffling in the rafters, and my father warning us children to stay away from the poison he had laid for them.

I thought of the cat then, its body rigid in an agonizing death.

I looked at the powder and I looked at the embroidered bag with its dangerous gift, and I understood what Lord Gerard had done.

8

Fenella

"OF COURSE JAKE HASN'T BEEN IN TOUCH asking about you," Pepper said, in answer to Fen's question. "I haven't heard a word from him for two years."

Pepper had picked up the phone on the thirty-second ring just as Fen had been about to cut the connection. It was the fifth time she had rung her sister. Pepper hadn't answered before, and now she had, she sounded as cross and harassed as she always did.

"Anyway, I thought Jake had gone abroad somewhere?" Pepper's voice was muffled. There was a ripping sound at the end of the line, then the sound of her chewing. "Sorry," she said. "No time for breakfast. This is the first chance I've had to eat."

Fen wondered whether her sister was deliberately rubbing in how busy she was. As a mother of three she already had her hands full. Sorting out their grandmother's chaotic affairs must have been an extra burden. But Pepper had never asked for help, just festered with the injustice of it all and grumbled snidely when she had the chance. It felt pretty much par for the course in their relationship.

Fen rubbed her forehead. She knew that she was culpable too; she had not offered Pepper any help. They weren't close—they never had been, both so preoccupied with their own lives that they had little time for sisterly support.

"Why do you ask?" Pepper said. "Has Jake been trying to find you?"

"Not as far as I know," Fen said truthfully. She was not going to tell Pepper that she thought she had seen Jake in Swindon, that she had even imagined he might be stalking her. Pepper would think that she was paranoid, obsessed. Her sister had told her often enough that she needed to move on. Not a single member of Fen's family had had the imagination to realize that between Jake's perceived behavior, the mirror he presented to the world, and the reality had lain an ocean of darkness. Sarah had been particularly susceptible to his old-fashioned gallantry.

"What a gentleman," she had cooed when Fen had taken Jake to visit. "One of the old school."

Fen clenched her free hand into a tight fist. Dark shadows moved in her mind, the same ones she had seen in the brightly lit bedroom two nights before. She shuddered.

"Never mind," she said, forcing herself to focus on Pepper, on the conversation. "I rang up to ask about the gown, really. The one you sent me in the post."

"Is that what it was?" Pepper spoke through another mouthful of biscuit. "I didn't know."

Fen looked at the box. She had taken it out of the wardrobe and put it on the table whilst she made the call. The label, with Pepper's scrawled handwriting on it, stared crossly at her in an echo of her sister's irritated tone. Fen had not opened it again. She had wanted to; she had felt almost driven to take the gown out and touch it and hold it, but she had resisted. The impulse troubled her because it was so powerful. It felt as though the gown was a presence at the back of her mind all the time.

"The box was already sealed up when I found it in Granny's wardrobe," Pepper said. "There was a sticky note from her on the top of it telling me to post it to you, so I did."

"Didn't you wonder what it was?" Fen asked. "I would have peeped inside."

"Of course you would." Pepper's voice dripped scorn. "I was too busy, Fen, with all this damned house clearance! Your parcel was just one of fifteen thousand other things I've had to do—"

"Sorry," Fen said quickly, to stem the flood. "It's just that there was a note in with it, and I wondered…" She stopped. There wasn't much point in asking Pepper any of this if her sister hadn't even known about the golden gown.

"Is it valuable?" Pepper sounded envious.

"No," Fen said. "It's just an antique gown. It's old and tattered, nothing special."

From inside the box came a faint sound, like scratching, claws on wood, as though in rebuttal of her words. Fen jumped, recoiling.

"If I'd know it was an antique I would have taken it out and asked the valuer to take a look at it," Pepper was saying. Then: "Fen? Are you still there?"

"Yes." The phone slipped in Fen's palm. She stared at the box. There was no sound, no movement. The sweat felt cold on the back of her neck. She must have imagined the noise.

There could not be anything living inside the box. Probably it was just a pigeon on the roof, or a tree tapping the window.

"I didn't realize you'd called in an expert to assess Sarah's collection," Fen said.

"I didn't," Pepper said. "He came to me. Said he'd seen the death notice in the paper and knew Granny had been a vintage dealer."

"How opportunistic," Fen said. "I wouldn't have trusted him an inch."

"He was nice," Pepper said, sounding surprised to be paying someone a compliment, "and there were a couple of things that were worth a bit of money."

"I expect he ripped you off," Fen said.

"He told me to take them to the local auction house." Pepper sounded smug. "They gave me a good price. There are good people left in the world you know, Fen."

Ouch. Fen winced. That had got straight through, and Pepper was right, of course. She was the one who was suspicious, who saw evil everywhere. Pepper was permanently cross, but not paranoid.

Pepper was still talking, but Fen tuned her out. If Sarah hadn't left any other details about the gown, such as its provenance or why it might be dangerous in some mysterious way, then there wasn't much else to be gained.

"Now I think about it, that must have been the gown that was on the inventory granny left." Pepper sounded aggrieved. "I looked for it everywhere but I never thought of your parcel. Damn."

"Granny left an inventory?" Fen's heart felt as though it had missed a beat. She could visualize the list, with its careful record of items bought and sold. Amongst the cameos and silver candlesticks had there been a line that read:

"One antique golden gown that Fenella stole when she was a schoolgirl. May possess dangerous qualities."

But no, that was stupid. It was her guilt and her imagination talking.

"What did the inventory say?" she asked.

"Hang on a minute." There was more rustling at the end of the line and a thud as Pepper dropped her phone, followed by some swearing.

"I've got it here..." Pepper cleared her throat. "'One lady's evening gown, mid-eighteenth century, gold silk decorated with silver thread, lace cuffs, fichu.' Is that the one?"

"Yes," Fen said. Her heart raced. "Is there any more detail?"

"No," Pepper said. "That's it."

Fen felt disappointed. She already knew what the gown looked like, and she could probably have guessed that it was eighteenth century from the style if she had consulted a few books. She wondered what she had expected to learn. Something useful that might explain Sarah's mysterious note, perhaps.

"Oh, wait, there is more." Pepper sounded as though she was enjoying keeping Fen in suspense. "I remember now. This was why I was so curious about the gown and wanted to find it. The inventory is typed but Granny has written a couple of notes in the margin. One is 'Fenella' then 'Lydiard Park' with a question mark after it. And then 'Lady Isabella Beaumaris.'"

"Who?" Fen said.

"Lady Isabella Beaumaris," Pepper said. "I looked her up when I found the inventory. She was married to Eustace Gerard who owned Lydiard Park back in the day. That's just down the road from you, isn't it? I think Granny thought the gown might have belonged to Lady Isabella and come from there."

"Lady Isabella Beaumaris," Fen repeated. She could hear the scratching again, louder now. She wasn't sure if it was in the box or in her head. She felt slightly dizzy.

"There's a pencil scribble here, as well," Pepper said. She spoke slowly. "It says: 'Danger: Existing personality traits are accentuated.' What do you think that means? It's written next to the description of the gown, but I can't see what it's got to do with anything…"

Danger. There was that word again.

Fen touched the box and felt a vibration through the cardboard, the sense of something moving inside. She withdrew her hand as though scalded.

"I suppose—" she started to say, but Pepper cut across her, her voice eager.

"Although when I think about it, it *is* weird because I did think Granny was getting more and more irrational in her old age. I mean, she always was a bit dotty—*you* know that—but she became…just… Oh, I don't know, more of everything, really. More drunk, more bitter, more bad-tempered."

"That's certainly true," Fen said. She groped for the chair and sat down. She was feeling light-headed and a bit sick. The scratching inside the box had stopped now, but it was as though she could still hear it echoing through her head.

"She was a bit of a caricature of herself by the end," Pepper said. "I wondered if she might have been suffering from Alzheimer's. One of the things that can happen with it is that your character traits can become more extreme. You know—more racist, or sexist, or obsessive, or whatever. It reminded me of Greg's mum—she began to develop early onset Alzheimer's eighteen months ago, and now she hoards so many cans of baked beans it would see us through a siege. She's convinced the Third World War is coming. Totally paranoid."

"Well, she could be right," Fen said, "but I still can't see what that has to do with the golden gown."

"No, but..." Pepper sounded uncharacteristically hesitant. "I know it sounds mad, but perhaps part of her paranoia was that she blamed the gown in some way for how she felt?"

Then, as Fen didn't immediately reply: "Look, forget it. Like I said, it's a mad idea. If she did change, it was only because of the drink—"

"It's not mad." Fen could feel the sweat chill on her forehead. She thought of the way in which she had suddenly and irrationally started to steal again after all those years.

Danger: Existing personality traits are accentuated...

"Whatever." It was clear, for whatever reason, that Pepper didn't want to talk about it anymore. "I've got to go, Fen. So much to do."

"Shall I come over at the weekend and help you with the rest of Sarah's stuff?" Fen said, on impulse. "We could catch up properly—"

"It's almost done now." Pepper sounded huffy. "There's no need."

Fen sighed, already regretting the momentary impulse that had made her reach out to her sister.

"I'd like to come and visit you anyway, Pepper," she said, after a moment. "Not just to help. It's ages since we saw each other."

There was a silence at the other end. "Oh." Pepper sounded surprised. "Well. I can't do this weekend, but I'll check my diary and get back to you."

Fen stifled another sigh. She knew it would never happen unless she pushed again. The truth was that neither of them wanted it enough. She did not want to spend a couple of days staying in Pepper's stifling little house on the out-skirts of Lincoln with her niece and nephews forever on their game consoles and Pepper's boring husband, Greg, bemoan-ing the cost of living. And Pepper... Well, she imagined that her sister didn't need her in her life, which was a tough fact to face but nonetheless true.

But at least Pepper seemed more animated now. "By the way, have you heard from Mother? Apparently she's coming back from Greece in a week or so."

"No, I hadn't heard," Fen said. "Is she staying with you?"

"God, no." Pepper snorted. "Can you imagine? She's rent-ing a flat in London until she heads off again."

"Which won't be long," Fen said.

"With any luck," Pepper said with feeling, and Fen laughed, and for a moment they were drawn into sisterly alliance.

"I'll be in touch," Pepper said. "Bye."

Fen picked the box up and carried it back to the cupboard in the spare room. There was no movement from inside it now, no scratching sounds, nothing. She still felt hot and shaky, and shoved it quickly to the back of the shelf, shutting the door tightly. Even so, her eyes were drawn irresistibly to the growing collection of items locked away in the dark with the gown. In the space of only two days, she had stolen quite a few things. There was Lucie's silver bracelet and also a watch she had pocketed the previous day, when one of the students in her design class had accidentally left it behind. There was a packet of sweets she had stolen from the corner shop, a beaded bag she had seen at a craft fair and a child's soft rabbit that had fallen from a pram. The mother and her friend had been chatting and had not noticed the little girl drop her toy. Fen did not feel it was her fault if they weren't paying attention. The child had screamed, but by then she had stuffed the rabbit in her bag and no one had noticed that she had taken it.

She knew that what she was doing was wrong, yet she felt helpless in the grip of the addiction. Years before, when she had moved to London and left her childhood impulse towards kleptomania behind, she had read about the condition and had been so ashamed and terrified that she had vowed never to steal anything again. The compulsion had diminished, then died. Yet now it was back, and it had metamorphosed into something far darker and more frightening than it had been when she was a teenager. She took no pleasure from stealing, but nor did she feel ashamed anymore of what she was doing. When the impulse gripped her, she was completely possessed by it. There was none of the heart-racing excitement she had read was associated with risk-taking, only a cold clear urge to steal. And afterwards there was an utter absence of emotion, no remorse, no guilt, nothing. In between the episodes she felt repelled and tried not to think about it at all, shying away from the locked cupboard when she went into the spare room to sort out her vintage stock. She wanted to pretend that it wasn't happening, yet at the same time she had to acknowledge it was.

She closed the wardrobe door, resting one hand against the panels for a moment. Perhaps she needed help. Perhaps it was the stress of her relationship with Jake and the move back to Swindon and the attempt to rebuild her life that was becoming too overwhelming. Jessie was a GP; when she saw her she could perhaps ask her to recommend a counselor. Except then Jessie would worry and want to know what was going on, and Fen cringed away from telling her about the stealing. It was too shameful.

Once the door of the spare room was closed behind her, she felt miraculously lighter and the nausea lifted completely. The day was bright and sunny and college was closed; she decided to go to Hungerford, to the arcade where she rented some sales space. She needed to review her stock and decide how she might refresh the display.

Rather than drive she took the bus. She was in no hurry and it was nice to have the leisure to look out of the window as the bus rattled through the pretty countryside and the chocolate box villages. It was surprisingly quiet in the town when Fen arrived, and the shops were almost deserted, unusual on a Friday. The heat pressed down from a cloudless sky and bounced back off the pavement in a suffocating wave. It was a relief to dive into the antiques arcade where at least it was shady and cooler. Only a few people browsed amongst the stalls, and they had the air of people who were too hot to be thinking seriously about spending money.

Fen went up the spiral stairs to the first floor. Magda, the owner of the building, was on the reception desk on the telephone, and waved at Fen as she walked past.

"Yes, of course," she heard Magda say. "Come on over."

Upstairs, Fen wandered into the big bow windowed room at the front, overlooking the High Street. There was a rail of clothes to one side: furs and linen and lace, a few dresses from the 1930s, some Victorian nightshirts. The rest of the room was taken up with some elegant furniture, silver and china. Terry, who rented the whole of the space, was what Fen would consider to be a "proper" antiques dealer rather than a vintage collector although he did mix some vintage pieces in with his older items. She stopped to admire a neat little inlaid table with a glorious green-and-gold paperweight sitting on it. Next to that was a canteen of cutlery, silver sparkling. The spoons were particularly pretty with a scalloped handle in the shape of a seashell. Fen picked one up and slid it into her pocket. There was barely a breath of time between the impulse coming into her head and the action. The arcade had CCTV in every room, but she thought her body was blocking the camera's view and she could hear voices from downstairs now. Magda's visitor had arrived. She would be too busy to notice what was going on upstairs.

Fen walked through the door into the next series of rooms, where she had her own items on sale. She thought her display looked a bit tired. It definitely needed refreshing with some new items and a splash of color to reflect the brightness of summer. Now that term had finished she would have more time to redesign it and to catch the summer trade. She came in to Hungerford at least once a week to collect her earnings and bring in new stock, take any messages and catch up with Magda and the other stallholders. Usually she would then go and browse the other Hungerford antiques arcades to see what other people were selling and the sort of items that were popular. Sometimes there was an antique fair on at the town hall, as well. It was fun, exciting, knowing that you might find the one item that would make you a fortune...

She waited for the buzz of anticipation she usually felt when she thought about the vintage trade, but this time she felt nothing. Nothing but the hard edge of the spoon in her pocket digging into her, a reminder of what she had done and the fact she had no remorse, only this strange sense of emptiness. A small shiver wracked her. It was no wonder that this morning she had brought no new stock with her and that she felt anxiety, not anticipation, when she thought about going to the fairs and markets. She no longer trusted herself. She could easily walk into an antiques fair and walk out with a whole load of contraband weighing down her pockets. She was not safe.

Realizing that she was shaking, she sank down onto an old oak chest on which she had piled some colorful throws and rugs. Overhead a fan turned lazily, but suddenly she felt too hot, the sweat prickling her neck. She remembered the inventory and its ominous message:

Existing personality traits are accentuated. Traits such as hoarding, or paranoia, or the inclination to steal… There was no denying it, the thefts had begun with the arrival of the gown. So had her escalating fears about Jake, her sense of unease, the sickness…

The clatter of steps on the iron stair to her left made her jump. Magda was coming, talking over her shoulder to a man who was following her.

"It's in the room at the front," Magda was saying. "I think your friend will find it the perfect addition to his collection—" She saw Fen and stopped, her sharp, dark gaze narrowing on Fen's face. "Are you all right, sweetie?" she said. "You look like death. Too hot?"

Fen smoothed her sweaty palms down her skirt. "I'm fine, thanks, Magda. I—" She broke off. Standing at Magda's shoulder was Hamish Ross.

Fen felt a paralyzing wave of mortification and horror. She could not have spoken had she tried.

"Hi. It's nice to see you again." Hamish filled the sudden silence with the conventional words. His tone was friendly but he was not smiling, and as Fen met his eyes she saw the mismatch between his words and his expression. He was angry about something, something to do with her. Her stomach dropped sickeningly.

"You know Fen?" Magda didn't sound thrilled.

"We met last week," Hamish said. He kept his gaze on her. "Fen, is it?" He cocked a brow. "You only told me your pen name last time."

A great wave of color swept up Fen's face, suffusing it with scarlet. If she had felt hot before, now she was sweltering. Damn and bloody hell. This was worse than bumping into him at Jessie's. This was ghastly.

"Fenella Brightwell." She thought about offering a hand to shake and decided against it.

"Pen name?" Magda was intrigued. "I didn't know you wrote, Fen."

"She writes science fiction," Hamish supplied. There was a glint in his eyes that could have been amusement—at her expense. "Under the name Julie Butler."

Magda looked skeptical. "Really?" she said.

"How are you?" Fen said hastily. "I didn't know that you were an antiques dealer."

"I'm not," Hamish said.

"Hamish is an academic," Magda said. "Dr. Hamish Ross. He specializes in art theft."

"How intriguing." Fen thought that if she got any hotter she would probably melt. She had no clue what to say—or how to extricate herself from such an awkward situation. This was emphatically not the moment to start trying to explain anything to Hamish, not with Magda eagerly listening in.

"Not just art theft," Hamish said pleasantly. "I'm interested in missing antiquities of all sorts. I'm based at Reading University, but I do some work for the Met."

"Super," Fen said. Her face felt stiff, her smile a rictus. "Well, don't let me keep you from tracking down whatever it is you're looking for in this den of iniquity."

"I'm not working today," Hamish said. "A friend of mine

is interested in buying a painting he saw here, and as I was passing I said I'd drop in and take a look."

"It's through here." Magda put her hand possessively on his arm, gesturing to the bay window room at the front.

"Thanks," Hamish said. He allowed her to precede him through the doorway, then stopped and turned back to Fen. He leaned in closer, so close she could feel his breath against her ear and smell a very nice fresh cologne that made her think of fresh air and the sea. Her heart rate increased.

"Put the spoon back where it belongs," he whispered.

He straightened up and followed Magda without a backward glance.

Shit.

Fen stood rooted to the spot. Hamish knew she had stolen the spoon. He must have seen her downstairs on the CCTV. No wonder he had been so angry when they had come face-to-face.

She dashed to the ladies and was promptly sick, shaking and cold now instead of the heat that had consumed her earlier. She had known that at some point she would be caught out, and now it had happened. It was almost as though she had been pushing it until she was caught, ignoring the risk, propelled onward by the same compulsion that had haunted her from the moment she had opened the parcel with the gown in it. She had been so reckless that it was bound to happen sooner rather than later.

If Hamish told Magda what had happened, she would lose her space in the arcade. She might be prosecuted. Worse, word would go round, her reputation would be in tatters and everyone in the vintage business would shun her. She would probably lose her teaching contract too. And then there was all the other stuff, the stupid lies about being a writer, the fact that she was Jessie's friend and hadn't told him... She felt sick all over again. What a mess, and all because of one silver spoon. Except it was not just a spoon. It was an illness, an obsession that was running out of control.

She hid in the toilets until she heard Magda going downstairs, still talking, and Hamish's low voice in reply.

Shit, she thought again, miserably. She couldn't bear that Hamish hated her. She had enjoyed the time they had spent chatting on the train. There had been a connection between them. It had been sweet and had made her happy in a way she had forgotten she could feel. She had liked him so much. Now she felt sick about that as well as everything else. She wanted to run after him and apologize. She wanted to try to explain. But how could she even start when she didn't understand it herself?

She took the spoon out of her bag and put it back in the canteen of cutlery.

"I thought you had gone," Magda said, when she crept down the stairs. "And what was that I saw you put on Terry's table just now?"

Typical that she had been caught putting the spoon back, Fen thought, when Magda hadn't seen a thing when she had taken it.

"One of the spoons was on the floor," she said. "It must have fallen off the table."

She waited for Magda to contradict her and tell her that she knew Fen had stolen it because Hamish had seen her, but Magda didn't seem interested.

"How did you come to meet Hamish, then?" Magda asked. Her eyes brimmed with speculation. "He wouldn't talk about it. Was it embarrassing or something?"

"Not really," Fen said. "We bumped into each other on a train, that's all. It was just a fleeting thing."

"And what was that about a pen name?" Magda was like a terrier with a bone. "You don't write, do you?"

"No," Fen said. She smiled weakly. "Misunderstanding."

Magda's phone pinged with an incoming text. She picked it up and smiled, instantly distracted. Fen grabbed her moment. "I'll see you next week, Magda."

Magda made a vague gesture of agreement combined with farewell. She was already tapping out a reply to her text.

The sun had gone when Fen stepped out into the street. Checking the time on the town hall clock she realized she had just missed the next bus and had a full hour to wait. Now that she knew Hamish hadn't told Magda about the spoon she felt relieved and lighter, as though the whole incident hadn't actually happened. She thought she might go and browse the other antiques shops after all, in case there was anything worth picking up for her stall. That had been the point of her visit after all. Or perhaps she would just go and find a café and have a cool drink whilst she waited. Even though it wasn't sunny anymore, it still felt hot and oppressive.

At the back of her mind was the thought that she should think about what had happened, about the thefts, about what Pepper had told her that morning, about Lydiard Park and Lady Isabella Beaumaris, and the gown, but every time she tried to focus on the thoughts, her mind seemed to slip away from them. There was a darkness there and a fear. It was far better not to think about it at all and pretend that everything was normal.

She crossed the road towards a café with tables on the pavement and chairs shaded beneath stripy umbrellas. At the next table a couple were taking coffee and talking animatedly. One of the men had left his camera carelessly slung over the back of the chair. Fen wondered if he would remember it when he got up. If not she could probably take it without anyone noticing...

She caught herself as the thought was forming. This was awful. She had to stop. She had to do something to halt this terrible journey she was on. She knew it. Yet at the same time she acknowledged that she simply did not know what to do. She might have gotten away with the theft of the silver spoon, but next time it could be different. For she knew there would be a next time, and one after that, until her destruction was complete.

9

Isabella

Summer 1763

I WAS DISAPPOINTED THAT EUSTACE HAD NOT yet come running in response to Constance's letter telling him I had gone to Lydiard. What was the point in manipulating a maid who was a spy for my husband if he did not rise to the bait? I had been sure that when he knew I was in Wiltshire he would return from Paris at once in fear of my meddling, for I knew all about the smuggling business he conducted here, and Eustace knew that I knew. Up until now it had been in my interests to keep silent on the matter of his lawbreaking, but that was no longer the case. There was so much that I could tell the authorities: how Eustace was in league with a criminal gang in Swindon who passed contraband goods from the south coast across Salisbury Plain and on to the northern towns. I knew all the hiding places, the sheepfolds and mill-ponds, the crypts of churches, the warren of tunnels beneath the town. I even knew the names of the people who plied the trade, Constance's father, Samuel Lawrence, for one. I was not sure how Eustace had originally become involved other than as a man who liked his brandy and was unwilling to pay the duty on it, but I knew he was up to his neck and I would use that knowledge to my benefit.

Blackmail was one option by which I might escape him, but murder was still my favorite course. I had no intention of killing Eustace myself. It was not in my nature to do such dirty work. I needed someone else to do it for me, and the law of the land would be the most satisfying executioner. It was notoriously difficult to persuade peers to condemn one of their own to death, but the recent case of Lord Ferrers had proven it was not impossible. So I could hope; and if that proved fruitless then there were other ways. But before any of them could take effect I needed Eustace to come home.

To pass the time as I waited, I painted every hour of the day, from dawn to dusk. It became an obsession with me. Sometimes I forgot to eat or sleep; occasionally visitors would call, and I told Pound to turn them away. I had no interest in seeing anyone. The social round held no curiosity for me. I was possessed, engulfed in the experience of the art. Sometimes I would take up my easel and paint box and strike out across the fields in search of new ideas. I worked until my arms ached and I could no longer hold a brush or pencil in my paint-stained fingers. I did not understand what impulse it was that controlled me nor did I like it very much, but I could not behave any differently. It was the same sensation that made me so passionately determined to bring Eustace down.

On the inclement days I went to the little dressing room that I had had converted into a studio. The light poured in through the stained-glass windows and reflected off the high white plaster of the domed ceiling, shining down on me as

I worked. The ideas came easily, too fast for me to capture them as quickly as I would have liked. It was a blessing and a curse at the same time to be so inspired.

One day, when the rain was pounding on the roof and running like tears down the window, I became aware that the light in the studio was fading so badly that I could no longer see clearly, even though it was only three in the afternoon. I put aside my brush and reached for the rag I used to clean the paint from my hands, standing a little stiffly for I had been at my easel since the morning.

On the threshold I stopped dead. The room ahead of me was in bright sunlight yet a fire burned fiercely in the grate. It felt airless and stifling, and I felt the sweat spring up on my skin at once. I did not recognize the arrangement of the furniture, or the decoration of the room, or the paintings on the walls, but over the high back of one chair, shimmering in the light with a soft, golden glow, was my gown.

I started forward towards it.

"Pound? Where the hell are you, man?"

I jumped almost out of my skin. It was Eustace's voice. He was sitting before the window, almost hidden by the high curved back of a wing chair, and he did not appear to have seen me. On the table in front of him stood a bottle of brandy.

Then I saw the girl. She darted forward from the shadows, grabbed the golden gown and ran, fumbling to push it into some sort of bag she was carrying over her shoulder. I heard the sound of her feet slipping and sliding on the wooden floor. I could even hear the sound of her panicked breath, loud in the silence.

"Pound!" Eustace roared. "Damn you, get in here now and pour me more wine!"

"Madam?" Constance's voice came from the doorway through to the drawing room. "Is something the matter?"

I turned to look at her. I was still standing in the door of my studio, and the room beyond was exactly as it always had been. Eustace was nowhere to be seen.

There was only one thought on my mind.

"The golden gown," I said urgently. "Where is it?"

I saw a frown touch her eyes. No doubt she thought me quite mad and perhaps I was. All that was important to me was that the girl I had seen had not run off with my gown.

"It is upstairs in my room," she said. "I am working on the repairs to it." Then: "Would you like me to fetch it for you, ma'am?"

"No," I said slowly. I blinked and rubbed my eyes. "Is Lord Gerard home?" I asked. "I thought…" My voice trailed off. The room, the girl, the gown, Eustace… Had they all been part of a dream, a vision such as I had had last time when I had seen my sketches and drawings from the future?

Constance's frown deepened. "There has been no word from Lord Gerard, ma'am," she said. She touched my arm gently. "Perhaps you should rest? You have been painting for hours."

"I will go outside," I said. "The fresh air will do me good." She looked dubious. "It has been pouring with rain, madam. You will be drenched."

"Nonsense!" I needed to be alone, to think and clear my head. Yet already I felt the urge to draw returning. It was like a burr against the skin, pricking me and forcing me onwards. I wondered if I could ever stop.

I decided to go down to the lake to draw the swans. The storm had passed, and the sun was out again. It felt humid. I sat with my sketchbook in the shade of the tall beeches and watched the birds as they preened and squabbled, stretching their wings to dry them. I concentrated hard on the composition and did not think about what had happened up at the house. Either I was mad or a visionary or something odd was happening, yet all that seemed important to me was the gown and the painting. I was like a woman possessed.

When I had captured the wildfowl to my satisfaction, I turned my attention to the rest of the grounds. Lydiard Park looked beautiful in the high summer, and I devised a few scenes, the long line of the kitchen garden wall, the face of Bacchus on a large stone urn, the horses that grazed in the fields beyond the drive, and a group of villagers gathering at the church gate, chatting in the sunshine. I liked the images of people best; expressions and gestures added life and animation to a picture.

"That's extremely good." Someone leaned over and plucked my sketch from in front of me. I saw nothing but a man's hand, a pristine white linen cuff, an arm in an elegant tasseled sleeve. I had not even known he was there.

I spun around. "Sir. You startled me."

"I apologize, Lady Gerard." He smiled at me. "You were quite engrossed."

I gaped at him. It was Dr. Baird, of all people. I had neither seen nor heard from him since our last, awkward meeting in London. Nor would I have expected to do so. It was not as though we occupied the same social circles.

"What are you doing here?" The words were out before I realized how ungracious and gauche they sounded. "Did you come all this way to see me?"

I saw him smile again. It was odd, but it felt as though somehow the relationship had changed between us, shifted in some way. He did not look the same here in Wiltshire as he had done in London. He was smoother, more assured, not so much the social inferior. He looked quite the gentleman, and when he spoke I felt it all the more.

"No, indeed," he said, "though it is always a pleasure to see your ladyship. I have family in Wiltshire, and whilst I was visiting I thought to look in on you to see how you progress. The servants told me I would find you out here."

I let the lie pass. I knew he would have had to ask in London as to where I had gone, and make a special visit to Lydiard to see me even if he did possess family in the region. It did not displease me to think that he had come here on purpose, quite the contrary. He looked most handsome in his fashionable apparel, with the sun shining on his chestnut hair.

Dr. Baird returned his attention to my drawing, flicking through the sketching book. There were earlier pictures there, caricatures of some of the people I knew. I felt a flash of shock that he would be so familiar and reached out to snatch it back, but I was too late.

"Hmm," he said. "Lady Frances Norton. You have captured all her sweet pretense at innocence. How clever to be able to convey in a few lines both her virtue and her deceit."

I blushed. I did not like Lady Frances. She hid a venal soul behind a pretty façade of being an ingénue.

"And Lord Gower…" He flicked over another page. "You must still hold a torch for him, I think. You have given him a distinguished air he does not deserve."

My blush deepened. The previous year all of society had been talking about my flirtation with Gower, and I concede that there had been fuel for their gossip. His attentions had been marked and I… Well, I had been angry and hurt by Eustace, and all too ready to take revenge on him for his infidelity. Gower had proven an accomplished lover, and I had enjoyed him but I had not loved him.

"He has a noble brow," I said. "All I do is reflect what is there."

"You see beneath the surface." Dr. Baird was frowning as he handed back the picture to me. "And you add to the image from your own imagination. A drawing is not a mirror."

"It is an interpretation," I agreed.

He sat down on the bench beside me even though I had not invited him. I found that I did not mind. The day was warm and I was drowsy now, and he was proving surprisingly pleasant company. More than pleasant, if I were truthful. It flattered me that he had sought me out, and his lack of deference intrigued rather than offended me.

"Why do you draw?" He seemed genuinely interested.

I put down my pencil and thought about it for a moment. "It makes figures beautiful," I said. "I like to capture the clean lines and the perspectives. It gives me pleasure. If I can capture something of the true character as well, that is even more pleasing."

He smiled. The sun was in his hazel eyes, and he shaded them with his hand as he looked at me. I thought then how delightful it would be to sketch him. He was very good-looking, and he also had the style of a man of fashion but without frippery, and a wit and incisive manner that was most attractive. Emotion stirred within me as our eyes met. He was so very different from Eustace.

He smiled at me again, very gently. "What would you see if you drew me?"

It was almost as though he had read my mind. I picked up my pencil and drew a few quick lines, and handed them to him. He looked startled, then he laughed. "Am I then so easy to divine?"

I smiled in return. "Perhaps my reading of you is superficial."

He looked at my picture again. "No," he said slowly. "You have captured me."

The day felt hot all of a sudden. I could feel his gaze on me. He picked up my hand, the one that was not holding the pencil, turned it over and pressed a kiss to my wrist.

"It is a pity your husband cannot appreciate the gift he possesses," he said. His lips were warm on me. I felt his breath send a shiver along my skin. I knew that I should stop him, but I did not want to, so I allowed my hand to rest in his. This was wrong for a great many reasons; I knew it and yet, as with the desire to paint, the urgency was in my blood and it drove me.

"Eustace does not care for beauty." I spoke lightly. Even though I trembled inside I would not succumb to him so easily. "He prefers his horses."

I thought Dr. Baird would make some light, flirtatious response, but instead he dropped my hand somewhat abruptly. There was a heavy frown between his brows. His mouth was drawn tight.

"It pains me to see the way he treats you." He spoke angrily. "He takes pleasure in breaking fragile things."

His words, their directness and sincerity, shocked me. I was aware that people knew that Eustace and I quarreled but not that anyone cared about it other than as fodder for gossip, or in the doctor's case, as a source of income. Then I remembered his visit to me in London and his impassioned offer of help. He did care for me, and now I stood on the cusp of something important, something dangerous. Doubly dangerous, in fact, for I realized with a flash of excitement that here was the ally against Eustace that I needed.

I locked my trembling hands together in my lap and spoke carefully.

"Eustace will not break me."

"Why did you marry him?" His hand now covered mine. His tone was urgent. I remembered Betty asking me the same question and implying that I must have been drunk. I remembered that night at Vauxhall Gardens. It had been seductive; there was something so raffish and exciting about Vauxhall, with its twinkling illuminations and its dark walks. Eustace had sat next to me in one of the supper booths, his leg pressed against mine in an intimacy that had been as enticing as it was illusory. I had been misled but not by drink.

"I was bored," I said. "I wanted more."

He nodded, understanding in his eyes, nodding towards the big house and all its burdens.

"More than this restricted life," he said. His tone was bitter. "Yes, indeed." His gaze came back to me. "But you would not find it with Gerard."

"That was my mistake," I said.

There was a soft hush between us. His hand still covered mine. I was alive to the sensation of his touch.

"He is still away?" Dr. Baird said, after a moment, and I understood exactly what it was he was asking. It felt as though the very air was holding its breath.

"He is still in Paris." I kept my voice light, though my heart pounded. "He is with his mistress."

Dr. Baird nodded. "Then perhaps..." He paused. "You might consider a commission to paint me—whilst he is gone?"

I thought about it then: about how it might be accomplished. With Gower it had been easy. I had visited his rooms incognito and the illicitness of the experience had added greatly to the excitement. Could Dr. Baird come to me? I could let him in late at night and sketch him in the light of the fire, all gold and shadows. I imagined him taking off those fine and elegant clothes to reveal the fine elegance of the man beneath. I think I must have made a tiny sound in my throat, for his fingers tightened on mine. He leaned closer.

"You will do it?"

"I..."

"Send for me." His grasp was so tight it was almost cruel now. "Isabella, look at me."

I looked up. There was such a blaze of desire in his eyes. "I'm not like Gower," he said. "I don't play by society's rules."

I gasped at his bluntness. Gone was the diffidence I had known in London, the urbanity of the society physician.

"It seems you are just like him," I said. "Perhaps you too have a reputation for distracting bored wives?"

He studied me thoughtfully from the knot in my hair to the tips of my slippers. There was no emotion in his gaze, only cold examination, and it felt as though his gaze stripped me naked, there, on Lydiard's immaculate lawns. It was intensely exciting.

"Is that what you are?" he mused. "Still bored, still seeking?" His hand came up to cup my chin and force me to hold his gaze. "I can give you whatever you want, Isabella. But I am not like the others. I take everything in return. I'm not civilized like Gower. Remember that."

I had no idea how the balance of power between us could have altered so radically, but I wanted him to kiss me then, even if all the servants were hanging out of the windows and watching. Instead he released me so abruptly that for a moment the whole scene spun before my eyes, such was my heat and desire. Then he was gone, striding away across the garden without looking back.

I realized that I knew next to nothing about him. I did not even know his first name. Yet I wanted him, and I knew I would send for him.

That was how it began.

10

Fenella

FEN ORDERED A CUP OF COFFEE AND WHILST she waited, she dozed for a little in the heat. She felt safe, as though for as long as she sat there the eerie sense of acting under duress was in abeyance. People passed by along the pavement. The tables around her emptied and filled up again. The sun came out. She ordered another cup of coffee but let it go cold. She did not know what to do.

A shadow fell across her, blotting out the sun. Immediately she felt cold.

"Did you put it back?"

Fen jerked upright, opening her eyes. The shadow moved. She squinted against the sunlight. It was Hamish Ross, and he looked formidably annoyed.

"What?" Fen gaped at him. She felt sweaty and at a disadvantage, made stupid by heat and sleep. She was almost sure there was a dent in her cheek where it had rested against the chair back.

"The spoon," Hamish said. "Did you put it back?" He sat down opposite her.

"Yes," Fen said. She struggled upright. "Of course I did! I always meant to, it was just—" She stopped. A plausible excuse didn't seem willing to present itself this time.

Hamish raised his brows, and she felt herself blush bright scarlet, heat and embarrassment combined.

"It's not what you think," she said. "I'm not a thief!"

"Right," Hamish said.

The very mildness of his tone caused something to snap inside Fen. She grabbed her bag from beside her seat and upended it onto the metal table. Everything fell out in an untidy sprawl: purse, phone, tissues, Tampax, lipstick, notebook, pens, an old bus ticket, unidentified fluff and half a dozen other things.

Hamish looked from the pile to her and said nothing.

Fen stood up and turned out the pockets of her jeans. Some change, more tissues. She looked at Hamish. There was still no expression on his face. Her hands went to the hem of her shirt and she started to tug it upwards.

"Is everything all right here?" It was the waitress, looking anxious. People were staring, conversations suspended.

"Fine, thank you," Fen said. She pulled her shirt down and subsided into her seat.

"Can I get you anything?" The girl seemed unconvinced, looking from one of them to the other.

"I'd like a flat white, please," Hamish said. "Fen? Another drink?"

"Lemonade," Fen said. "Still. With ice, please."

The waitress nodded and backed away, casting one uncertain look back over her shoulder at them.

"How far were you prepared to go?" Hamish asked.

"As far as it took," Fen said. She stared at him defiantly. "I don't have it."

"Okay," Hamish said. "I accept that. But you did mean to steal it. I saw you put it in your pocket."

Fen ignored him. She started to shove all the stuff back into her bag. The lipstick fell off the edge of the table and rolled away. Suddenly she wanted to cry and had to bite her lip hard to stop herself. How stupid it all was, how pointless. She felt lost and trapped at the same time, not her true self at all. That was the feeling she hated more than anything.

Hamish bent down, picked up the lipstick and handed it to her.

"Thanks," Fen said. She didn't look at him.

"Do you do this sort of thing often?" Hamish asked. "Steal things?"

Fen flinched. "No," she said.

There was silence. She had the sense that he was waiting for her to contradict herself and would be prepared to sit there in silence for as long as it took. Well, she would not do that, but there was one thing she would tell him before she walked off out of his life.

"Look," she said. "There's something you should know. It's nothing to do with this and it's not important, but you were right on the train the other night. We have met before."

She saw that at last she had surprised him.

"I'm a friend of your sister," she said. "Jessie," she added, just in case they had another sibling she had forgotten. "We were at school together. I only remembered when you told me your name, and by then it was too late to tell you."

Hamish looked rueful. "I knew you seemed familiar."

"Anyway," Fen said, "like I say, that's nothing to do with anything." She wondered if it were possible for things to get any more excruciating between them. "I just wanted you to know." She stood up. "Actually I won't stay for the lemonade, but I'll pay for it, of course—"

"Please sit down, Fen," Hamish said. The words were too courteously spoken to be an order, but it still felt like one.

Fen hesitated.

"Please," Hamish repeated.

She sat.

"You were saying," Hamish said, "that you don't steal stuff normally."

"Not until recently," Fen muttered.

The waitress came back, lemonade in one hand, coffee in the other. "All right?" she said brightly.

"Great, thanks," Hamish said, smiling at her. He waited until she was out of earshot and then leaned forward. "What do you mean, not until recently?"

Fen gave a half shrug. "I could tell you, but you wouldn't believe me."

She saw his gaze narrow on her. "Try me," he said.

"Why?" Fen stared at him. "I hardly know you. I don't see why I should tell you about all the weird stuff that's going on in my life based on twenty minutes' acquaintance."

"All right," Hamish said equably. He sat back, lifting his coffee cup. "It's up to you."

A bus rumbled down the High Street. Fen took a long gulp of lemonade. She realized that her throat felt parched.

"I used to take bits and pieces when I was a child," she admitted, after a moment. "You know the sort of thing—sweets from the corner shop, small stuff, like kids do just for fun."

"I didn't," Hamish said.

"You don't surprise me," Fen said. She remembered that whilst he might not be a police officer he did work with the police, and she wondered why she was telling him anything incriminating at all. "I don't suppose you even had a library fine," she said.

Hamish smiled. "I think I was once warned for covering the entrance to the old railway tunnel at Grimes Cutting in graffiti." He shrugged. "I always did like art."

"And you needed a big canvas," Fen said.

Hamish smiled at her. She felt the connection between them then, just as she had that night on the train, direct, undeniable, enough to make her feel a little bit dizzy. She drank some more lemonade and tried to stay cool.

"I had you pegged as a 'brown furniture' person really," she said. "Rather than an urban artist."

Hamish looked startled, then he laughed aloud. "Brown furniture? You mean someone who's into the proper antique stuff? Well, yes, I suppose I am. I do specialize in seventeenth and eighteenth century stuff. The graffiti was just a phase." His smile faded. "Anyway," he said, "we were talking about your crimes and misdemeanors, not mine."

"Yeah," Fen said. "So we were. Well, the stealing stopped when I got older, but then, a week or so ago, I started to take things again."

She saw a flicker of interest in Hamish's eyes. "Do you know what prompted that?" he asked.

"Oh yes," Fen said. "It was after I got a parcel from my sister. Well, technically it wasn't from her. It was a dress I'd forgotten I had, and when my grandmother died and Pepper was clearing her house she sent it on to me..." She stopped, making a vague gesture with her hands. "I can't see how this could be of any interest to you at all."

"It's curious," Hamish said. He played with the spoon in his saucer, not looking her. "And I like puzzles."

THE WOMAN IN THE LAKE

"More to the point," Fen said, "I don't see why the way I behave interests you."

Their eyes met again, and she felt the little shiver of awareness down her spine. She knew she was going to have to be careful. Instant attraction was not her thing. Not that she was any better at relationships that developed slowly over time. The disaster that was Jake had proven that.

"I've no idea why you interest me," Hamish said. "But you do."

There was silence. Fen drained her glass.

"The thing that *is* curious," she said, "was that I had stolen that gown in the first place. I took it from Lydiard Park when Jessie and I were on a school trip when we were about thirteen. If I was a psychiatrist..." She shifted uncomfortably, "I'd say that perhaps the fact that I had taken it in the first place somehow kick-started the habit again and prompted me to start stealing again."

"It's an interesting theory," Hamish said, noncommittally. Fen immediately felt irritated, with him, with her, with the fact she had told him in the first place. She put the empty glass down with something of a bang.

"I'll figure it out," she said, wanting to dismiss the conversation, dismiss him.

"It sounds like kleptomania to me," Hamish said. "How do you feel when you are stealing? Excited? Reckless?"

Fen's irritation flared into temper. "No," she snapped. "I feel possessed. I feel as though something or someone is controlling me against my will. It's frightening. And if that sounds melodramatic, or if it sounds as though I can't take responsibility for my own actions, then I'm sorry but you did ask."

She stood up. "I need to go. I've already missed one bus."

"Wait a minute." Hamish put out a hand to stop her. "I apologize. I didn't mean to sound judgmental—"

"Oh yeah?" Fen said. "Next you'll be telling me it's an illness and I need help."

Hamish smiled. She liked his smile a ridiculous amount and could feel her temper easing, and that annoyed her even more.

"Why don't you sit down again, and we can talk about it some more?" he said. Then, as she glanced at her watch, "I'll run you back to Swindon afterwards if you'd like me to as you haven't got your car."

Fen did like that idea and the fact confused her. She sat down slowly. "Well..."

"So this dress," Hamish said. "You say you took it originally from Lydiard Park? I think I remember that trip. Jessie said it was boring."

"Well, she never enjoyed history, did she," Fen said. "Physics and chemistry was more her thing. It's no wonder she became a doctor."

"What about you?" Hamish said. "Did you enjoy history?"

"Not really," Fen admitted. "I wasn't interested in much at school in those days. Typical teenager, I suppose. I couldn't wait to leave."

"So you didn't take the gown because you liked it," Hamish said.

Fen shook her head. "Not in that sense. I wasn't interested in its history." She shifted a little in her chair. "It sounds bad, I know, but I just saw it there and felt this huge compulsion to take it. It was so beautiful, but it wasn't the sort of thing I'd ever wear. I was a teenager, you know, and it was old, a proper antique..." She shrugged. "The whole experience was just weird, so I shoved the gown in a cupboard and tried to forget about it, and for years I did."

"And then your sister sent it back to you out of the blue just a few weeks ago," Hamish said.

"Yes," Fen said. "And immediately I felt the same sensation—the urge to steal. When it strikes me it's so strong and uncontrollable. It takes me over. I'll take anything—children's toys, silver spoons." She met his eyes. "It doesn't matter what the item is. That's not important. I never do anything with them, but…" She shuddered, wrapping her arms about her even though the sun was still high and bright. "It frightens me. I know it has to stop, but I don't know *how* to stop it."

The waitress drifted over, clearly wanting them either to order something else or free up the table.

"Let's take a sandwich and something to drink down to the water meadows," Hamish suggested. "Unless you need to get back urgently."

Fen thought about the flat, sealed up tight, hot and stifling, with the spare room sheltering the golden gown. She did not want to go back there. She realized that it was mid-afternoon and she'd missed lunch.

"Okay," she said. "That would be nice."

They walked slowly down the High Street, past the bookshop, the antiques arcades and the elegant Georgian houses with their cobbled paths, over the bridge and along the canal.

"I'm not sure why you're doing this," Fen said suddenly. "Why you're being so kind, I mean. I—" She stopped. "It's not because of Jessie, is it?" she said. "Because I'm her friend?"

Hamish laughed. "Do you realize how lame that sounds? I don't have a particular sense of responsibility towards my sister's friends."

"Sorry." Fen blushed. "I just didn't want you to feel any obligation."

"I don't," Hamish said.

That, Fen thought, was unequivocal. It led back to the fact that Hamish was here because he wanted to be, because he was interested in her. She was not sure how she felt about that. She did realize, though, that she had been totally wrapped up in herself.

"Didn't you come to the gallery on business today?" she said. "I hope I'm not taking you away from something important."

Hamish shook his head. "It's fine. All you're taking me away from is marking student assignments on art thefts, frauds and forgeries."

"So you're based at Reading Uni," Fen said. She glanced at him sideways. "With forays into the world of crime?"

Hamish grinned. "That makes it sound much more exciting than it is."

"Then I wasn't the only one spinning a fantasy that night on the train," Fen said. "You told me that you wanted to be made redundant. Would that be from the university or the police?"

"What? Oh…" Hamish had the grace to look slightly embarrassed. "In a way it was true," he said. He gestured to the long shimmering stretch of the water meadows basking in the sun. "I'd love to have some time out to walk, and take photos, and to paint, maybe, although I'm pretty bad at art these days. The graffiti was probably the high point of my career. Anyway—" he shot her a look "—what's your excuse? What was all that stuff about writing science fiction, and the false name?"

"Yes," Fen said. "Sorry. I…" She paused. She didn't want to tell him anything about Jake or her disastrous relationship history. Hamish no doubt already thought she was certifiable.

"I have a vivid imagination," she said. "I didn't think I

was going to see you again, so I thought I could be anyone I wanted. It was…liberating."

"Hmm," Hamish said. "But do you really want to be a sci-fi author called Julie Butler?"

"No," Fen admitted. "Actually I like what I do, teaching, and buying and selling my vintage stuff. But…" She hesitated. "Look, I don't want to lie to you. It's complicated. I was in a bad relationship, and I kind of reinvented myself after I came back to Swindon. Sometimes I just get a bit carried away."

"You certainly have an interesting relationship with the truth," Hamish said dryly.

Fen stole a look at him. His expression was dark, unreadable. "I am sorry," she said. "Really. It was stupid of me to pretend."

"Forget it," Hamish said. "Shall we sit here?" He indicated a peeling wooden bench set back from the towpath. "Are you hungry?"

"Yes," Fen said, her stomach rumbling. She burrowed in the paper bag. "I chose cream cheese and smoked salmon. You?"

"Bacon, lettuce and tomato," Hamish said. He took a bite. "It's good." He shifted, turning towards her on the bench. "So tell me more about this stolen gown of yours. What do you know about it?"

"Not much," Fen said. She threw a few crumbs to the ducks. A cacophony of quacking filled the air as a dozen more scrambled in to forage. "Pepper—my sister—said it was mid-eighteenth century, it had belonged to someone called Lady Isabella Beaumaris, according to my grandmother's inventory. I was going to try and find out a bit about Isabella. She lived at Lydiard Park, apparently."

"I didn't know that," Hamish said. "I mean I've heard of Isabella Beaumaris. She was one of several aristocratic women who designed patterns for Wedgwood, along with Emma Crewe and Elizabeth Templetown. She was a talented artist. I suppose it makes sense that the gown was hers if it came from Lydiard in the first place and is the right date and style."

"I don't know where Granny got that information from," Fen said, "but she did enjoy researching her finds."

"Perhaps there's a record of the gown somewhere, or a portrait of Isabella wearing it," Hamish said. "It certainly should be easy enough to find about Isabella's connection to Lydiard Park."

"There was something else," Fen said, remembering. "Pepper said that Granny had written a note in the margin that said: 'Existing personality traits are accentuated' or something like that." She frowned. "I don't know whether that was supposed to refer to the dress or if it was just random, but it's a bit weird, given that as soon as I got the gown I started taking stuff again."

"An existing personality trait in your case being the inclination to steal?" Hamish raised his brows.

"I guess so," Fen said. "It seems absurd to suggest that the gown itself could have such an influence on anyone, and yet…" She paused, remembering the fierce grip of obsession that took hold of her whenever she was near the gown. "It does feel as though it has some sort of malign energy."

"What you're talking about is possession," Hamish said slowly. "An object that has the power to make you behave in a particular way."

"Possession," Fen said. "That's just…medieval."

"But not impossible," Hamish said. "If one is open-minded about the supernatural."

"Which I am," Fen said, "but not to that extent. Sorry,

but it sounds as though I'm making up some feeble excuse for bad behavior."

"Okay, then." Hamish rested his elbows on his knees and looked at her sideways. "Do you feel you have any control over this phenomena when it happens to you?"

Fen was silent for a long time, looking out across the wash of the river, where the water shone with a dull silver glitter in the sun.

"No," she admitted. "I feel as though I'm impelled to act, as though something or someone is making me behave in a particular way." She took a deep breath. "I feel as though it fills me, takes me over. If I try and fight it, it completely swamps me." She looked down at her hands, then up to meet his gaze. "It's pretty scary, actually, but that doesn't mean that it's not some sort of mental illness."

"Okay," Hamish said again. "Perhaps you should go to see a doctor if you think it would help. But don't discount alternative theories." He saw her look of surprise and smiled. "It would be arrogant to imagine that everything in life could be explained by science, wouldn't it? Or at least by the science we already know."

"I suppose so," Fen said. She smiled back. It was odd, but his matter-of-fact acceptance made her feel much better, lighter somehow and reassured.

"Perhaps we need find out more about Lady Isabella," Hamish said, "and see whether the same thing happened to her. Or to anyone else who might have had some connection to the gown. Did they also have some sort of character trait that became exaggerated or obsessive? It would be interesting to know."

"That's a good idea," Fen said, wondering about his use of the word "we." Was he offering to help her?

"Pepper thought it might have affected Gran over the years," she said thoughtfully. "She became much more of a hoarder as she grew older. It might have been a natural thing, I suppose—she always was a collector—but she would always sell stuff as well as buy it. Then at some point she just gave up the selling and accumulated more and more items, and when we suggested she sell them on she got really angry."

"How long was the gown in her possession?" Hamish asked.

Fen did some quick mental arithmetic. "About twelve years. I left it behind when I ran away from home at sixteen."

"I'd forgotten that you lived with your grandmother when you and Jessie were at school," Hamish said. "I'm not sure I ever met her." His gaze narrowed on her. "Why did you run away so young?"

"I was sick of being Gran's carer," Fen said bluntly. "She had an alcohol problem, and no one wanted to know or to help us deal with it."

Hamish's hand covered hers briefly. "I'm sorry. That must have been tough for you. Where were the rest of your family— your sister?"

"Pepper's older than me," Fen said. "At the time she was working as a dig assistant on one of my mother's excavations."

Hamish's brow cleared. "Your mother's the archaeologist Vanessa Brightwell?"

"I'm afraid so," Fen said. "Speaking of obsessions, she's completely obsessed with her job. I don't think that's anything to do with the gown," she added. "It's just the way she's always been. She was never around."

"And the rest of your family?"

Fen shrugged. "I don't know what's happened to my father. He's a well-known academic too, but my parents divorced when I was young, and he and I aren't in touch. I have a couple of brothers, but we're not close. That's why I used to love coming round to Jessie's. You were all so normal." She emptied the last of her crumbs out of the bag and the ducks gobbled them up. The sun had dipped behind the willows now, and there was the first hint of coolness in the air.

She saw Hamish glance at his watch and quickly got to her feet. "Sorry," she said, "I've taken up a lot of your time. I can get the bus back in fifteen minutes."

"The offer of a lift still stands," Hamish said. "I'm heading off to Bristol to see some friends tonight, so I can drop you in Swindon on the way."

Fen hesitated. Hamish seemed safe and sane, but how could anyone really know what was at the core of another person?

"That's very kind of you," she said cautiously. "Thank you."

"Difficult decision?" he said quizzically.

"The bad relationship," Fen said, by way of explanation. "Sorry. It makes me wary."

Hamish didn't say anything, just nodded, and she was grateful for his easy acceptance.

"I don't remember seeing you at Jessie's wedding," Fen said as they retraced their way along the towpath. "That was the last time I met up with your family, I think."

"You were pretty preoccupied with being a bridesmaid that day, as I recall," Hamish said. "Jessie was a bit of a bridezilla, wasn't she? Very demanding."

"As was her perfect right as the bride," Fen said, grinning.

"Very loyal of you," Hamish said, "but I remember what it was really like. Hard hats for all the family in the run-up to the big day."

"I'm not going to side with you against my best friend," Fen said primly.

"I'll remember that." Hamish held open the car door for her. It was a convertible of some sort, very sleek, the top already down, something of a contradiction of Hamish's apparent steadiness.

"Clearly you're not as boring as you seem," Fen said, "if your car is anything to go by."

Hamish gave her a look that made her feel quite hot. "I'll let you be the judge of that," he said. He slammed the door and walked round to the driver's side.

"Speaking of Jessie's wedding," he said, "what happened to that very good-looking guy you were with?" An edge had come into his voice. "Was he the bad experience you mentioned?"

"He was," Fen said. "We're divorced."

Hamish's hand checked on the ignition. "Hell. I'm sorry to hear that." His expression went blank for a moment, then he shook his head slightly. "Actually, no, I'm not sorry. He seemed rather controlling."

To put it mildly, Fen thought.

"I didn't think anyone realized," she said. She'd always thought Jake hid his behavior very cleverly from everyone except her. It had been part of his skill, the charming exterior masking the ugly truth beneath.

"I noticed him because I was looking at you," Hamish said.

Fen's heart jolted. Her gaze flew to his face. He was smiling, and there was something in his eyes that looked like tenderness. She'd forgotten emotions like that if she had ever experienced them at all. She felt ridiculously happy for a moment—and then she felt panicked.

"I'm not surprised you noticed me," she said lightly, tearing her gaze from his. "Pink ruffles have never suited me."

Hamish laughed. He turned on the car engine. "Don't worry," he said. "I'm not going to rush you. It sounds as though you've been through some tough times."

"You're very direct," Fen said, grimacing. She was not used to such honesty. With Hamish there was no hiding, no pretending.

"It's the way I am," Hamish said unapologetically. "I've never seen any point in playing games."

He pulled out into the traffic. Fen stole a glance at him and felt her heart turn over. She had had no idea that integrity—honor, she supposed was the old-fashioned term for it—could be so attractive. God help her, she'd done a U-turn from the bad boy to the knight in shining armor.

Then with a sick jerk of emotion she remembered just how dark and twisted the whole relationship with Jake had been, the depths they had plumbed and the grotesque, misshapen thing her life had become. She didn't want Hamish to know about that. She was ashamed of that phase of her life. It didn't matter how much people told her that it had not been her fault—it didn't matter that she told herself the same thing—the guilt and the shame were difficult emotions to shift. They stalked her, and she was always fighting them. Besides, when it came to men, her judgment sucked. Hamish could be a serial killer and she would be the last to realize. She had to ignore the instinct to trust that had gotten her in such terrible trouble before.

She thought Hamish must have sensed her mood because he turned the conversation back to how much she had enjoyed his mother's cooking when she had been a teenager, and they talked about simple things on the way back to Swindon—

favorite food, music, books, the pleasures of teaching. They had absolutely no tastes in common, which Fen thought was funny.

"Our interests are totally incompatible," she said to him as they came into Old Town and passed the ruin of the Locarno building and the columns at the entrance to the park. "I expect you think vintage is kitsch and of no real value."

"I think the value accorded to any of these things is a matter of fashion," Hamish said, "whether antique, vintage or whatever. The real value comes from what they mean to people."

"That's not a bad answer," Fen conceded. "You can drop me off here," she added, as they passed the Goddard Arms. "There's no parking in front of my flat." It was true, but for reasons of caution, self-preservation, whatever she wanted to call it, she was not going to tell him where she lived.

Hamish pulled over into one of the car parks that backed on to the park. "This is pretty," he said. "I had no idea there was anything so historical here."

"There's a lot of fascinating stuff," Fen said. "I grew up just down the road from here. My grandmother was a mine of information about Old Town. Not that I was interested in those days."

Hamish hesitated. "Would you like me to help out with some research into Isabella Beaumaris and the gown?" he asked.

Fen felt some of her lightness of spirit drain away. For a short while she had forgotten about the gown and the thefts and the weirdness of those scratching noises that had come from the box... She thought of going back into the flat and being alone, and she shuddered.

"Are you okay?" Hamish had seen her shiver.

"Yes, of course." Fen pulled herself together. "Thanks for the offer of help, but it's better I sort this out on my own."

Hamish nodded. "Okay."

Paradoxically, his acceptance of her decision made Fen feel miserable. She'd turned down a number of dates since she split up with Jake, and none of those rejections had caused her a moment's difficulty. This wasn't even a date, just someone offering his help, and yet she felt wretched.

"I'm sorry," she started to say, but Hamish cut her off.

"Don't worry," he said. "I can see you don't want to get involved. It's not a big deal."

That was that then.

"Thanks for the lift," Fen said, awkwardly. She got out and watched as he pulled out into the traffic and disappeared. She knew she had made a good decision, a safe decision. She had expected to feel reassured and happy, but she felt disappointed and dissatisfied.

The flat was silent, antiseptically clean, bright and modern. Yet it felt threatening. Fen could not shake off an overwhelming sense of unease. There was an exhibition at the art gallery that evening that she had planned to go to, so she did not stay home for long, stopping only to have a shower, get changed and have a bit of salad to eat. She went nowhere near the spare room. The bland wooden door was closed, holding its secrets within. It was another warm evening as she slipped out on to the street and headed through Old Town. The shop frontages spilled their light across the pavement. Like the flat they looked new and modern, but they hid their history behind the façade.

It was as she was crossing Albert Street that she caught sight of a couple walking down the alleyway to her left, their backs to her, their arms about each other. They were walking slowly, dreamily, laughing together, seemingly completely wrapped up in one another. There was something so familiar about the set of the man's shoulders and the way his head was inclined towards the girl, something that Fen recognized immediately and instinctively.

Jake.

She stopped dead, the group of people who were walking along behind her almost cannoning off her as a result.

"Sorry," Fen said. "I..." But her voice trailed away. She had no thought for explanations. All she could think of was that Jake really was back, that he was here, in Swindon, a mere step away from her. She had been right when she had thought she'd seen him a couple of nights ago.

She started to shake, with shock, with confusion, disbelief and fear; she felt a huge uprush of nausea. All the months of living on the edge, of coping with that gut-wrenching sense of danger, the unsettled sense that nothing in life was certain anymore. It all coagulated into one hard, cold terror that consumed her.

She looked back along the alley. The couple had just reached the end and were disappearing from view, oblivious to anything external to them. The street lighting illuminated the girl's fall of long fair hair as she reached up to kiss the man on the cheek, sliding her hand around his neck to bring his mouth down to meet hers. Fen stared. Surely that was Lucie? And it was definitely Jake. She knew him too well to be mistaken. Two years apart could not wipe out ten years of bad memories.

The couple turned a corner and vanished, and Fen found that she was huddled deep within a shop doorway, her palms pressed against the glass, her back against the hard wooden frame as though she were trying to melt into the shop to escape. Someone walked past and glanced at her curiously, and she thought she must look like a drunk searching for shelter or someone who had lost their mind. She was trembling. That was how she felt, within an inch of madness.

Her first instinct was to seek the comfort of home, and it was only as she inserted her key in the lock at Villett House, her hand still shaking, that she realized what waited for her in the flat. The gown. More weirdness. More stuff she could not compute at all.

The light flooded the entrance hall, so bright she blinked. It should have felt reassuring, but all Fen felt was cold.

Jake was here. He had found her.

Or had she been mistaken?

It had only been a moment in the half light.

The doubts were creeping in. She did not know what to believe, what to do.

"Alright, luv?" Dave had appeared in the hall to see who had come in. Behind him the television blared, a reality show, music and cheers. "I thought you were going to the exhibition?"

"I'm feeling a bit poorly," Fen muttered, shooting past him and up the stairs. "Think I'll have an early night instead."

"Good idea." Dave was watching her, a frown between his brows. "You look like death."

The flat did not feel like home. It was a place Fen could go, four walls and a roof, but it no longer felt like *hers*, a bolthole. She poured herself a glass of orange juice, gulping down the cold liquid greedily as though she had not drunk in days, then went and sat down heavily on the sofa. The sick feeling twisting her gut felt like despair. For twenty-four months she had struggled towards change, freedom, the shedding of her past life. Her progress had been slow, but she had thought she was getting somewhere.

One minute had undone everything.

She groped for her phone. She wanted to talk to someone. She wanted to make human contact. Yet there was no one she could talk to. No one really knew about Jake. No one understood. They thought they did, they thought they had the facts, but unless they crawled inside her mind they would never know the darkness there. If she tried to explain about seeing Jake they would think she had imagined it, that she was obsessed. They would say she needed help—justifiably so. First there had been the gown, the thefts, the strange shadows, the noises. Now there was this. She could not hide any longer how close to the edge of sanity she had come.

Her phone rang, the bell jarring in the quiet. She did not recognize the number and could not have answered it even had she wanted. She felt paralyzed.

"Fen, darling?" It was her mother on the voice mail. Fen had forgotten whereabouts she was at the moment—Zanzibar, perhaps, or Madagascar. "Wonderful news! I'm coming home. Can't want to see you! I'll call again soon. Ciao, darling!"

Silence again. But no... A faint scratching sound, the brush of wings, a scrape of claws...

Fen jumped up, grabbed her phone and ran down the contacts list, pressing a button.

"Please be in..."

"Hello?" Jessie's voice. Fen felt such a huge relief she almost cried. The lump in her throat was momentarily too big for her to speak.

"Fen?" Jessie had seen the caller ID. Then more sharply, "Are you okay? What's going on?"

Fen heard voices in the background, laughter and the clink

of glasses. She felt simultaneously a sharp stab of jealousy that she was not there doing something as normal, as enjoyable, as meeting with friends, and complete mortification that she was interrupting Jessie's dinner party. She could not do it. She would have to pretend she was fine.

"Hi, Jessie," she said. Her voice sounded odd to her ears, too high-pitched. "Sorry to bother you—I was just checking what time you wanted me to come over tomorrow?"

"Make it about twelve-thirty." Jessie's voice hadn't lost its wariness. "Fen, are you sure you're okay? You sound—"

"Half twelve," Fen said brightly. "Great. See you then."

Her hands were still shaking as she pressed the button to end the call. She dropped the phone on the table and wandered through into the bathroom. It was still humid from her shower earlier, the windows steamed up. So was the mirror, and in the condensation on its surface someone had written one word. The name "Jake."

11

Constance

1763

FIVE WEEKS AFTER WE ARRIVED AT LYDIARD
Park I went to visit my family in Swindon. It was only a few
miles distant but so very far in my mind.

"Don't trouble to show me in," I said to the little maid
who stood in the hall of my parents' house by The Planks,
staring at me as though I were some exotic being. "I can find
my own way."

She bobbed a curtsey. The maid was new, as was the polished mahogany table by the door and the narrow runner on
the hall floor. It had an intricate pattern woven in orange
and pink and gold. It looked French to me, and expensive.
Though I was no expert, I had seen sufficient grand houses
to know quality when I saw it.

The walls had been painted too. It did not sit well with the
old, lumpen stonework of the ancient cottage. Lime wash had
been better; this was an unpretentious worker's house trying

to masquerade as a gentleman's residence. Perhaps that was why Mother had covered most of the wall with an ugly old hunting tapestry that clashed terribly with the carpet. Poor Mother. She had neither taste nor style.

"Connie!" She met me in the parlor doorway. "I thought I heard your voice. You should have written that you were coming."

It would have availed her little even if I had. Mother was illiterate, one of the many reasons she had insisted that father have me educated alongside my brothers. I was grateful to her for that surprising show of strength, and now I played along with her pretense as I bent to kiss her cheek.

"There was no time," I lied. "I have been so busy since we arrived." I stood back a little, still holding her hands. "You look well, Mother."

In truth I thought she looked dreadful, all preened and powdered in the latest fashion, and wearing pink, which she had always loved and I had always thought too old for a woman of her years. She patted her hair.

"There is a new modiste in Wood Street. French. She has all the latest styles." She drew me into the room. "You will find Swindon has changed."

"I had already noticed." I sat down on the overstuffed sofa. It was new—and very uncomfortable.

"They are building again on Brock Hill." She wanted to tell me all about it anyway. "Mr. Harding has erected a fine house there. Apparently Mr. Villet is most put out. He covets it."

"Of course he does." I knew of the Villets, gentlemen who were second only to the Goddard family in Swindon. Each town, each village, had its hierarchy, just as the nobility did. Mr. Harding had knocked down an old inn and built a brick monstrosity in its place, and Mr. Villet envied him because it was his place to show off his status, not Mr. Harding's place.

She nodded. "They are such elegant houses there. Your father is hoping to buy in a year or two. We will be more comfortable amongst the right sort of people."

"Business people?"

Her nose wrinkled. "And the gentry."

"What would Swindon have to offer them?" I had not intended to sound sarcastic, but she flushed red.

"Are you grown too good for us then?" she asked stiffly.

"Of course not." This has always been the trouble for Mother and me. We did not understand one another and never had. I sighed, looking around at the old cottage. I had grown up here, across the road from the mill that had started Father on the road to fortune. It was home to me, recognizable still even under its heavy disguise, but my parents had moved on, and up. They had outgrown their origins. They wanted to live on the west side of the hill now and leave their past behind.

"You will have a good view from the top of the hill," I said. "And clean air." But my words could not appease her. I could see the stiffness lingered.

She clapped her hands. I jumped. "Tea, Dorcas!" Her formal smile was in place for the maid; she turned it back on me. "How is Lady Gerard?"

"She is well."

"Is there another child on the way?"

"I doubt it," I said.

Mother's face fell. She loved talking about babies. "We had thought that was why she had come to the country," she said. "It is health-giving, unlike London."

"It's true she came for her health," I said, "whilst Lord Gerard is abroad."

"We heard about that, as well," Mother said. "He has a new mistress and lavishes all his money on her."

"All his debt," I said. It never ceased to amaze me how London gossip ran ahead of people even as far as their country estates.

Mother's brow had puckered. "It puzzles me," she said, "how a man can be married to a beautiful woman such as Lady Gerard and yet seek his pleasures elsewhere."

"Was Lord Gerard not ever thus?" I asked. "Before his marriage? Most men are." To my mind it was naïve of Mother to think that a man would ever be satisfied with one woman even if she were the most beautiful in the world. Too many times I had seen them stray simply because they could.

"It takes more than beauty," I said, "to hold a man."

Mother looked blank. I sighed.

"Lady Gerard paints," I said. "She is quite fascinated by it. Every day she is at her easel, or out in the grounds. Flowers, people, the view from the gardens…cows grazing, sheep munching the grass, it matters not to her what the subject is. She draws it anyway."

Mother looked startled. "Good gracious," she said. "Drawing."

"It is what ladies do," I said. My gaze fell on her embroidery bag, lying beside the foot of her chair. "It passes the time."

Mother's gaze fell too. Now that father was rich and she did not have to work anymore, I suspected she did not know what to do with herself either. It was one of the few things she had in common with Lady Gerard.

The tea arrived. Poor Dorcas was holding the tray as though she was terrified. The china rattled with the shaking of her hands.

"Put it down before you break it," Mother said sharply. I

could see how flustered they both were for the tea set was new, like everything else.

"It is Meissen," my mother said proudly. "From Germany."

It was too fine for the house, of course, and sooner or later one of them would break a cup and my mother would treat it as a disaster. The tea was good though. Dorcas evidently knew how to brew a strong cup. We talked of the family, my brothers and their broods of children, and the news from the village. There was very little to interest me, and my attention wandered out on to the shady lane where the ducks and geese squabbled on the pond and the occasional cart rolled by. The walls of the cottage were so thick that I could not hear the turn of the mill wheel or the splash of the water even though it was close by. The mill would be as I remembered it. That would not have changed even if my father now left the work to others. The mill would echo with the turning of the wheel, the bare boards would be coated with dust and the air thick with it, the rats would be scratching amongst the grain sacks. One of my younger brothers ran the place now that Father was a businessman and my elder brother had bought one of the inns in the old town. All of them were involved in the smuggling business as well, of course. It touched every man.

"You should go to see your father before you return to Lydiard," my mother said, reading my mind. She half looked at me as she spoke, pleading, for she knew what had happened between us, that we had argued when father had sold me to Lord Gerard as his spy. She wanted to pretend it had never happened, wanted me to maintain the pretense that all was well in our family. Such secrets and lies there were in that house—in every house! I thought of Lord and Lady Gerard. They were no better.

This time, however, I was happy to oblige my mother. There was something that I needed to discuss with my father.

"Yes." I put down my cup. "I should. Where will I find him?"

"He has an office in Wood Street," my mother said proudly. "He needs suitable premises now that he is so influential."

I went out blinking into the bright sunlight and stood for a moment looking around. My father's circumstances might have changed, but the view was the same one I remembered. To my left I could see the high wall of Mr. Goddard's gardens and the roof of the manor soaring beyond. Ahead of me the tower of Holy Rood church looked down over the houses, watchful and dark, a shadow cast over sinners, of which I knew there were many, mostly in my own family. To my right was the mill, rumbling and creaking like a laboring man. After a moment I turned my back on it and picked my way along the planks and back into the market square, turning right, passing the tall entrance pillars of the manor gate.

My father's office was in a new building, smart and prosperous. A clerk showed me into his room with the deference due to the great man's daughter. It was a new sensation to be treated with respect. My father was writing a letter when I entered and did not immediately look up. I imagined it was a ploy he used often to make himself appear important. His desk was vast, of the same shiny wood as the paneling on the walls. To the side was an ornate marble fireplace with a mirror above. It would be fearsomely hot in here when the fire was lit.

When he did eventually stand up to greet me, there was a wary look in his eyes. Unlike my mother, my father and I understood one another perfectly, which was more of a curse than a blessing.

"Constance." He kissed my cheek. "What a pleasure to see you. You have been to visit your mother?"

"Of course," I said. "And now I have come to speak with you."

He gestured me to the chair. "Please…"

I looked around the office, taking my time. "You are very well set up here," I said. "And the house…so many new and expensive items. The mill must be doing well."

"It is." He sat back and laced his fingers over his stomach. It was a very well-filled stomach straining against his embroidered waistcoat. "I have expanded my business into ironmongery and upholstery, and have taken a share in the stone quarries."

"Mother said that you are lending money, as well," I said. I smiled at the flicker of annoyance that crossed his face. He did not appreciate her indiscretions, even within the family. "She is proud of your achievements," I said. "She thinks you might even open a bank in the near future?"

He made a noncommittal noise. "Perhaps."

"And buy one of the new houses on the hill," I said. "She is very excited at the prospect of moving in with the gentry."

He smiled. The genuine affection my parents had for each other was sweetly touching even as it baffled me. "Clarice deserves all good things that I can give her," he said.

"It is a pity then," I said, "that the money that funds such happiness is so tainted. We all know it does not come from the mill, Father. Nor from the limestone quarries, no matter how popular Swindon stone may be to line the halls of London."

A change came over him at once. He sat up straight, rigid, eyes narrowed as he watched my face. "You have always known of my additional sources of funds," he said softly. "It is no secret within the family."

"No," I said. "Of course it is not. And Jack and Billy and Sam... I assume that they are all involved with the Moonrakers too."

My father sighed. "There is no shame in it in this town."

That was true. Being one of the Swindon Moonrakers conferred a certain respect in the town, for such was the contrary admiration men had for lawbreakers. There was a long tradition of smuggling in this part of the world. It had started at least a century before when French and Dutch merchants had settled in Swindon and, not unreasonably, missed the brandy and gin distilled in their own countries. The trade was lucrative for those prepared to take the risks of running contraband. My father had been one such as a young man, making connections with the free traders of the south coast to bring their goods across the barren reach of Salisbury Plain to safe storage in the town.

My father, though, being an ambitious man, had not stopped there. Soon he was running a network of smugglers northwards to the new cloth towns whose need for refreshment was as great as those in the south. And so his business had grown, and he had brought in new investors, people such as Lord Gerard and Mr. Goddard and Mr. Villett, even the vicar of Holy Rood, gentlemen, men of the cloth, happy to turn a blind eye for the sake of cheap brandy, even if they were magistrates.

"Have we not spoken of this before?" My father added, impatient, when I did not reply, "That it is better for you and your mother to look the other way and say nothing when it comes to matters of business?"

"I can see why that would suit you," I said, "but I am beginning to wonder what benefit the smuggling business brings to me."

My father made an impatient gesture. "What is it that you want, Connie? Money?" He was already reaching into his drawer. I heard the chink of coin.

"No," I said, and his hand stilled. "I want to be free," I said. "It ill becomes a successful businessman to have a daughter in service even if it is with the Gerards of Lydiard Park. I want a business of my own. You know I would be good at it. I have a sharper mind than any of my brothers."

I saw the spark of interest light his eyes, the excitement of the true speculator as he considered the idea. Then it was doused as he sighed.

"You know that is not possible."

"I am tired of being Lord Gerard's spy," I said. "I did not like it when first the idea was suggested, and I like it even less now."

My father sighed again, leaning back in his great chair in such a manner as to make me fearful for its survival beneath his weight. "You know the reasons he chose you."

"He has a hold over you," I said.

His face puckered as though he had bitten on a sour fruit. That was not at all what he had meant.

"He wanted someone quick and clever," he said. Still he was trying to flatter me.

"And he has a hold over you," I repeated, "and you must do his bidding, and therefore so must I."

This time my father was silent. I could tell he did not wish to see his weakness exposed in such stark terms, but it was the truth. At some point in his criminal career he had made an error and lost control of the smuggling trade. Oh, he still held high office in the organization, but he no longer called the tune. In his place was Lord Gerard's man, Mr. Binks, a man of ruthlessness and cunning that went beyond the ordinary. No one knew him; no one had seen his face, except perhaps Lord Gerard who pulled his strings.

Father had given up the pretense. "You understand the circumstances precisely," he said. "At present it suits my situation to agree to whatever Lord Gerard demands, and therefore so must you."

"Unless the balance of power could be changed," I said.

His gaze fastened on me fiercely. "How might that happen?" he asked. As I said, he and I understood one another, and he knew I was offering him something infinitely precious: freedom.

I smiled. "It will happen like this," I said.

I opened my bag and took out a small glass vial that I had stoppered very tightly. In it were collected a few, a very few, white flakes that I had taken from the golden gown that Lord Gerard had ordered me to destroy. I nodded to father to hold out his palm, and I tipped the powder on to it. He sniffed, dabbed a finger in it, tasted it. For a moment his expression was blank, and then he looked up, sharp and swift as a hunting dog getting a scent.

"This is…"

"Poison." I nodded. "We would need an apothecary to examine it to be sure, but I believe it is."

"Where did this come from?"

"It was in a gown that Lord Gerard gave as a gift to my lady," I said. "The material is laced with it."

He stared at me as though he could not understand what I was saying. "He gave her a poisoned gown?"

I nodded. "Exactly so."

He looked bemused. "How might such a thing be accomplished?"

I felt a flash of irritation. What did it matter how the gown had been made or how the poison had been added to it? It was the chance it offered us that was important.

"I have no notion," I said. "Don't you see what this means?" Impatience gripped me. "We know Lord Gerard tried to murder his wife. Now *we* have a hold over *him*. We can make him do what *we* want instead of the reverse."

Father shook his head. "You could never prove it."

"I have the gown," I said. "It is full of this powder and I know it to be lethal. It has already killed a cat. Besides—" I enlarged on my plan. "I know the dressmaker. She could be persuaded to speak if we offered her sufficient inducement. I am sure of it. Lord Gerard owes her a great deal of money."

Father was shaking his head. His reluctance puzzled and disappointed me, for I was so fired up by the thought of being free of Lord Gerard that I had no patience for discussion. I had not thought my father was a timid man, and this cautiousness confounded me.

"I don't understand," I said, after a silence in which my father had refused to meet my eyes. "This could buy you your freedom from Lord Gerard, from Mr. Binks, from all of them. And for me too—"

"Lord Gerard is a dangerous man to cross." My father interrupted me. He fidgeted with the items on his desk, the inkstand, the quill and the paper. "Perhaps you have not seen it, but there is a violence in him."

"Oh, I have seen it," I said, thinking of the way he had treated my lady and remembering too the harshness of his grip on me. "I know he can be both cruel and violent." I took a deep breath. "But, Father, I believe he is also a lazy man. He likes matters to go his own way of course, but when they do not, he does not wish to trouble himself. He would let me go easily in the end because it would not matter enough to him."

I stopped, waited. Father was still silent.

"You're afraid of him," I said, and it came out like an accusation.

"Not of him." My father was still shuffling his papers and avoiding looking at me. "I am afraid of Binks. I do not pretend otherwise. Binks is dangerous in a different way. He is cold and merciless—and he has a long reach. We could never truly be free."

"So you are not even prepared to try," I said. I was trembling now but with anger, not fear. All I could think was that Father had failed me for a second time. First he had sold my services like a whore, and then when I offered him the chance of freedom, he had not the courage to take it.

"I shall just have to fend for myself then," I said.

He reached out a hand to me across his desk. There was fear in his eyes now. I saw it and despised him. "Connie. You do not understand. I beg you not to go against Lord Gerard. Binks will crush you."

"I understand perfectly," I said. "Whatever you pretend, you are not concerned for me. Your profits are more important than your daughter." I thought of my mother sitting so proud amongst her ugly new possessions, and my heart clenched with love and pity. "Have no fear, Father," I said. "I shall do nothing to hurt my mother even if I could happily send *you* to perdition."

I took the vial of poison from his desk and pushed it down into my bag beside the golden gown. I had folded the gown small and sealed it tight to contain its evil, yet still I felt its power. There was a malevolence about it that crept into the room with us, sowing discord. If it had not been so fanciful I would have imagined that it had worked on my father's weak spirit and made him even more of a broken reed. As for me, it made me shudder and look over my shoulder in suspicion. I am not a person who believes such far-fetched things normally. My grandmother, who was a laundress for the Goddards, once said that only the rich and idle have time for fanciful feelings and emotions. The rest of us are too busy doing to be thinking.

As I went out, my father had not moved, as still as the marble carving above the ornate fireplace, his expression closed, fear in his eyes.

12

Fenella

"YOU LOOK TERRIBLE," JESSIE SAID, OPENING the door to Fen the following day. "Come in and sit down before you fall down."

"I don't look that bad," Fen protested. She peered in the hall mirror. "Do I?"

"Pretty bad," Jessie said with all the bluntness of an old friend. "I was worried about you when you rang last night," she went on, closing the door behind Fen and leading her through to the huge open living area of the barn conversion. "If I hadn't had a few drinks I would have driven over to see you. What was that phone call all about?"

"Oh... Nothing." Fen felt awkward. She had hoped that Jessie had forgotten about her panicked call the previous night. She had tried to forget it herself. An entire bottle of rosé wine had been the means she had chosen to blot out her febrile imagination: the conviction that she had seen Jake that night and the terror she had felt to find his name written on the glass in the bathroom. The evening was something of a blur to her now, but she remembered turning the TV on and watching mindless program after program with the sound turned up. The rosé had finally softened the edges of her fear until a sort of resigned acceptance had taken her over and she had fallen asleep. It was no wonder she felt like hell now. The only good thing to come out of the entire experience was that she had decided to take the gown back to Lydiard Park. She planned to go the very next day. Somehow it felt as though that might make a positive difference.

Jessie went across to the worktop and picked up a frosted glass, handing it to Fen.

"It clearly isn't nothing," she said. "What's up?"

"I'm sleeping badly," Fen said, truthfully. "Bad dreams, that sort of thing."

It was true that Jake was a bad dream, but was he more? She could not tell. It terrified her that she might be imagining all the Jake-related stuff that was happening. She didn't want even to think about it.

Jessie gave her a searching look. "Remember my advice? You're not going to be able simply to dismiss the past without experiencing some resonances, Fen. I know you saw a counselor for a while but go back if you need to. Or see a doctor."

"I will," Fen said, thinking that if Jessie knew even a half of what had been going on, she would be getting hold of a psychiatrist on speed dial. She took a sip of her drink. "Homemade lemonade? Oh, that's so good."

"I thought we could have lunch outside. Isn't this weather bliss?" Jessie took the hint of a change of subject, unusually for her. Fen felt a rush of gratitude. She followed her friend through the big glass doors and out onto the terrace. It faced south and was in full sun, but a striped umbrella shaded the table where Jessie had already set out a picnic.

"Guacamole!" Fen said, subsiding into a deck chair. "And sour cream dip. You are an angel."

Jessie looked smug. "I think I've remembered all the stuff we used to take on those picnics we had with Kesia and Laura in the school holidays."

"Cucumber sandwiches?" Fen said. "They need to be curling at the edges to be truly authentic."

"Funny how we used to love those," Jessie said, picking one up and biting into it. "They don't really taste of much, do they?"

They chatted for a bit about Jessie and Dev's trip to Paris and Fen's plans for the following term at the college and any number of other inconsequential things that cropped up. It didn't feel like a day for serious conversation, just a lovely relaxing day in the sun, the sort of day Fen had almost forgotten existed. Jessie didn't mention her family at all and Fen didn't ask, and it was the only small shadow in the sky because she felt bad about holding out on her best friend.

"I'm so glad you came back," Jessie said. They had cleared the lunch away and brewed some tea and were sitting in the deck chairs in the shade of the apple tree now. "It feels right, somehow. As though we belong here, as though we have roots going back a long way."

"I don't really belong anywhere," Fen said. "I never have."

"Here is as good as anywhere then," Jessie said contentedly. She turned her head slightly towards Fen. "Will you stay, do you think?"

"I don't know," Fen admitted. "I still feel a bit..." She made a slight gesture with her hands. "Restless, I suppose. I haven't really found myself again yet. I have plans for what I want to do, increase my vintage sales and maybe open a shop one day, but whether I'll stay in Swindon to do that, I don't know."

"Perhaps if you meet someone new..." Jessie sounded hesitant.

Fen thought of Hamish. "I don't want to build my life around a relationship," she said. "Not again. I need to work things out for myself first before I get involved with anyone else." She settled her sunglasses more firmly on her nose and smiled. "Oh, Jess, this is so *nice*."

Jessie smiled too, but she still had a faintly anxious crease between her brows. Fen watched her for a moment, then said: "So what is it you're not telling me?"

Jessie jumped, then blushed guiltily, reminding Fen forcibly of the times they had been caught doing something naughty at school. Jessie had been such a good girl it had always mortified her to be told off. Fen had hated it too, but she had pretended she didn't care. Unlike Jessie there had been no one at home to be disappointed in her.

"I know about you and Hamish," Jessie blurted out.

Fen sat bolt upright, spilling her tea. "What? I mean... How? There is no me and Hamish!"

Jessie paused from mopping up the tea to give her a very hard stare. "Fenella Brightwell, I never thought you would lie to me." She shook her head slightly. "I've been waiting all afternoon for you to tell me. I even gave you a chance just now, but you wouldn't take it. It's lucky I like you so much, or I'd be really annoyed with you."

"I wasn't holding out on you," Fen said, blushing. "There's nothing to tell."

"Right," Jessie said. "Of course not. So how come Laura saw the two of you together in Hamish's car in Old Town? He was just dropping you off by The Lawns."

"Laura Pye?" Fen said. "Laura who we went to school with?"

"Who else?" Jessie said. "She couldn't wait to tell me. She was full of how thrilled I must be that my brother and my best friend had got together. I felt like a fool not knowing."

"God, it's like living in a village," Fen said involuntarily. "I had no idea."

"If the two of you want to have a secret affair, you should be more careful," Jessie said piously.

"Now you really are leaping ahead," Fen said. "We've only met twice."

Jessie grinned. "At last—some information. So... Tell me more." She poured another cup of tea for them both and settled down with a biscuit, pushing the tin towards Fen.

"There really isn't anything going on," Fen repeated. "I met Hamish on the train that night I came back from the get-together in London. We got chatting. I didn't realize who he was at the time."

"Then what happened?" Jessie said.

"Nothing," Fen said. "I met him again in Hungerford yesterday when he thought I had stolen something."

"Okay, that's different and original," Jessie said. "What was that all about?"

"It was just a misunderstanding," Fen said evasively. "We had a picnic together down by the canal—" She broke off as she saw Jessie smiling.

"What?" she demanded. "Hamish gave me a lift home, that's all."

"When are you seeing him again?"

"I'm not," Fen said. "It isn't like that. We just bumped into each other a couple of times, that's all."

Jessie ate a third biscuit. "But has he asked you out?"

"No," Fen said. "Well, yes, I suppose... He offered to

help me with something to do with work. But I turned him down."

Jessie's face fell.

"What?" Fen demanded again. "I can't go out with him just to make *you* happy!"

Jessie giggled. "But you do like him."

Fen pulled a face. "Don't put me on the spot."

"So you do." Jessie smiled, closed her eyes and tilted her face up towards the sun. "That's okay then."

"You look as smug as the Cheshire cat," Fen said crossly.

"Whatever," Jessie said. "You'll see."

There was silence for a little while, the birds calling, a tractor passing by away over the fields. It was so different from London and the other cities she had made her home. Fen wondered whether she could ever settle for this sort of life, ever settle at all.

"I thought I'd go to Lydiard Park tomorrow," she said. "I haven't been since I came back to Swindon. Do you remember that school trip all those years ago—" She broke off as she heard Jessie give a gasp. Her friend had turned chalk white. Fen took the tilting mug from her hand before more tea could be spilt.

"Are you okay?" she said. "Jessie?" She put a hand on Jessie's arm. "What's wrong?"

"Sorry." Jessie was recovering a bit of color. She sat back in the chair, rubbing a hand across her forehead. "You startled me, that's all. I hadn't thought about that day for so long, and then suddenly out of the blue a couple of weeks ago there was something about it in the paper and it reminded me—"

"Slow down," Fen said. She frowned. "What are you talking about? What was in the papers and what has this got to do with the school trip?"

Jessie shuddered. "You remember! That horrible day! You got locked in the toilets and we all had to search for you."

"Well, I didn't really," Fen said. "I made that up because something weird happened. But more importantly, what happened to *you*?"

Jessie gripped her hand. "Ugh, I'll never forget it," she said. "I'd seen you going into that little room off the state bedroom, the one with all the china and paintings. So I followed you, but you weren't there. I was kind of spooked that you'd just disappeared into thin air—" she shivered again "—so I ran back out into the next room. Do you remember it? There was a horrible man there all drunk and abusive, and he yelled at me."

"You saw him too?" Fen said. "So did I. I thought they were filming a TV program or something."

Jessie shook her head. "They weren't. Anyway, he shouted at me to get out and to take the box with me. I... Well, I was so scared I just did what he said. I grabbed this box that was sitting on the table next to him and I ran all the way back to the coach."

"You should have said something," Fen said. She squeezed Jessie's fingers. "I had no idea."

"I didn't want anyone to know," Jessie said. She gave Fen a watery smile. "You know what a wuss I was. I hated causing trouble, so I was really pleased everyone was still looking for you and not taking any notice of me. And when I realized I still had the box with me I felt awful. I didn't know what to do. I thought I'd be arrested for stealing it."

"Oh, Jess." Fen hugged her. "What was it—some sort of antique?"

"Sort of, I suppose," Jessie said. "I opened it when I got home and it contained a jeweled pin, the sort people used to put in neck cloths in the eighteenth century."

"That sounds lovely," Fen said.

"It was horrible," Jessie said. "It was made of a picture in a small oval frame with a drawing of a hanged man and next to him a coffin. They're called memento mori, apparently. They were very popular as keepsakes in Georgian times." She pushed her hair back from her face, and Fen noticed that she was shaking slightly. "That was what was in the paper a few weeks ago—an article about a collection of memento mori, including the one I'd taken all those years ago. It brought the whole horrible day back to me."

"I'm sorry," Fen said. "It sounds awful and such a weird thing to have as a keepsake. More like a threat or a warning, like something the mafia would send."

"That's what the curator said when she saw it," Jessie said. "I took the box back to Lydiard Park the weekend after, and explained that someone had asked me to take it out of the drawing room that day and that I had forgotten to hand it back. The staff seemed pretty surprised, actually, and said the pin wasn't on their inventory. They had no record of it. But they took it anyway, and said they would try and find out about it."

"You took it back," Fen said. "Yes, you would. You're not like me."

"I know you used to steal stuff all the time when we were at school," Jessie said candidly, meeting her eyes, "and you never seemed bothered. We all thought you were very cool. But I wasn't like that. I was scared."

"Oh God," Fen said. "I was scared too. I might have seemed cool, but really I was horribly mixed up. All I really wanted was to be like you, with your lovely family and your...your principles, I suppose...and everything."

Jessie squeezed her hand. "I think I realized that when we

got older," she said. She smiled at Fen. "You know, we should have had this conversation a long time ago."

"Yes," Fen said. "Perhaps we should have. I took something that day too," she added. "A golden gown."

"The one that was lying over the back of the chair?" Jessie said. "I saw it. It was glorious." She did a double take. "You stole it? Why?"

"I don't know," Fen admitted. "It kind of called out to me and I took it. But unlike you, I didn't give it back. I've still got it. That's why I was planning on going to Lydiard tomorrow. I'm taking it back."

"Better late than never, I suppose," Jessie said. "Wow. What a weird day that was."

"How do you know we hadn't stumbled on to a TV or film set?" Fen asked, remembering Jessie's earlier comment. "You seemed pretty certain."

"I asked," Jessie said simply. "When I took the box back. They said there was no filming taking place that day."

Fen sat back. "Then what was going on? Did they have room guides dressed as historical reenactors or something?"

"Apparently not," Jessie said slowly. "When I took the box back I told the curator what had happened. She seemed really surprised. I described the old man, and she said there was no one like that on the staff. She seemed very concerned and I was afraid she'd start asking awkward questions in case he was a child molester, or that she'd tell the school or something—" She caught Fen's glance. "Like I said, I hated causing trouble. So I just said he must have been a visitor, and then I shut up about it and went home." She paused for a moment. "I've no idea what happened that day," she finished. "If it didn't sound so ludicrous I'd say we must both have seen a ghost. Not that my scientific mind agrees with such phenomena."

"Whereas my considerably less scientific one thinks there must be plenty of things that science can't explain," Fen said. "The dress, for example, and the jeweled pin. They were real, not a figment of our imaginations."

Jessie nodded. Her expression was still troubled. "So you're implying that the man might have been real as well in some way? That we were *there* somehow, rather than that he was in our time?"

Fen took a deep breath. "I hadn't thought of it in those terms," she admitted, "but we did take something away, something tangible. How could we do that if..." She allowed her words to tail off. There was a silence, loud with the chirping of birds and the unmistakable twenty-first century sound of an airplane overhead.

"Do you remember the entrance hall, with the family portraits?" Jessie said suddenly.

"Yeah," Fen said. "They all had long noses and no chin."

"He was there," Jessie said. "The drunken old man. I recognized his portrait on the way out. Last week, when I saw the newspaper article about the memento mori, I looked him up on the internet. He was the fourth Viscount Gerard and he died in 1787."

Fen checked her watch. "It's nearly four o'clock. Do you think they'll still be open now?"

"Who?" Jessie looked mystified.

"Lydiard Park," Fen said. She took out her phone and tapped into Google, pressing the link for the telephone number. It was answered on the fourth ring.

"Hi," she said. "This is a rather odd enquiry, but I wonder if you can help me? Do you have a catalog there of the items in your collection?"

She waited whilst the receptionist at the other end passed

her on to someone called Dr. Teal, the curator, and repeated her enquiry. It was all very swift and efficient. Yes, there was an online register of all the items that were, or had been, in the museum collection for the past seventy years, since the house had come into the ownership of the council. No, there was no record of a golden gown embroidered with silver thread, circa mid-eighteenth century, ever being a part of the collection. No, they probably would not want the gown donated as it had no proven link with the house and they did not have the means to conserve textiles anyway. She would need to contact a specialist such as the Victoria & Albert Museum.

Fen thanked Dr. Teal and ended the call.

"There's no record of Lydiard Park Museum ever having the golden gown in their collection," she said slowly, "just as there was no record of your memento mori and its box."

"Which means," Jessie said, "that they weren't officially part of the contents of the house that day we went on the school trip."

"Right," Fen said. "Just as the fourth Viscount Gerard presumably wasn't officially part of the contents of the house that day either."

Jessie giggled. "Which means…" she said again.

"I don't know," Fen said. "If it wasn't so utterly bizarre, I'd say that it means we weren't there in the 2000s." She shook her head. "For that moment at least, we were in a different time entirely."

13

Isabella

Summer 1763

"I HAVE SEEN THE FUTURE," I SAID. "IT APPEARS delightful. I am a famous artist respected for my designs and I am married to someone other than Eustace, someone by the initial *B*."

I looked at Dr. Baird—John—under my lashes as I spoke, hoping that he might take the hint. We were lying in the hay in one of the barns tucked away on the edge of the estate. It had been John's idea; I think he liked tumbling me like a milkmaid, and I must admit that I liked it too, although the hay was rather too prickly.

John was stroking my bare arm thoughtfully, watching the play of his fingers over my skin, rather like a connoisseur admiring a precious object. For that was how he viewed me, as something infinitely rich and valuable that he possessed, at least for now. It was very agreeable to be treated like rare china, but there was a darker strand to his obsession with me too. Often he would make me strip off my clothes and simply lie naked, exposed to his gaze. Sometimes he would touch me at will whilst I must stay quite still and silent beneath his hands and his mouth. His greatest satisfaction was to make me abandon myself to him in wanton delight, begging like a harlot to be pleasured. He loved to shock me, once undressing me in the gardens in full daylight and taking me standing against one of the statues of Eustace's worthy ancestors. How that rough stone scored my skin. How much he enjoyed having me literally under the nose of my husband's ancient family.

He never hurt me, as Eustace had been wont to do, but even so there was an intensity in his possession of me that disturbed me. Gone was the sincere and respectful man I had known in London. Now, for example, it was as though he was not even listening to me as his hands swept over my bare body and he studied me absorbedly, as though I were a marble statue or a work of art.

"What an imagination you have," he murmured.

I immediately felt irritated that he was not listening to me properly. He was like every other man I had known; he could think only of one thing when he was in the throes of desire, and it was not conversation.

Truth to tell, the affair had already lost a little of its charm for me. I am fickle, I know, but I cannot seem to help myself. Once the initial thrill of a liaison has faded, I soon find myself finding fault. With Gower, for example, I soon noticed that his breath smelled of wine and although he was an accomplished lover, he would always relieve himself loudly in a piss pot immediately after we had coupled. Then there was the Earl of Farne. I do not believe that Eustace knew of my dalliance with Farne because it was a matter of a few nights

only. I fled his bed when I discovered he could only rise to
the occasion if he spanked me first.

As for John, he might worship my beauty and long to own
me, but he did not value me for my mind as well as my body.
He was as dismissive as most men are of a woman's intelli-
gence. This could be useful at times, of course. It is an easy
way to trick men and use them to my advantage, and that
was why I needed John.

"It seems that Eustace must die," I said. "In order for me
to wed again."

"It is entirely possible that he will," John said, "given the
grave nature of his excesses."

I played with a blade of straw, avoiding his gaze. "I am
not so sure," I said. "Sometimes I believe he will survive me
just to spite me."

John smiled but said nothing, and again I felt irritated, pa-
tronized, not taken seriously. I remembered that he had once
praised my drawing and asked that I paint him. It had not
happened, other than a few pencil sketches of him that I had
snatched once whilst he was sleeping. In fact he had mentioned to me that he had had a portrait done recently by no
lesser artist than Joshua Reynolds, a man very much on the
rise, and I had thought this was a ridiculous affectation for a
doctor. It was as though my art were inferior, and only Mr.
Reynolds could do him justice.

"You may remember," I said, "that once you offered to do
anything in your power to help me."

He made a noncommittal sound and moved closer to me.
I moved a little farther away, making sure that as I did so I
afforded him a pretty view of my breasts just to keep his attention.

"It seems to me," I continued, "that it would be useful to

speed the process a little so that Eustace may leave me a grieving widow. We cannot rely on fate alone."

I had his attention now. There was no doubt about that. John Baird was not a stupid man, and he understood me exactly. His gaze came up to mine, vivid hazel eyes fixed intently on me.

"What are you suggesting?" he said softly.

"Eustace has to die," I said again. "And you have the means to make that happen. You are a doctor. There must be ways..."

He was utterly still, his gaze shuttered, expression blank. It unnerved me. I wondered if I had misread him, if he would recoil from me in shock and horror, if the ruthlessness I had sensed in him was an illusion.

"If you provide the means," I said, "I will administer it."

I held my breath and waited. All on this one gamble...

He laughed.

I was taken aback and then I was angry. "If you are seeking to make a game of me—" I started to say haughtily, but he reached for me and tumbled me beneath him, holding me tightly.

"Isabella." He brushed the hair tenderly from my flushed cheeks. "It seems I have misjudged you. Who would have guessed that you had an appetite for murder?"

Then he smiled, a brilliant smile, hard as diamonds, and with a rush of relief I saw that I had not mistaken him after all. This was the ruthless man I had known that day when he had pressed me to take him as my lover. I could see that the idea of a conspiracy against Eustace excited him.

"And what would be my reward for such a service?" he asked.

"Anything that it is in my power to give," I said. My voice

was shaking. I could not quite believe the enormity of my plans, nor that he would help me. What had been a dream, a longing, had abruptly transformed into reality as soon as the words were spoken.

"There is one thing that I want." He was watching me, a curious look in his eyes. I could not read it. "There is a gown in your possession, silver and gold. I would like you to wear it for me."

I was puzzled for a moment. Odd as it seemed, it was almost as though I had forgotten the golden gown once I had handed it over to Constance to be mended. It felt as though it had passed completely from my mind, subsumed like almost everything else in my desire to paint. The art was my obsession now and, I blush to admit it, so were the carnal delights John gave me. I was insatiable that summer.

"I did not know you had seen the gown." I spoke slowly, some strange emotion stirring in me. Had Constance shown the dress to him? I knew she had a fancy for him. It showed in her face every time she looked at him.

"I saw it in London," he said easily, "that time I came to visit you after Gerard had left for Paris. I thought then how divine it looked and how beautiful you would look wearing it."

Such flattery. Yet still the doubts disturbed me. Something felt awry here, though I was not quite sure what it was.

"I might not have it here with me," I said. "I did not bring my entire wardrobe from London."

He looked surprised as though this had not occurred to him. "Oh. Well, if you do not have it with you—"

"As it turns out," I said, "I do have it here. And of course I will wear it for you."

He smiled brilliantly again. "Wear it for me with nothing beneath so that I may pull up your skirts and have you in it," he said.

"I will," I said, "but not until Eustace is dead."

His gaze sharpened on me. "You strike a hard bargain, madam."

"No more than you do," I said.

He lowered his mouth to mine. "Then we are well matched," he said, when he broke the kiss. "So be it."

Constance

I knew all about their affair from the first. I was not the sort of servant to spy through keyholes or indulge in gossip, but I did not need to be. Lady Gerard was blatant. She sent for him almost every day:

"Send a boy to fetch Dr. Baird from Brinkworth, Constance. I have the headache."

"Call Dr. Baird for me, Constance. I need a tisane to help me sleep."

It was not a tisane she was wanting. She took me for a fool if she thought I believed that. No longer was I required to stay with her when he visited. She would see him alone and lock the door behind them too. Afterwards she looked all bright and glowing and happy. On the fine days she would take her sketching book outside and disappear into the grounds for hours. I imagine he met her somewhere and tumbled her in a barn like the village drab.

I envied her, trysting with him whilst I laundered her clothes, sewed buttons and stitched seams. She knew that I knew what was going on, just as I had when she had been Lord Gower's mistress. We never spoke of it, of course. That was the unwritten rule between mistress and maid, and she assumed I was on her side. I hated her for that, for taking my complaisance for granted. I also hated her being able to command him where I, a little dab of a girl, had not been able to hold him for more than a few moments. I hated her for a vast number of other things besides. My resentment devoured me whole that summer.

Every so often I would take out the golden gown and stroke it, and promise myself that soon—very soon—it would make my fortune. Lady Gerard had said no more about my mending it, and I had no intention of returning it to her anyway. As Father had not dared to blackmail Lord Gerard I thought that I might do so myself when I had the chance. I had a mad idea of persuading him to pay me off so that I could go wherever I pleased, far from him and his murderous plans, and his unfaithful wife and her dangerous games. But Lord Gerard was reputed in Italy now, according to Pound, the butler, and he showed no inclination of returning to Lydiard. I thought this would suit her ladyship since her indiscretions became ever more barefaced, but in fact she mentioned more than once that she could not wait for his lordship to return.

"Should you have means to contact Lord Gerard," she said to me one night, "I pray you might appeal to him on my behalf. I miss his company."

"Why would you imagine I should have the least influence with Lord Gerard, madam?" I asked, feigning astonishment, and she gave a heavy sigh.

"Oh, I know not, Constance, other than that you always seemed to deal well together."

"You are mistaken," I said. "His lordship pays no attention to me." I felt chilled to think she might have guessed that I spied for him, and yet did it truly matter? Soon, I thought, I would be free of them both.

One evening, I was in Lady Gerard's dressing room tidying

away her clothes from that afternoon. She had had grass stains on her gown when she came back that day, which she had told me had been caused when she knelt to draw a very pretty marguerite growing down by the lake. She even showed me her sketch of the flower as though to give credence to her tale, and it was indeed a pretty little innocent-looking plant with its open white petals and its slender stem. The grass stains had been nigh on impossible to remove as they had set themselves in the very fibers of her gown, and I thought she would probably discard it when she saw the shadow of the marks were still there. However, I would launder it again, to prove that I had tried.

I closed the drawer of the chest quietly so as not to wake her for she had retired early with another sick headache. I had thought this one genuine since she had been out in the sun so long this afternoon. However, I was about to go out onto the landing when I heard her laughing, softly, with such pleasure, and then a sigh. There was no mistaking that.

I froze. So now not only was my lady consorting with her lover during the day under the pretense of his visits to check on her health, she was secretly smuggling him into her chamber at night. I was not sure why I felt shocked; it was not at her behavior but perhaps I was surprised at the risks she was prepared to take. This was too blatant. Then the anger took me, and I wondered why she had not simply asked me to bring Dr. Baird to her via the backstairs. Perhaps I should suggest it, and then we could be done with all pretense.

I have said that I was not one to look through keyholes. I lied. The fury in me felt like a creature possessing me, and I knelt down and pushed aside the keyhole cover to peer into the room beyond.

I saw them then, in the candlelight. She was on hands and

knees on the bed, stark naked, head thrown back in ecstasy, her breasts bouncing as she was taken from behind. But the man so lustily ravishing her was not the good doctor. I recognized those buttocks as belonging to Jim, the second footman, who was a well set-up lad who frequently took the maids' fancy and, it seemed, also appealed to my lady's taste.

I realized I *was* shocked now, though perhaps only because I was surprised that my lady had stooped so low as to invite a servant to her bed. But barely had I registered the shock when it was superseded by another, far greater one. There was movement in the room beyond the bed hangings and Dr. Baird stepped forward into the candlelight. I realized that he had been standing beyond my vision, watching as I was. Unlike the naked footman, he was fully dressed in breeches and shirt. His waistcoat was open, his neck cloth undone.

"Very nice," he said, reaching out to stroke my lady's breasts. "Don't stop." His hands went to the buttons on his breeches as he stood before her.

If eavesdroppers never hear good of themselves, what do Peeping Toms see? I did not know how I felt to witness such depravity. I should have been appalled, horrified. Instead, to my utter mortification, I felt a burning excitement and lust, frustration and anger, fury and desperate longing. I wanted to be in there with them. I imagined that I was.

And as I stared, Dr. Baird looked up and he saw me watching and smiled at me, intimate, beckoning. I backed away and stumbled to the dressing room door, crashing out onto the landing careless of who heard me.

I did not sleep that night but lay awake in a fever of lust and jealousy, tormented by what I had seen. In the morning I was tired and bleary-eyed, and when Lady Gerard showed no signs of stirring I decided to go outside in the hope that the fresh air might banish my headache and restore my good spirits. It was a glorious summer day, the sun high and bright, the sky a clear sharp blue, and yet it felt as though the beauty of it could not touch me. As a child I had loved the outdoors, the splash of the water in the mill pool, the wind through the trees of the Goddards's parkland. I wondered when I had lost that pleasure. It felt as though everything was tarnished now.

Down by the lake I saw a figure loitering beneath the trees by the bridge, and recognized it, a moment too late, as Dr. Baird. I had no wish to speak to him and paused on the edge of flight but realized that I would have looked foolish in the extreme if I turned and ran away. So I raised my chin and made to pass on by with only a brief nod of the head. However, he stepped directly into my path.

"Miss Lawrence."

"Dr. Baird." I could not look him in the eye, not after what I had seen the previous night, not knowing that he knew I had spied on them all.

There was a silence, hotter than the sunshine. After a moment he said gently, "You really should not watch, you know. It only serves to upset you."

That brought my gaze up to his and made my fury burst through.

"How could you do it?" I demanded. "How could you treat her so? I thought you cared for her, but I know now that you do not."

"She likes it," he said, with a careless shrug. "It pleases her. You are a little innocent, are you not, Constance, to imagine otherwise."

"I may be naïve, but you willfully misunderstand me," I said hotly. "Perhaps I should have asked why you do it?"

"Ah." He seemed amused. He turned away from me to gaze

out across the expanse of lawns running down to the lake. "I do it because I can," he said, simply, after a moment. "Don't you find, Constance, that it gives satisfaction for people like us to take what we may from people like them?"

I looked at him with loathing, because of course he was right and I hated that he could see that I felt the same way. I felt transparent to him, vulnerable. After a moment I forced myself to break away and walked off down the path, my head held high. I could hear his laughter following me.

That night he did not come to my lady's chamber, nor as far as I am aware, did the footman. Lady Gerard seemed in a distracted mood.

"Constance," she said, as I was replacing one of her empty vials of orange blossom cologne with another, freshly made. "The golden gown, the one I entrusted to you to repair? Is it ready?"

I floundered a little. It had not occurred to me that she might ask for the gown back, for it seemed she had quite forgotten about it.

"I… No, madam," I said. "I have almost finished it, but I discovered that it requires some special silver thread. I thought perhaps I might visit the modiste in Swindon to find a match—"

She waved a hand to stop my rambling. "Go tomorrow. I want it ready at once."

She dismissed me on the words, seeming very displeased, so I went out into the corridor to think and draw breath. All I knew was that I could not give the gown back to her. I would not. It was the key to my freedom, and I would not give that up. Shockingly it did not occur to me to share the truth with her, or warn her that Lord Gerard had wanted to poison her. The gown's secret had become mine alone to use to my benefit. I would take it to Swindon and hide it in a safe place and then, somehow, I would think of a lie to tell my lady as to how I had lost or destroyed it.

I found my fists were clenched tight and I was pacing from one end of the landing to the other. How I must have appeared, I had no notion. I tried to calm my breathing and relax my frame. If anyone had seen me, I feared I would look crazed.

The lamps were lit, but the corridor was in shadow. The window at the end, which gave a view across to the church, was wide and dark. Automatically I raised shaking hands to draw the curtain across, my mind still occupied with how I might deceive madam and keep the gown safely hid. As I pulled the curtains closed a movement caught my eye; the south door of the church was opening silently, furtively.

I stepped back into the shadow of the window embrasure where I could still watch but remain unseen. A sliver of light showed below, spilling across the uneven flagstones by the church door. Moonrakers, I thought. Who else would be so stealthy? I knew too that they hid their contraband in churches, using the supposed piety of the priest as a cover for their criminality. I waited to see who it would be, whether I would recognize any of my father's associates or even my father or brothers themselves.

The line of light widened, and a man stepped through the doorway, followed by another. The second man held a lantern high, and by its light it was possible to see both faces illuminated against the darkness.

I stared. I almost rubbed my eyes in disbelief. For it was Lord Gerard, nowhere near Italy but here at Lydiard. And behind him was Dr. Baird.

14

Fenella

"THANK YOU FOR SEEING US AT SUCH SHORT notice," Fen said. She was sitting on the edge of a leather sofa in a warehouse conversion high above the Bristol docks, the box with the golden gown in it perched awkwardly on her knees. The sofa faced a window that spanned the whole of one side of the flat, and the view was stunning. Hamish was standing gazing out across the river, where the seagulls whirled against a moody gray sky.

"It's a pleasure," Augusta Monday said. "When Hamish called me I was quite intrigued. It isn't often that my newspaper articles cause such a stir. Usually they sink without trace."

She said it without resentment, reaching for the china teapot and pouring for them all into old-fashioned chintzy-looking porcelain cups. The whole flat, and indeed Professor Monday herself, with her *broderie anglaise* dress and severe statement glasses, was a clash between the ultramodern stripped-back style and what Fen would have called vintage chic. It worked brilliantly.

Hamish came to sit beside Fen on the sofa. She felt glad he was there, relieved in some obscure way to have allowed Jessie to persuade her to tell Hamish at least a little of what they had discussed the previous afternoon. It didn't make the situation less bizarre, but it did make her feel a little less isolated.

The newspaper article about the memento mori was on the table in front of them, alongside a number of laminated photographs of examples. One was of the tiepin and box that Jessie had described taking from Lydiard Park.

"Memento mori are odd things," Augusta said, as Fen picked up the photo and studied it. "To our eyes they seem quite grotesque with their images of skulls and gravestones, but to the Georgians the symbolism was quite different. They were sentimental items worn to remind you of a loved one and that mortality is something none of us can avoid. Some of the brooches and rings included locks of hair or other personal items."

Fen felt a rush of repulsion. The drawing on the tiepin was crude, in black and white. She could immediately see why it had disturbed Jessie so much. The face of the hanged man was a rictus of agony, his body, suspended upside down, a twisted wreck. The coffin beneath him bore the letters *EG* and 1763. The bright blue jewels of the oval frame seemed almost offensively pretty to encircle so horrible a picture.

"Yet this one really is gruesome," Hamish said. He was looking at the picture over Fen's shoulder. "It feels as though there is something malevolent about it rather than comforting."

Augusta nodded vigorously. "This item is unusual. I've never come across a memento mori quite like this before. It does appear to have a macabre purpose, as I discovered when I dug into the story behind it."

"That's the story that was reported in the paper," Fen said. She passed the laminated photograph to Hamish and picked up the copy of the *Swindon Advertiser.* "Mystery of the Swindon Moonrakers," the headline read. "Ten years of research has led Professor Augusta Monday of Bristol University to a remarkable story of murder and madness relating to the dark history of the Swindon Moonrakers."

"Very sensationalist, I'm afraid," Augusta said, with an apologetic shrug. "But it sells papers."

"I've heard of the Moonrakers," Fen said. "There's a pub called that in Swindon, isn't there? I remember my grandmother telling me they were smugglers of some sort, which always struck me as odd since Swindon is so far from the sea."

"Distribution networks," Hamish said briefly. "It wasn't just the seaside towns and villages who benefited from smugglers. There was a lot of money to be made from passing the goods on."

"Well, who knew?" Fen said.

"A number of years ago I was browsing in the Swindon Museum when the tiepin caught my eye," Augusta said. She looked at Hamish. "Of course I didn't know its provenance then—" she smiled gently "—or that your sister had taken it from Lydiard Park."

"She didn't steal it," Fen said, immediately defensive of Jessie. "It was given to her—" She broke off as Hamish squeezed her hand.

"Augusta knows that," he said. "I told her what happened."

"Sorry." Fen subsided.

"The card in the display case simply stated that it was eighteenth century," Augusta said. "The picture is so monstrous that it caught my interest, and having made a study of eighteenth century keepsakes, I asked if I might do some research on it. I hadn't realized…" She paused, sighed. "It's not often one uncovers such an extraordinary story."

"'A tale of feuding and murder to rival any contemporary TV drama,'" Hamish quoted, his lips twitching. "Or at least that's what it says in the paper.'

"I know." Augusta sighed again. "I suppose it is rather melodramatic. The fact is that smuggling was not the glamorized profession that history has made it out to be. It was rough and brutal and violent."

"And lucrative," Fen said, with feeling, "or so we're led to believe from this." She tapped the article.

"Samuel Lawrence was a rich man," Augusta agreed. "By day he was a respectable businessman with an office in Swindon Old Town, but by night he was a free trader who supplied not only the people of Swindon with duty-free brandy but also arranged its onward shipment to the growing industrial towns of the Midlands and the North. Swindon was the focus of considerable trade in this era," she added, "hard as that is to believe. Both the foreign merchants who settled there and the local population benefited from the smuggling, or 'moonraking' as it was known in the area. Samuel Lawrence's gang controlled a large network of contacts from the south coast up to Birmingham and Manchester."

"And then they had some sort of falling out," Hamish said.

"So it seems." Augusta took the photograph of the memento mori from him and studied it, a frown between her brows. "Both Lawrence and his wife were found dead, drowned in the millpond. It was reported to have been a domestic tragedy, that Lawrence had killed her in a rage and then drowned himself in a fit of remorse. But there were other rumors too, darker ones. It was said that they were both murdered as a result of a feud within the moonraking gang."

"God," Fen said blankly. "What a ghastly story."

"They were all very unpleasant people," Augusta said crisply. "I can't bear the way that smugglers and highwaymen and pirates are romanticized as heroes." She opened a folder and passed Fen another laminated photograph. Fen saw it was titled "The Moonrakers." It reminded her of a lineup for a police identification parade. A woodcut print of the Moonrakers from 1762, read the attribution. Six men in a row, cloaked, some bare headed, some in stovepipe hats, all looking sinister. Their names were engraved over their heads: Stratton, Digby, Hicks, Tilling, Beynon, Binks.

"It's like that famous picture of the Gunpowder plotters, isn't it?" Hamish said. "A sort of rogues' gallery. They were creating a legend."

"The most interesting thing I found," Augusta said, "was the way in which the story was covered up. The newspapers all dismissed it as a domestic incident, and there's no record of it being reported beyond the local area. It seemed to me that the papers at the time were under pressure from someone influential to drop it as quickly as possible."

"Who owned the papers?" Hamish asked.

Augusta smiled at him indulgently as though he was a particularly clever pupil.

"The Goddards, the Villets, respectable families who knew all about the cellars and tunnels that had been carved out under the old town to store contraband."

"Well then…" Hamish let the implication hang.

"Plus Lord Gerard, of course," Augusta said. "As you know, he was the local aristocrat, the man who owned Lydiard Park. It was rumored that he had a very expensive mistress and racehorse habit, and financed it through the proceeds of smuggling."

Fen immediately thought of Jessie—and the drunken old man they had both seen on the school trip that day. This was the one bit of the story that they had agreed not to tell Hamish or Augusta.

"Eustace Gerard," she said. "EG, like the inscription on the memento mori. But he didn't die until the 1780s, did he?"

Augusta turned her benign smile on her. "Very good! Yes, those are Eustace's initials, but not his death date. This is where the story takes a particularly interesting turn." She rummaged through the folder to take out another document, this time a scan of what looked like a handwritten accounts book.

"I can't decipher that," Fen said regretfully.

"It's from the 1763 account book of a local jeweler, Jeremiah Day," Augusta said. "I matched the description to the tiepin. He made the pin—and incorporated the drawing into it—and had it delivered to Viscount Gerard of Lydiard Park."

Hamish sat forward. "Who is recorded as commissioning it?"

"No one," Augusta said regretfully. She passed him the scan of the document.

"A private commission," Hamish read. "Damn. And it doesn't say who drew the picture either."

"It's all very secretive," Augusta agreed. "I think that rather than a commemorative piece, the pin may have been commissioned as a threat to Lord Gerard. It has that appearance to it."

"The eighteenth century equivalent of a horse's head in your bed," Fen said. "A sort of 'watch your back—we're coming for you.'"

"Exactly," Augusta said. "Although that's pure speculation on my part. I can't prove it." She brightened. "Still, now that I know the tiepin definitely came from Lydiard, I will research it some more. And I understand there is a gown too?" She looked at Fen expectantly. "I'm no expert on textiles but I'd like to see it."

"Thank you." Now that the moment had come to take out the golden gown, Fen felt uneasy, not for any specific reason, simply the deep visceral disquiet that the gown always brought with it. It felt as though the room was a little darker, the wind buffeting the outside of the building a little stronger and the gray waves of the harbor more sharp and spiteful.

"Hamish will have told you that it was taken from Lydiard Park at the same time as the tiepin and box," she said a little awkwardly. She wasn't sure just how much Augusta knew about her kleptomaniac habit.

"I told Augusta that your grandmother wondered if it had belonged to Lady Isabella Beaumaris, previously Lady Gerard," Hamish interjected smoothly, covering her embarrassment. "Which would, of course, fit the same time frame as the tiepin. Lord and Lady Gerard separated in 1763."

"I hadn't realized that," Fen said. She opened the lid of the box. As always, the gown seemed to light up the room with its radiance, dulling the surrounding day to even darker tones of black and gray. She heard Augusta's exclamation of surprise and pleasure:

"Oh, how beautiful it is!" And then Augusta had snatched the gown from her and was cradling it close, and in the same moment Fen saw the stiff corpse of a mouse tumble from the folds on to the floor.

"Oh my God!" she said, recoiling. "I'm so sorry. I can't imagine how that got there." Dave, she thought, would be absolutely appalled to be told there was a rodent problem in Villet House. He prided himself on the cleanliness of the building. And how the hell had a mouse gotten in the box anyway? It hadn't been there when the dress had arrived, although that probably explained the weird scratching noises she'd heard.

A cat leaped gracefully down from the windowsill and padded across the room to investigate the corpse, sniffing at it and then drawing back, its lips curled in a grimace.

"Quick," Fen said to Hamish. "Don't let it eat it—" She stopped. Hamish wasn't looking at the dead mouse. He was looking at Augusta who had dropped the gown on the floor as though it had burned her and was pressed back against her chair with her hands braced in front of her as though to ward off some unknown evil. She was frozen into a grotesque, misshapen form and did not move.

"Augusta?" he said. "Are you all right?" Then, when Augusta did not answer, did not even glance up: "Augusta!"

Fen saw Augusta jump. Her head came up jerkily. There was blankness in her eyes, a terrifying emptiness like a dark abyss, devoid of life. At the same time Fen was swept with a feeling of paralyzing cold and a sense of evil as old as time.

Fen heard Hamish give a sharp exclamation and then he had leapt up and grabbed the gown. She wanted to yell at him not to touch it but it was too late. She saw him freeze for a moment, the gown in his hands, and then it was as though he broke free, thrusting it into the box and slamming the lid down on it. Augusta made a tiny sound, and her body crumpled like a marionette when the strings were cut.

"Call an ambulance," Hamish said. He was kneeling on the floor next to Augusta's still body. "Fen—" He looked at her over his shoulder. He was very white, but Fen realized with intense relief that he was recognizably himself.

"Yes," she said shakily. She fumbled for her phone, her

fingers slipping on the touch pad. But Augusta was already stirring, straightening up and putting a hand to her head.

"What happened?" she said. "Did I faint?" She looked around, bewildered. "I've got a terrible headache."

"I'll get you some water," Fen said. She put the phone back in her pocket, surreptitiously retrieving the dead mouse on her way to the kitchen. The cat had vanished.

The kitchen was state of the art with a huge fridge, acres of stainless steel and pale wood cupboards. Fen eventually located a glass, but she couldn't find a bin anywhere, so she threw the dead mouse out of the window and washed her hands with meticulous care.

Back in the living room, Augusta was sitting bolt upright now and chattering as though she had a temperature.

"I'll be fine," she kept repeating, when Hamish suggested they should take her to the ER. "I'll sleep it off. It's just a migraine." It was clear she wanted them gone. Her gaze kept darting to the box and then skittering away as though she dared not quite look at it.

"Is there someone we could call?" Fen said. "I don't like the thought of leaving you here alone."

Augusta gave her a wan smile. "Bless you, don't worry. My cousin's popping in later for dinner. I'll get him to take me to the hospital if I'm feeling any worse." She closed her eyes. Her skin was translucently pale, and there were purple bruises beneath her eyes. "I just feel exhausted," she said. "Sorry to throw you out so abruptly."

Nothing more was said about the gown or the memento mori. Fen had the distinct impression that Professor Monday would not be rushing to offer them help in future. She and Hamish were silent as the lift took them down to the ground floor and out onto the cobbled quay. It felt a huge relief to take a lungful of fresh air, as though she had been locked away in a suffocating small room.

"I hope Professor Monday will be all right," she said as they walked back towards her car.

"I'll ring later to check," Hamish said. He had his hands deep in his pockets and his shoulders were hunched. There was a deep frown on his brow.

"What do you think happened?" Fen said slowly. "She looked as though something had sucked all the life out of her."

She glanced sideways at Hamish. He didn't answer.

"I know you felt it too," Fen said. "I saw what happened when you picked up the gown."

Hamish stopped walking. His gaze was opaque, shuttered. Fen had never thought to see him like that; Hamish had seemed so open, so direct. Now she saw that he too had his secrets and his darkness.

"I always wondered what would happen if the gown exerted its power over you," she said. "I thought that if existing habits were accentuated, you would probably suffer from an excess of niceness."

Hamish's expression lightened. "Unfortunately not," he said. He took her hand and drew her over to sit on one of the benches that looked out across the river. Fen rested the box and its dangerous cargo on the seat beside her.

"I felt possessed," Hamish said, after a very long pause. "There's no other way to describe it. You know what I mean anyway—you've told me yourself how it makes you feel. I felt a furious, tormented anger and hatred, and it was appalling. It wasn't me and yet it was in me, a part of me. It took every last shred of willpower I had to fight it."

Fen expelled a long breath. "Oh my God."

"I had a temper when I was younger," Hamish admitted. He rested his elbows on his knees, looking out across the river. "The psychologists called it anger issues. It started when I was in my teens and I fell out with Jessie. We weren't always close as siblings, you know. There was a time when we couldn't stand each other."

"I had no idea," Fen said. "Jessie never said." She thought of all the times she had envied Jessie her perfect childhood. It felt naïve now. Perhaps no one's life was entirely free of pain.

"I can remember exactly when it started," Hamish said. "I had a watch, one of those digital monstrosities that was so geeky and cool when we were young. I loved it and then Jessie broke it and threw it away. I was livid with her."

Fen felt chilled. She hadn't thought about it for years, but now she remembered that night at Jessie's house when she had raided the cloakroom. What was it she had stolen—some charms off a bracelet and a watch? She couldn't remember precisely, it was so long ago, but she felt sick.

"Hamish…" she said.

"Jess always denied she'd done it," Hamish said, "but I didn't believe her. I almost hit her, I felt so angry and frustrated." He swallowed hard. "God, it was horrible. I felt so out of control. I got into fights at school and was vile at home. Everyone said it was just teenage boy stuff, but it felt much worse, much more violent and dangerous. In a weird sort of way I almost wanted something terrible to happen just to stop me."

"And did it?" Fen asked.

Hamish shook his head. "No. Nothing dramatic happened, anyway. I got cautioned for graffiti-ing the railway tunnel, just like I told you, and I was caught smoking weed a few times. I moved on to MDMA, and then I had a bad experience with the drugs and scared myself." His mouth turned down at the corners. "So I stopped. And that was the end of my teenage rebellion."

Fen took his hand and entwined her cold fingers in his. "Thanks for telling me," she said. "It helps to know you weren't always a saint."

Hamish's smile was rueful. "Hell, I'm as flawed as anyone else."

"I still think I can give you a run for your money," Fen said. "I was the one who stole your watch."

She felt Hamish go very still at the bald admission. "Oh Fen, no," he said. "Please tell me that's not true."

"I'm really sorry," Fen said. She freed her hand from his. "If I'd known it would cause such trouble between you and Jessie…"

"You would have reined in your dishonest tendencies?" Hamish said. He rubbed a hand across his face. "Damn it, Fen…"

"I know," Fen said miserably.

"Oh well," Hamish said, after a moment. "If it hadn't been that, it would have been something else. I can't blame you for my anger management issues."

"Only for contributing to them," Fen said. Hamish took her hand again, and she tried to control the leap of her heart.

"I suppose we could just leave the gown here," she said, glancing at the box. "Then it couldn't cause any more trouble."

"Not for you, at least," Hamish said, "but what about the person who found it? Wouldn't you feel guilty if something bad happened to them?"

"Not really," Fen said. Then, catching Hamish's look: "What?" She gave a sharp sigh. "You know, I really hate the way I seem to need your good opinion. It's like you're the headmaster, or something—"

"That's not the relationship I was aiming at," Hamish said.

Fen carried on as though he hadn't spoken. "Just knowing you makes me want to be a better person—"

She never got the chance to finish the sentence. Hamish leaned forward and kissed her.

"Sorry," he said, as he let her go. "I promised not to rush you."

"I'll let you off," Fen said a little shakily. "And I take back what I said last time we met about you being boring."

Hamish's smile made her feel hot all over. He touched her cheek. "So are we good then?"

"Very," Fen said. She thought he was going kiss her again, but her mobile rang, the sound jarring through the happy little bubble that had surrounded her for a moment. She ignored it.

"It could be important," Hamish said mildly.

Fen glanced at the caller ID. Katie Barr.

"What is it?" Hamish was watching her face.

"It's Jake's sister," Fen said. She felt a horrible welter of emotion. "I don't know… I mean, she never rings…" It wasn't that she and Katie had ever had a problem, she thought. For a while they had been friends as well as sisters-in-law, and that had been one of the few nice aspects of her relationship with Jake. Except, like everything else, it had been tainted by his presence, and in the end it had been a relief when they hadn't had to pretend any more.

The call had gone to voice mail. Fen waited for the text telling her that there was a message and then dialed in to see what Kate had said.

"Fen." Katie's voice was soft and hesitant, just as she remembered, so different from Jake's smooth, confident charm.

"I…er… I wasn't sure whether…" Fen heard her voice break. "I thought I should tell you," Katie said, more strongly, "in case no one else had." There was a long pause. Fen wondered if the message had run out. Then: "Jake's dead, Fen," Katie said. "He died a few months ago in that horrible train crash outside Berlin but they've only just identified his body." There was another pause. Fen thought she heard a muffled sob. "He's dead," Katie repeated. "I thought I should let you know."

15

Constance

1763

THERE WAS NO SIGN OF LORD GERARD THE following morning, nor any indication that he been at Lydiard the previous night. I began to think that in my half-crazed state I had imagined seeing him emerging from the church with Dr. Baird. Yet I knew that I had not. I had seen him with my own eyes. He was here no matter that Pound maintained he was still abroad.

I thought about what I had seen as the carriage took me into Swindon village that morning. My lady had been most insistent that I go straightaway to find the silver thread I had said I needed to mend the golden gown. She even ordered Farrant to drive me.

"The horses will break their legs on these godforsaken roads," the coachman had grumbled. "You'd be better off in a cart."

He was right, for the journey was devilish uncomfortable

bouncing over all those ruts, but I knew the good people of Swindon would be set by the ears to see me arrive in a coach with the Gerard crest on the side, and I was vain enough to want to enjoy that.

So I mulled over Lord Gerard's presence at Lydiard as we crawled along, and wondered at the secrecy of it. It might be Moonraker business, of course, but why would he trouble to keep that hidden? Everyone at Lydiard knew about the smuggling. I wondered if it was that he did not want my lady to know he had returned. That was more plausible, especially as I had seen him in company with Doctor Baird. What business could the two of them have together? Did my mistress know of it, and did Lord Gerard know about the affair between his wife and her doctor? Could I turn his lordship's presence to my advantage now I knew the secret of the poisoned gown? I had so many questions and no answers.

More pressing was the story I must concoct for my lady to explain why I could not give the gown back to her. I had it with me, tucked away in the blue bag, and I was going to place it safely where no one would think to look. It was my pension, the promise of my future. I had to use it well.

My arrival into Swindon was all that I might have wished. The people on the streets fell back as the carriage, a great deal more impressive than that of even Mr. Goddard himself, swept through their midst. I heard the whispers and saw the stares, and if the crowds were disappointed that it was I rather than Lady Gerard who alighted, it still pleased me very well.

I knew that my mother was watching but the door of the house remained closed, so I sent Farrant to knock for me. He did it with an ill grace but at least he went, and I followed him up the path to the door.

"Thank you, Farrant," I said. "Please meet me in Wood

Street in an hour's time. I will go directly to the haberdasher once I have paid my respects to my family."

Farrant muttered something ungracious and drove off, but I was well pleased. I knew he would have been set to spy on me, and I did not want him reporting back to Lady Gerard that I had not purchased the sewing thread. He must believe I had tried to fulfil my errand.

My mother's maidservant dropped a curtsey when she saw me, slightly less clumsily than the first time. My mother must have been training her up. She was bursting with excitement to see the carriage and be the one to greet me. Mrs. Lawrence, she told me, was in the parlor, and would be very happy to receive me.

I had assumed my mother would be alone, sitting in lonely splendor because through my father's dealings she had climbed higher than her friends and neighbors but not high enough to make new ones. However, as I entered the room I saw that there were a couple of other people there, the elder a woman whose vinegar face was unflatteringly framed by a puce-colored bonnet. She rose when she saw me, and a wintry smile touched her lips. It did not reach anywhere near her eyes. I was as little pleased to see her as she appeared to be to see me. It was essential that I should talk to my mother alone, and I had not reckoned on visitors.

"This is my daughter, Constance," my mother said. I could tell she was nervous. She was fidgeting with an embroidered rose on her gown, picking at a loose thread. "Connie, may I present Mrs. Hicks—" she indicated the vinegar woman "—and Mrs. Beynon? Their husbands are business associates of your father."

I felt the hairs rise on the back of my neck. So these were my mother's new friends, women who also owed their livelihood to the Moonrakers and their dark deeds. Mrs. Beynon, the younger of the two, smiled at me but it was a smile shadowed with strain, and looking at her I could see she was heavily pregnant. She was small and pale and anxious-eyed, and I wondered if she felt trapped by the fear the Moonrakers seemed to trail with them. I could almost scent it in the room.

"We have been speaking of you, Miss Lawrence." Mrs. Hicks sounded most genteel. I wondered at her origins. They were hidden behind several layers of elocution lessons. "It is a pleasure to meet you when I have heard so much about you… From your mother, but also from Mr. Binks, as well."

Her words held the faintest emphasis, and her pale gaze rested on me unblinking. I kept my expression bland whilst inside I felt my stomach churn. I had never met Mr. Binks, but I knew everyone was afraid of him. He was a whisper, a shadow against the wall, a threat. Why would he pay any attention to me? Or was Mrs. Hicks lying just to scare me? I did not know.

"I understand you are lady's maid to Viscountess Gerard," Mrs. Hicks continued. She examined the seam on her glove before raising her eyes to my face in a look as bland as mine. "It seems a rather…menial…position for the daughter of so successful a man as Mr. Lawrence, but I daresay there is a good reason for it."

"Connie and her ladyship are close as peas in a pod." My mother poured tea jerkily into a cup and held it out to me. The spoon tinkled on the china as her hand shook. "They are more like friends than mistress and servant. Why, you saw just now how she sent Connie in the carriage! It is her ladyship who will not hear of Connie leaving her even though it would be my greatest wish to have her home with me." Her eyes pleaded with me to support her, but I said nothing.

I wanted nothing more than for my mother's guests to leave so that I could talk to her alone, and silence was the quickest way to achieve that.

Mrs. Hicks said nothing for a moment either, betraying only with the flicker of an eyelid that she was irritated that her barb had missed its mark. With exaggerated daintiness she helped herself to another pastry.

"I hear that your father had you taught book learning," she said. "Such a waste not to use it. But then—" She paused. "No lady should work, of course. My daughter would not dream of it."

"I am sorry she does not feel herself capable of it, madam," I said. "But not all of us have the ability, of course."

Mrs. Beynon looked from Mrs. Hicks to me. Her eyes were even more frightened now.

"You mistake Mrs. Hicks, Connie," my mother said. "She meant—"

"I understand Mrs. Hicks very well, Mother," I interrupted. I turned to Mrs. Hicks. "We understand one another, do we not, madam?"

Her teeth showed in a smile. "I believe we may do, Miss Lawrence."

I nodded. I knew her type well enough, the ambitious wife who even now was planning for her husband to replace my father in Lord Gerard's empire. No wonder she was hand in glove with Mr. Binks. She would know that my mother was no obstacle to her plans, but what about me?

"I see you bring gifts from Lydiard." Her gaze had fallen on my basket. "Something for your mother, perhaps? How charming and dutiful. May we see?"

It was then that I knew. I am not sure how, but the thought slid into my mind like the serpent in Eden.

My father had betrayed me. He had told Lord Gerard and Mr. Binks that I knew about the gown—and the poison. He had warned them that I planned to use the knowledge for my own ends.

I do not know how long I sat there whilst the conflicting emotions chased through me in a huge ungovernable spiral of anguish and fury. I saw it so clearly now. Once again my father had sacrificed me to his business interests. He had thrown me to the lions.

I saw all of this in Mrs. Hicks's implacable gaze as she watched me, waiting for me to give myself away. Panic bloomed inside me. *They cannot kill me. Not yet. They want the gown back and they do not know where it is.*

I heard myself speaking and my voice sounded quite steady.

"I have marmalade from Mrs. Pound, Mama, made in the Lydiard kitchens, and a beautiful herbal cream for your hands that I made myself in the stillroom." I threw back the cover on my basket and took out the pots, handing them to her.

"Marmalade," Mrs. Hicks sniffed. "Fit only for country people."

"Lady Gerard takes it with her breakfast roll," I said mildly. I could see Mrs. Hicks's gaze scouring the inside of the basket, which was now completely empty.

Mother looked gratified. "How lovely."

Mrs. Hicks stood up. "Perhaps you would care to visit for tea one day soon, Miss Lawrence," she said to me. "When your duties allow it, of course." She drew on her gloves.

"Mrs. Hicks has Royal Worcester porcelain," my mother said unhappily, toying with her German china. "And *two* maidservants."

My mother's solitary maidservant escorted the ladies out. Mrs. Beynon had not said a word throughout and now looked equally as unhappy to leave as she had been to call in the first place. I thought of the painful world of social visiting that was a lady's lot and felt grateful that it was not mine.

"Mrs. Hicks worked in the haberdasher's in Wood Street before her marriage," my mother said suddenly. "And her daughter is an ill-favored girl in temper as well as looks."

I squeezed my mother's hand. I knew she was trying to comfort me.

"Mrs. Beynon is very quiet," I said. "What is she afraid of?"

My mother avoided my eyes. "She fears for the babe, I think."

I knew it was a lie. Mrs. Beynon was afraid of the same things my mother was afraid of, the dangerous business their menfolk engaged with. Every day it haunted them. Between the excise men and Mr. Binks, they had no peace.

"What does Mr. Hicks do?" I asked.

My mother's eyes darted about the room as though she might find the answer in a corner of the wainscot. "He works for Mr. Binks, of course, just as your father does."

"But what does Mr. Hicks actually *do*?" I asked.

"He arranges business dealings." My mother knitted her shaking hands together in her lap. "Ring the bell, Constance. I need Dorcas to clear these dirty dishes."

I did as she asked. I had no desire to upset her any further, and I could see that any reference to the Moonrakers' business distressed her. It was something she would far rather pretend did not exist. Besides, she might be stupid, but she had native cunning and she knew that Mrs. Hicks was a threat to her in some way. She was like an animal sensing the hunter.

"Come upstairs, Mother." I took her arm. "There is something I want to ask you. I need your help."

She brightened at the intimation that she could be useful and led me eagerly enough up to her new boudoir, all tricked out in swags of pink silk and embroidered rosebuds. I listened to be sure that the maid was about her duties downstairs and then closed the door very carefully.

I took the linen bag out from beneath my skirts where I had hidden it for the journey from Lydiard. My mother's eyes bulged with surprise and apprehension.

"Connie. What have you stolen?"

"Nothing." I was exasperated. "Why would you assume that? It is a gown, a gift to me from Lady Gerard."

"A gift!" She was wreathed in smiles now, as changeable as a weathervane. "From Lady Gerard! How wonderful!"

"It is," I said, "but therein lies my difficulty. There is a jealous housemaid at Lydiard who has tried to take it from me." I had devised my lie in the carriage on the journey. "She resents that I have my lady's favor. She has already searched my room looking for the gown, so I need you to keep it safe for me and hide it until the time when I can alter it to fit me." I placed the bag in her outstretched hands, and she held it reverentially. For a moment she did not speak.

"Mother?" I was afraid that she had not heard me. "This is important to me. Tell no one you have it. I want it to be a surprise, to wear it for a grand occasion when you and Father will be proud of me."

I thought I might have gone too far, for I had never shown any interest whatsoever in attending the tedious provincial balls and parties that my parents enjoyed, but my mother did not question. She had heard only the words "gift" and "Lady Gerard" and "my lady's favor."

"Mother?" I said again. "You must not tell anyone Lady Gerard has given me this present. It is to be a surprise. Especially do not mention it to Mrs. Hicks," I added. "She is another who is eaten by jealousy. Imagine her face when I wear it!"

She nodded, smiling. In her mind it would be the greatest triumph for me to appear at a country assembly clad in a cast-off, cut-down golden gown.

"And don't tell Father either," I said as an afterthought.

"Of course not." She sounded scornful now. "What would your father care for women's fripperies?"

I squeezed her hand where it clutched the edge of the bag. "That's good then. This is to be our secret. Keep it safe for me."

"I will hide it in the chest in the red room with my tammy cloth and linings," Mother said. "No one will look for it there."

"Thank you," I said. I kissed her cheek. "I love you."

I do not know what prompted those words. We were not a demonstrative family. Love was shown, grudgingly perhaps, with an edge of embarrassment. It was sincere but it was never spoken of. This time, though, I spoke it and I was glad I did, for her face lit with pleasure and she held me close.

The last time I saw her she was standing in the middle of her boudoir surrounded by acres of pink silk and painted rosebuds.

16

Fenella

"JAKE?" PEPPER SAID BLANKLY. "HE CAN'T BE dead! That's impossible."

"Jake was many things," Fen said, "but immortal was not one of them."

She was alone in the flat. Hamish had not wanted to leave her, but she had needed time alone, time to think, time to work out how she felt. She had rung Katie back on the journey home from Bristol and heard her halting account of what had happened, what little she knew. The German police were still investigating the circumstances, but there seemed no doubt that Jake had been one of the victims.

"I can't get it out of my mind," Katie sobbed. "They could only identify him by his watch. It was engraved. And there were a couple of other personal items that weren't destroyed by the fire. It ripped through the first three carriages. Jake didn't stand a chance."

Fen hadn't known what to say. She had felt quite numb. She could not commiserate with Jake's sister because she wasn't sorry he was dead, no matter how horrific the circumstances. She thought that she should feel something—some regret for the way things had gone so abjectly wrong between them, for the wasted opportunities or the harsh words. No sorrow came. There was nothing.

Fortunately Katie only wanted to talk. "I didn't even realize," she said. "I feel terrible now. You know we weren't close… I didn't think anything of it when I hadn't heard from him in months." This had prompted a fresh bout of crying, and in the end Fen had suggested that they talk again in a few days when the news had had time to sink in.

"I didn't mean that," Pepper said now. She sounded irritated. "Honestly, Fen, making an irreverent joke at a time like this! Are you even sorry at all?"

"I have no idea," Fen said truthfully. She felt exhausted all of a sudden and so weary she could barely stay awake.

"I don't suppose you can be sorry," Pepper said waspishly, "since you once tried to kill him yourself."

Fen's throat closed. She could not reply, could not even begin to frame a response.

"Sorry." Pepper sounded scared. She knew she had gone too far this time. "I'm just upset. And now I've heard about Jake's death, I'm confused, as well."

"Why?" Fen managed the one word. Not that she was certain she wanted to continue the conversation. "What do you mean?"

"I was going to ring you before," Pepper said. "But I forgot. It was after our last conversation, when you thought Jake might have been asking after you. It was odd because only a day or two later Mrs. Briggs, next door to Gran, mentioned his name. We were chatting over the fence, and she said she'd seen him visiting Gran just before she died."

Fen sat down abruptly on one of the dining room chairs. "That's impossible," she said. "Jake would have been dead by then. The train crash was four months ago, and Gran's only been dead since May."

"I know." Pepper sounded subdued. "Mrs. Briggs must have been wrong. Old people do get muddled about dates and stuff. She probably saw him visiting months ago, or perhaps confused him with someone else."

"Right," Fen said. It wasn't just old people, she thought. She had been convinced she had seen Jake, not once, but several times in the last few weeks. She had even started to believe he was stalking her. But not even Jake was capable of cheating death. All the time she'd imagined his malign presence, thought she was being watched, he had been dead and gone.

Like so many other things, it could only be a product of her imagination. She felt scared that her grasp on reality seemed so fragile. Had she written Jake's name on the glass mirror? Why was her instinct still telling her he was a threat when she should be feeling relief that he was dead?

"I've got to go," she said to Pepper, and cut her sister off in the middle of her renewed apologies.

It was a beautiful evening. Sunset was painting the sky with pink and gold over to the west as Fen went into her kitchen. She had already locked the golden gown back in the wardrobe. She found she couldn't seem to frame any thoughts about that either, about Augusta and Hamish and the violent possession of the gown.

She poured herself a glass of orange juice from the fridge and leaned against the counter to look out over the grassy lawns of what had once been Swindon House. They sloped away down the hill towards the new town. All that murder and evil they had talked about with Augusta had happened here, she thought, only a stone's throw from where she was standing. She thought of the Moonrakers and the references to the old town and to Samuel Lawrence's offices, to the mill-pond, just along from where she and Sarah had lived.

She tried again to work out how she felt, but her mind felt light and empty. She could not pin down a single sensation or feeling. It was as though she was watching herself, knowing she should feel some sort of emotion but unable to connect to anything. She decided to have a bath and go to bed.

The plunge, when it came, was sudden and terrifying. One moment she was walking towards the bathroom, the next she had bumped against the wall, aware that her legs felt like rubber and she could no longer walk in a straight line. Her head spun sickeningly as though she were on a merry-go-round. There was a buzzing in her ears: Voices? She didn't know. She could not see properly. The corridor seemed dark. She could feel herself sliding down the wall to crumple on the floor like a rag doll. The darkness pressed in, suffocating her, and then the dreams came.

The dreams were not coherent. They were ragged banners of thoughts and images chasing each other through her head. She could hear Jake's voice, the lazy, smooth tones that had seduced her when first they had met. His charm had seduced so many people: Sarah, her mother, her friends. Everyone had liked Jake. It had only been slowly, oh so slowly, that she had realized what he had been doing.

"Your career will never amount to much, will it, darling?" he had said once when she had picked up some college bro-chures with the intention of returning to study. "I think it would be a waste of time and money."

"Fen's still trying to work out what she's good at," he had

told Sarah over an uncomfortable Sunday lunch. "Perhaps one day she'll find something."

She could hear that voice in her head now: "Wear this for me... You look terrible in that... Be back for eight... Call and cancel—I want us to go out together tonight..."

By the end of the nightmare, just as in their life together, his voice was screaming in her head, and she did not believe in anything anymore, least of all herself.

"I love you..." The shreds of darkness parted, and in the dream she saw Jake's face. He was smiling. "I'll always love you. We'll always be together." It was a trap, of course; he seemed to offer her everything when really all he wanted to do was control her. Yet no one seemed to understand why she would reject such a life. They all conspired against her. She was struggling, drowning...

It was the buzz of the entry phone that woke her. She fought her way out of the nightmare, wrestling with the darkness that wreathed her as though it were a tangible force. Consciousness returned. For a moment she was completely confused. Something sharp was digging into her cheek; the corner of the sofa cushion. She sat up. Her mouth felt dry. Her head ached. What had happened to her? For one terrifying moment she couldn't remember anything at all, not even who she was or what she was doing there. It felt as though her mind was in freefall.

The entry phone buzzed again.

"Fen!" It was Jessie's voice. "Are you there?"

The clock on the mantelpiece said one-thirty. Bright light streamed in from the open curtains. Fen dragged herself across the room and pressed the button to unlock the main door, then bolted for the bathroom. It looked spotlessly clean and bright. She paused on the threshold, trying to remember.

There had been something about the bathroom, something terrifying... But that had been days ago. What had happened in between? It was something to do with Jake. She knew it, she sensed it, but the feeling slid away into the cobwebbed shadows of her mind.

By the time Jessie was knocking on the door of the flat she had at least brushed her hair and washed her face, not that it was much improvement.

"I knew you shouldn't have been left on your own." Jessie bustled past her into the flat, all bouncy dark hair and bossiness, making Fen feel even more like a limp dishcloth. "Hamish rang me. He told me what had happened to Jake. Oh Fen!" Jessie hugged her, her eyes full of concern. "How are you?"

Fen felt helpless, lost. "I don't know," she said. She put a hand up to her head. "I've only just woken up. I feel weird, as though I've been drugged." There was a dull ache behind her eyes but far more worrying was the blank in her memory. What the hell had happened to her the previous night? She tried to draw together the events, but it was like trying to catch the shreds of clouds.

"I wanted to be on my own," she said slowly.

Jessie nodded. "That's what Hamish said."

"I wanted to think," Fen said, "only I couldn't think about anything at all. I couldn't *feel* anything."

"Shock can do that," Jessie said.

"No." Fen shook her head. "It wasn't shock. It was... I don't know what it was. Like I was standing outside myself, watching, unable to connect to any emotion at all." She pressed her palm to her forehead, trying to remember. "I came in and had a glass of juice, and then I was going to have a bath. I was just going down the corridor when I started to feel dizzy and faint."

I can't remember anything else… She shuddered.

There was no glass on the table in the living room. Walking through into the kitchen she realized that there was no orange juice container out on the counter either. The place was spotlessly clean and tidy and certainly not the way she had left it the previous evening. Or at least she thought not, but she wasn't sure.

It must be her. She was losing her mind.

"I heard Jake's voice," she said. "In my head."

"Whoa." Jessie had been putting the kettle on, but now she turned back to Fen, her eyes wide and anxious. "What do you mean, you heard his voice?"

"I've seen him too," Fen said. She knew her brain wasn't working properly and that the words weren't coming out right, but her mind was too woolly to form ideas and sentences properly. "I caught sight of him in the street a few days ago," she said. "He was with a girl. Lucie, from work…"

She saw a different expression cloud Jessie's eyes and realized that her friend thought she was sick, or hallucinating, or obsessed. Which was not unreasonable. Jessie didn't speak for a moment, as though she was trying to find the right words, and in that silence Fen said: "I know you'll think I'm mad. It seems mad to me too but I'm sure I'm right. It definitely was Jake. I know he's dead, but—" She stopped, feeling despairing. There was no *but* when someone was dead. It was a fact. She wrapped her arms about herself, feeling increasingly frightened, trapped in some way and yet at the same time adrift.

"You didn't say anything about this when we met up, Fen," Jessie said carefully. Fen recognized that tone of voice. Jessie was worried about her but didn't want to sound either bossy or condescending.

"I didn't want to," Fen said. "There was enough weirdness going on with the gown and the other stuff."

She wished Jessie would go. She only wanted to sleep. "I'm fine," she said rapidly. "Really I am—"

"You said you had a drink when you came in," Jessie said. "How much did you have?"

Fen jerked back. "Not that sort of drink! It was orange juice. I didn't pass out because I was drunk!"

"Okay." Jessie's voice was soothing. Fen could see her looking around the kitchen in the same way she had, for a glass or a drink carton, or anything that might support her story.

"I'm sorry to have to ask this, Fen," Jessie said, "but did you take anything—for your headache, or to help you sleep? I know you said that you weren't sleeping well—"

"Don't forget I've been on antidepressants, as well," Fen snapped. "You might as well section me now. I know I sound mad."

Jessie raised her hand in a gesture of appeal and for a moment Fen thought she would simply turn and walk out of the flat, and she was glad. Everything felt distorted, spiraling away from her. Then Jessie hugged her tightly. Fen resisted for a moment, then relaxed into it.

"Fen," Jessie said, "last time we met, we were talking about ghosts, and I was the one who was haunted by a creepy jeweled tiepin. You're not mad at all." She tightened the hug for a moment, then let Fen go. "I just wish you'd told me about Jake, that's all."

"Thanks." Fen eased back and wiped the tears from her cheeks. She felt pitifully feeble. "Sorry," she said. "It's just all completely bizarre."

"Why don't you go and have a shower," Jessie suggested, "and I'll put the kettle on and then we can talk about it."

"Okay." Fen ran a hand through her hair. It felt greasy and unkempt. Very probably she smelled, and Jessie was just too kind to say so. She wandered down the corridor towards the bathroom, stopping dead in the doorway. She remembered now, remembered the steam and the humidity and the writing on the mirror... The terror rushed back in, making her so light-headed she thought she would faint again.

She must have made some noise because she was suddenly aware of Jessie standing behind her. Her friend was looking over her shoulder towards the mirror where the letters spelling JAKE were still very faintly outlined on the glass like a ghostly presence.

"I didn't write it," Fen said quickly. "It appeared a couple of nights ago. I remember now. Jake must have got in here. I don't know how, but he must." She was talking too quickly. She knew she was. She felt so odd, shaky and exhausted but at the same time exhaustingly wide awake. "So many weird things have happened since Pepper sent me the golden dress," she said. "I saw Jake, and there were noises, and then I was stealing things again..."

Jessie's expression morphed into outright alarm. Fen spun away from her and almost ran down the passage to the spare room. "I told you about the dress," she said. Her words were tumbling out now as though she had no control over them. "I've locked it away because it's dangerous. Hamish knows all about it, though. It got to him too, and Augusta Monday. It's not just me! It's in here—" She flung open the bedroom door. "So is all the stuff I've stolen. You'll see..."

She unlocked the wardrobe, noticing as she did so that her

fingers were shaking. She grabbed the handle and wrenched the cupboard open.

There was nothing there, nothing at all. The dress, the box, and all the stuff she had stolen: it had all gone.

17

Isabella

1763

JOHN BAIRD AND I SAT IN THE BLUE DRAWING room, conversing very properly over a cup of tea, he on the sofa and I in an armchair. The reason for our formality sat across from me too, an awkward third. Eustace had returned from Italy that morning in high good humor and a new silk waistcoat. I had been surprised when he had indicated that he would join me for Dr. Baird's visit.

"I have the greatest desire to hear from the good doctor how well you progress, my dear," he said. "I was grievously sorry to see how unwell you had become in Town."

Since Eustace had been responsible for my sickness this seemed a little rich, but no doubt he had forgotten that along with everything else, or rewritten his memory of it, more likely. In his eyes I was always the one at fault. I was the errant wife, a disappointment to him in a multitude of ways. He had offered me the golden gown, and I had clumsily rejected his peace offering and spurned his gift. How long ago that seemed! And now the same gown was gone, lost, destroyed, and I would have to find another way to repay John for the service he was about to do me. I was, however, sure I could come up with something that would satisfy him.

A rustle of sound drew my attention to the window, where Constance was fussing around tidying the newspapers Eustace had brought back with him. That was the housemaid's task, but poor Constance did not appear to know what to do with herself and so was looking for jobs to perform. I had not offered her tea; she was not a guest and I thought it odd that Eustace had requested she join us. Her presence made me a little uneasy. She was Eustace's spy—was she about to reveal to him the detail of my affair with John, here in front of us all? I hoped that gratitude might hold her silent, for she was lucky I had not turned her off after the accident with the gown.

"When do you return to Town, Dr. Baird?" I asked as I passed John his cup.

"Very soon, madam." There was some constraint in John's manner and certainly not the slightest hint of familiarity in his words. He was a good actor, that was for sure. "I have some small business to attend to in Swindon, and then I will go on the morrow." He stirred his tea thoughtfully and fixed me with his bright hazel gaze. "I was hoping," he said gently, "to have the pleasure of seeing you in your golden gown at tonight's assembly before I leave. You would be such an ornament to our little town, Lady Gerard."

I jumped, almost spilling Eustace's tea, which I had been handing him in that moment. I had not expected John to make even a veiled reference to our agreement.

"Alas, I do not attend any of the local assemblies." I glanced modestly at Eustace under my lashes. "As you know, Doctor, I have lived quite retired during my husband's absence. There have been no balls or excitements for me."

"I am aware," John said, smiling gently. "Which is quite appropriate for a wife alone."

"Besides," I added sharply, irritated by the complicit look he exchanged with Eustace, "the golden gown you mention has been lost in an unfortunate accident. I am afraid that Constance took it to Swindon for some repair, and it was ripped to shreds beneath the wheels of a carriage. She slipped in the street and dropped it. Foolish girl, so clumsy."

Out of the corner of my eye I saw Constance shift on the window seat, turning her face away so that her embarrassment was hidden from us. I felt a sharp stab of spite. She deserved to feel ashamed. She had returned home filthy with mud and damp; Tarrant had refused her the carriage because she was so dirty and had made her walk, and it served her aright.

John, for some reason, seemed to find the news of the golden gown's demise rather entertaining. I saw his shoulders shake with the effort of repressing his amusement.

"Run over by a carriage!" he murmured. "How fortunate that it was only the gown's fate and not Miss Lawrence's!"

Eustace looked bored. Having inflicted his presence on us he was making absolutely no effort to join in any conversation. Now he yawned ostentatiously. Sensing the awkwardness, John addressed him directly.

"Do you intend to be fixed at Lydiard for a while now, Lord Gerard?"

"God, no," Eustace said. "Ghastly place. No, dear Doctor, I too will be returning to Town just as soon as my business here is complete."

I took that to mean that Eustace intended to stock up on illicit brandy and other smuggled goods whilst he was in the country. I wondered whether he intended for me to return to Town with him or whether I would be left to rusticate here indefinitely. Not that it mattered; if John was true to his word, within a day or so Eustace would be dead.

"You are looking very well, my dear," my husband said, condescending to glance in my direction. "The country air has been beneficial for you, I think."

"Thank you, my lord." I looked down at my lap. That definitely meant he would be leaving me in the country.

John drained his cup. "You must excuse me, Lady Gerard, Lord Gerard." He reached into his pocket and took out a small vial of liquid, placing it on the table beside the teacup. "Before I leave, Lady Gerard, I must give you this. It is to help with your sleeping, as we discussed."

I swallowed hard, looking at the innocuous little flask of clear liquid, handed to me in full view of my unsuspecting husband.

"Thank you, Doctor."

"Just a few drops," John said. "That is all you will need."

I did not dare to meet his eyes. My mind had already sprung ahead; hopefully Eustace would not wish to bed me tonight for he had probably contracted the clap once more from his woman—I had seen him scratching beneath the fine new silk. In the morning, though, I would persuade him to breakfast with me before he went down to the plunge pool at the lake, which was his habit at Lydiard. I would add some drops from the vial into his hot chocolate and watch him go. Then I would imagine his slide into the deep green waters of the pool, his sudden lassitude as the effect of the drug took him, the waters closing over his head... It was deeply pleasing to think of him drowning in his own lake.

I realized that Doctor Baird had gotten to his feet and was

waiting politely for me to rise and bid him farewell. I walked with him to the front door and gave him my hand, which he kissed very tenderly.

"Goodbye, Lady Gerard," he said. "It has been my pleasure to serve you."

"Goodbye, Dr. Baird," I said. "Will I see you again in Town?"

He shook his head. "I doubt you will be in need of my services again."

"But—" I started to say, but he pressed a finger fleetingly to my lips. "It is sufficient for me to know that you will be safe and well, my dear."

He smiled at me and turned away, running down the steps, heading towards the stables, calling for his horse, a vital man, a very attractive man, a man who had served his purpose and, astonishingly, asked nothing of me in return. I felt a moment's pang of sadness that our affair was over. Not that he could have been the "B" who would be my future husband. He was not a gentleman, after all.

I walked slowly back into the drawing room. Eustace was sitting in the armchair where I had left him, reading one of the newspapers. Constance was sitting in the window seat. She looked downcast. I remembered she had always had a fondness for Dr. Baird. Having him laugh at her must have been hard to bear, but the silly child had deserved it for such a disaster as she had had with the gown. I had seldom been so angry.

"Constance," I said sharply, an echo of that anger once again lighting my blood, "I want you to go and wash all of my muslins. It is a fine day to dry them all."

She looked appalled, as well she might. It was a hard task, and she would be up to her elbows in suds for most of the day. I looked at Eustace, who was ignoring us both. That, I thought, is how I treat your spy, and soon I will deal with you too.

I felt full of decisiveness and strength. I walked over to ring the bell for the footman to clear away the tea tray. Then I went back to the table, oh so casually, to pick up the vial of precious liquid that Dr. Baird had left.

It had gone.

18

Fenella

FEN WONDERED AT WHAT POINT SHE SHOULD stop believing in her sanity and simply let go. Her mind was a scramble of fear and confusion. She didn't want to try to sort it out anymore. She wanted to sleep and never wake up. Had she imagined all those sightings of Jake? Had she written his name on the mirror herself? Had she taken the gown and destroyed it to pretend that someone had broken in, as a plea for attention or out of a need for drama, or some other weird and twisted behavior? She didn't know anymore. She did not know what to think, what to do. It was terrifying to imagine that she might have such a twisted distortion of reality.

"Here you are." Hamish placed a mug of tea in her hands and a plate of toast on the table in front of her. She had had a shower and was wearing clean clothes, but she still felt soiled in some way, as though Jake had reached into her life and had put his vile fingerprints all over it. It was impossible; Jake was dead, and no one could get into Villet House and certainly not into her flat. Yet the only other explanation was that she had lost the thread of her sanity.

Jessie hadn't said anything at all since the moment in the spare room. She had scrubbed the mirror in the bathroom so that the letters had completely gone, propelled Fen into the shower and gone out leaving the door ajar. Fen had showered as though in a dream, wrapping herself in the towel, automatically selecting clean clothes from the drawer in her room and coming out to find Hamish waiting for her. He hadn't said anything either, but he had wrapped her in a hug. It was wonderfully comforting, and Fen had felt herself soften inside and some sense of normality return. Hamish smelled of fresh air and faintly of citrus soap and his hair was mussed by the wind, and she wanted to hold on to him indefinitely but she wasn't quite ready to analyze why.

"Thank you," she said now. She didn't really want to eat or drink, but perhaps it might make her feel more normal.

Hamish watched her for a moment, a frown between his brows, then went out again into the kitchen. A moment later, Fen heard Jessie speaking. She had her doctor's voice on.

"Fen's sick..." Jessie's voice fell. Fen strained to hear. "Possible psychotic episode... She needs help—"

Hamish said something Fen missed, his tone low but insistent.

"I've checked the whole flat," Jessie said. "All the doors and windows are secure. There's no sign of forced entry. No one has been in here and even if someone had... Well, it can't be Jake, can it?"

"You can't be certain that no one broke in," Hamish said.

"It's all in her mind." Jessie's voice had sharpened. "That's my clinical diagnosis, Hamish. We need to get her to hospital."

Fen got up and pushed open the door. "Don't talk about me as though I wasn't here."

"Sorry." Jessie had the grace to look ashamed. Hamish was standing leaning back against the counter, arms folded. His body language was not difficult to read. Fen's heart, already in her boots, tumbled lower. The last thing she wanted to do was force a wedge between brother and sister again.

"Jessie, I hate that you think I'm delusional," she said wretchedly. "You're probably thinking that I've imagined all the stuff about Jake and that I made up the story about the dress that I told you yesterday—"

Jessie's hand squeezed hers. "I don't think you're delusional," she said. Then, as Fen gave her a look, "Well, perhaps you are when it comes to Jake but even if that's the case, there's a reason for it and we'll sort it out." She scanned Fen's face. "I do think it would be better if you went to hospital, though."

"I think it would be better if you called the police and reported a burglary," Hamish said. His jaw was set hard, and he looked determined and impatient.

"I'm not going to do either of those things." Fen felt better wresting back control. A new determination, a new sense of self, possessed her.

"Jessie," she said. "I probably have taken something by accident but I'm feeling better now." Then, as Jessie opened her mouth to argue: "Don't make me remind you that the day before yesterday you were chattering on about ghosts, time travel and haunted tiepins. *Neither* of us is going out of our minds."

She heard Hamish give a snort of laughter and turned to him. "Hamish, I'm not going to report a break-in. For a start I can't be certain that's what really happened. There's a small chance I could have had some sort of memory lapse, just as Jessie suggested. Besides, can you imagine how that would sound? Me reporting someone stealing a load of stuff I stole in the first place?"

Hamish sighed, running a hand through his hair. "At least take a look at the CCTV. That's why there are cameras in the building."

"Okay," Fen said. "I'll think about it." She knew there would be nothing to show on the CCTV. She just knew it, just as there were no signs of forced entry or even any real evidence that someone else had been in her flat.

Jessie checked her watch. "I have to go. Afternoon surgery. I'll ring you later and we'll talk more about this Jake thing." She gave Fen a quick hug. "And for God's sake go to hospital if you feel ill." She scowled at her brother. "Look after her."

"I'm so sorry," Fen said to Hamish as Jessie clattered off downstairs. "I don't want to cause trouble for you two."

"It's no big deal," Hamish said easily. "We've got past all that." He smiled at her. "What do you want to do? Talk? Sleep? Or go out somewhere?"

Fen didn't need to think about it. "Go out," she said, with a shudder. The less time she spent in the flat, the better. She wasn't sure where that left her future, but it probably meant she would be looking for a new place to live very soon. She drove her hands into her jeans pockets. "Let's go to the park. I could do with some fresh air, and I did promise you the history tour."

"Okay." Hamish grabbed his jacket.

The lens of the CCTV camera winked at them as they went down the grand staircase and into the hall.

"This is quite some place," Hamish said. "Early eighteenth century?"

"I believe so," Fen said. "It's called Villet House now, although I think it was built for someone else before that family lived here. It's very grand, isn't it? A bit of a show-off house."

"New money, I expect," Hamish said, "or someone wanting to keep up with the Joneses."

"Or the Goddards in this case," Fen said. "They were the lords of the manor of Swindon."

She turned to look back at the façade. "What do you make of the weird stone faces? They're a bit odd, aren't they? Like gargoyles."

"Strange stone carvings of mythical or fantastical beasts were usually used to educate as well as decorate a building." Hamish squinted up at the faces staring down at them. "On churches it's supposed to be illustrations of creatures in the Bible and folklore but here... Hmm. Maybe someone was caricaturing some of the villagers."

"Perhaps they represent the Moonrakers," Fen said. "I wonder if Mr. Villet was one of the patrons?"

They turned left through the park gates, leaving the high street and the traffic behind.

"According to my Gran there were gatehouses here, back in the day," Fen said. "This was the carriage drive for the big house, the Lawn."

"You used to live just around here somewhere, didn't you?" Hamish said. "I remember coming with Mum and Jessie to collect you for tea once."

"Just round the corner in The Planks," Fen said. "We'll walk back that way."

"I guess this was all the grounds of the Lawn at one time?" Hamish said. "Very nice for Mr. Goddard. It must have been very rural before the arrival of the railway and the new town."

"It still looks very pretty," Fen said. She had stopped on

the edge of the hillside where the trees fell back and the land tumbled away to endless streets and houses, row after row of roofs marching into the distance.

"You're a true Swindonian," Hamish said, smiling, "to see beauty here."

Retracing their steps beneath the planes and beeches and pines they found a series of low walls poking through the grass and a formal garden laid out with flower beds and neat paths.

"This is all that's left of the manor house," Fen said. "It was demolished sometime last century."

"It's odd, isn't it…" Hamish was walking around the edge of the building, studying the layout in the grass. "The footprint of a lost house is all that's left."

"And the memories," Fen said. She shivered a little although the sun was hot. "Let's sit down for a bit," she said. "I'd like to tell you about Jake."

Hamish stilled, looking at her. "You don't have to do that."

"I want to," Fen said. "If you want to hear."

"Yes, I do," Hamish said, with emphasis.

Fen nodded. She perched on the edge of a bench, knitting her hands together. It was easier to talk outside than in the claustrophobic confines of the flat. The sky was high and wide; it did not press in or confine. There were no ghosts here, no echoes, or at least nothing to threaten her.

"We met when I was about eighteen," she said. "He was a businessman, importing glass and furniture, really nice stuff. I was drifting from one waitressing job to another. He was older, good-looking, confident, you know…" She looked down at her fingers clasped so tight they showed white. "Although I'd run away from home I hadn't much confidence myself, or experience. I thought he was wonderful." She glanced at Hamish. There was a concentrated stillness to his listening that seemed relaxed, but she sensed tension under the surface. He held it tightly, though, under total control, very different from any man she had known.

"We married when I was twenty. It was great at first, lots of money, fast cars, champagne." She shrugged awkwardly. "I liked all that stuff."

"There's nothing wrong in that," Hamish said expressionlessly.

"Only if it comes at the expense of other people," Fen said, "or if it breeds arrogance and cruelty." She moved her shoulders again. It felt as though there was a weight on her pressing down. But she wanted to continue.

"Jake started to take on some work that seemed a bit dubious," she said. She swallowed hard. "I wondered if it was legal, to be honest. He was moving artworks out of the country without the proper licenses and stuff. I wasn't sure what was going on—I didn't really understand the paperwork, but it seemed a bit suspicious so I asked him about it." She curled her body in more tightly. "He was shocked, I think. Shocked I'd questioned him. Then he was defensive. And when I didn't have the sense to back down, he got angry."

She stopped. The distant traffic hum filled her ears overlaid with the chirp of birdsong.

"Did he hit you?" Hamish asked quietly.

Fen shook her head. "Not that time. He just demolished me verbally, if you know what I mean. He was very articulate and I wasn't, and by the time he'd finished I felt limp and stupid and utterly useless. And that was the start." She looked at Hamish. "It wasn't aggressive most of the time. He just chipped away at my confidence and my life until there was nothing original of me left, until I was an empty shell and didn't have an identity anymore. It was weird, but I didn't see myself how I was unraveling over time. It was such a slow process and such a subtle one."

Hamish's hand covered hers. He didn't say how sorry he was or any of the other well-meaning phrases people had used before, but his fingers tightened over hers and he smiled at her. Fen intertwined her fingers with his.

"In the end I left him," she said, "as you know."

Hamish turned their joined hands over, opening them up, running his fingers gently over her palm. "Did he ever hurt you physically?" His tone was conversational, but the emotion she sensed in him was fierce.

"Only once," Fen said. "That was what made me snap."

"What happened?" Hamish asked softly.

"One night Jake came in late just as I was about to go out to a club with some friends," Fen said. "I'd had my hair done specially and chosen my favorite dress, and I was feeling almost normal for once..." She swallowed. There was a hot, panic-stricken feeling in her chest even though she was relating old history. Her heart had started to race.

"Jake was drunk. He didn't want me going out and leaving him on his own. He told me he'd call a hooker to keep him company if I went out and when I told him how horrible he was being he went mad. He took a pair of scissors and held me still, trapped against the kitchen door, whilst he cut off all my hair."

She stopped. Her entire body was tense. She had learned over time that it had a visceral memory of that night that could never be erased. "I remember trying to get away, but he was strong and his grip was so tight and I was completely trapped. It was a horrible feeling, that sense of physical powerlessness. I was afraid that if I struggled the scissors would slip. He had already cut my neck…" She shivered convulsively. "Then he started on my dress, ripping it off me… I can still hear the sound of the scissors, the snip, snip, snip—" Her voice cracked. "My dress, my underwear, he sliced it all straight off and dropped it on the floor. I was so scared and so angry. I thought he was going to rape me." She freed herself from Hamish's touch and stood up. She could not be close to him now, could not even look at him. She had always been alone in this. She still was.

"I grabbed a knife from the block on the counter and I stabbed him with it," Fen said. "I wanted to kill him, but unfortunately I wasn't accurate enough." She folded her arms tightly about her. It was all there, trapped in her head: the blood, on her hands, splashing on the floor, Jake screaming in pain and fury, and the darkness in her mind lifting as she stood there, naked, staring at him in his agony before scrambling for her phone to dial for an ambulance.

"I can't imagine how it must have felt," Hamish said, after a moment, his voice snapping her back to the present. He looked tense, cold, but Fen knew those feelings were not directed towards her. Hamish's anger was protective, she thought, not destructive.

"I won't even pretend I could imagine it," Hamish said, "but it must have been a living hell."

"The most frightening thing," Fen said, "was discovering that I was capable of murdering him." She glanced up. "It's a figure of speech: 'I could kill him.' We all say it. And then I found I could. That was a shock, to realize that I had the capacity for such violence." She shuddered. "It wasn't even in the heat of the moment either. It was a cold, fierce determination to protect myself."

"The survival instinct," Hamish said. He nodded. "Thank

God you found you had that strength in you." His voice changed, hardened. "I don't suppose he pressed charges either."

"No, he didn't," Fen said. "He told the police it was an accident. How did you guess?"

There was such darkness in Hamish's eyes that she could not read them. "Firstly because he wouldn't have wanted all his vile behavior to come out and expose what a bastard he really was," Hamish said. "I'm guessing he took pleasure in people thinking how friendly and charming he was. But also because he would want to use it as another way to manipulate you." He clenched his fists. "I bet he planned to threaten you that he would go to the police if you stepped out of line in future."

"He did try that when I said I was leaving him," Fen said. "He threatened to lay a charge of assault against me. But I went anyway. At that stage even prison would have been preferable to living with Jake, and I'm not being flippant when I say that."

She took a shaky step forward. "So now you know," she said. "I tried to murder my ex. I really wouldn't blame you if you walk away right now."

A smile lit Hamish's eyes like sunlight on water. "I'll take my chances," he said.

Fen took another step towards him, and his arms closed around her.

"I'm doing this all wrong," she said, muffled, against his chest. It was blissful being there, being held.

"I'm not sure there is a wrong way." Hamish ran a hand over her hair.

"I like you too much, too soon," Fen grumbled.

"You're not alone in that," Hamish said. He pushed the loose strands away from her face. "Fen, look at me. Please."

Fen tilted her chin up. "I'd rather kiss you," she said.

She saw his mouth curve into a smile. "Okay." He took a breath. "Thank you for telling me about Jake," he said.

"You've killed the moment," Fen grumbled. She felt sleepy all of a sudden, there in the sun, in his arms. It was the reassurance, she thought, and the sense of safety. It was not familiar to her.

"Wake up," Hamish murmured. He kissed her gently. "We haven't finished the guided tour."

Hand in hand they wandered down the path away from the old house, past the ruins of a church that were locked away behind an iron gate.

"The Church of the Holy Rood," Fen said. "Before they built Christ Church on the main road, this was Swindon's parish church. It's ancient. Gran said there was once a monastery here and that the crypt is still there with a load of tunnels that run from here under the town."

"It's a shame it's not open to look around," Hamish said. "It looks fascinating."

"We used to sneak into the graveyard for a fag sometimes when I was at school," Fen said. "I tried my first joint there too." She caught Hamish's glance. "Small stuff compared with your experience, I'm sure, Dr. Ross."

Hamish kissed her again, and she grabbed his jacket and held him tight against her.

"Do you really want to finish the guided tour?" she said, when she finally drew back.

"Yeah," Hamish said. His voice sounded rough. "Damn it, Fen…"

"All right." Fen grabbed his hand again. "This way."

She pulled him down a narrow path leading away from the church. The park wall soared above them to the right. To their left, a grassy space opened up, neatly cut and edged with flower beds.

"This was once the upper millpond," Fen said. "They piped all the spring water underground years ago, and it dried up. That's why this is called The Planks. It used to be so wet underfoot that they had to put down a wooden pavement for people to walk into town. Our house was over there—" She pointed to a set of gates on the corner. "Behind the old mill cottages."

"I remember this," Hamish said, looking around. "You wouldn't even know there had been a mill here, would you? No water left, just that dip in the ground to show where it once was."

"There are a couple of small lakes in the park," Fen said. "I guess they must still be fed by the springs and are all that's left from when the mill was here. It's odd, isn't it? As though history gets tidied away sometimes. It only survives in the street names and the lumps and bumps in the ground." She stood with one hand on the railings, looking out across the hollow that had once held the mill and its pool. "This must be where those people drowned," she said. "The ones Augusta talked about, Samuel Lawrence and his wife."

Hamish nodded. "The mill would still have been operating in the eighteenth century and the pool would have been quite deep enough to drown in. Horrible stuff."

Fen felt an unpleasant ripple of sensation along her skin, not fear precisely, but something like familiarity, recognition. She did not understand it.

"I wonder what happened to the rest of the Moonrakers,"

she said, "and to Lord and Lady Gerard, for that matter. I'd like to find out if we can."

"We will," Hamish said. "Fen, about the gown—"

Fen immediately felt defensive and tried not to let it show. "What about it?"

Hamish's expression softened. "Relax. I don't believe you imagined any of this stuff. I saw the gown myself, remember—and saw what it did to Augusta."

"So where is it now?" Fen said wretchedly. "There was no evidence of a break-in, Hamish. I must have destroyed the gown myself." She rubbed a hand across her forehead. "If only I could remember what happened last night! All this stuff about Jake too…" Her shoulders slumped. "I'm scared Jessie's right, and it's all part of some sort of psychosis."

"If it is, then I'm suffering some of the same delusions," Hamish said roughly. "I don't know, Fen. I can't explain, but you've got to hang on in there until we can work it out."

There was silence between them as they walked back to Villet House. Fen fumbled in her back pocket for her key.

"Would you like to come in?"

"Yes," Hamish said, "but I'm not going to."

"Jessie said I wasn't to be left alone," Fen said.

Hamish groaned. "Help me, Fen. I'm trying to do the right thing here."

Fen giggled. "We're not teenagers."

"It would be more straightforward if we were," Hamish said. He ran a hand through his hair. "Look, I need to go and check something out. It's an idea I've had and it might come to nothing, so I'm not going to go into details now. Can I come over later? There's something else we need to talk about, as well."

"We can talk now," Fen said, with her hand on the doorknob.

Hamish hesitated. "Later," he said. He gave her a quick, hard kiss. "Is seven good for you?"

"I'll see you then," Fen said.

"Don't open the door to anyone until we get all this stuff sorted out," Hamish said, "and if anything happens, call me at once."

"All right," Fen said. "It all sounds ridiculously melodramatic, but I will."

Up in the flat, she opened up her laptop. She typed "Lady Isabella Beaumaris" into the search engine. It was somewhere to start her research, and it gave her something to concentrate on. It was better than sitting around wondering if she was going mad or if someone was about to break in again.

A number of pages came up relating to Lady Isabella, and a number of images. Fen chose the first encyclopedia page and clicked on it.

Lady Isabella Beaumaris (née Lady Isabella Cavendish) other married name Isabella, Viscountess Gerard, 1734–1801, was an English noblewoman and artist.

Fen scanned down the details of Isabella's birth (the daughter of a duke) and her childhood on a large country estate where she had first been introduced to the artist Sir Joshua Reynolds, a family friend. There was a painting of Isabella by Sir Joshua dated 1765. In it she was wearing a golden gown, although not the one that Fen recognized.

Her first marriage was unhappy and Gerard notoriously unfaithful, Fen read. Hmm, that reminded her of Jake, with his little "flings" at the Christmas party and when he was away on conference. She had only found out about them after she'd left him. Bastard.

In 1763 her husband petitioned for divorce on the grounds of Lady Isabella's adultery, she read. She was starting to dislike Viscount Gerard more with every sentence. A notorious philanderer, yet he blamed his wife for her infidelities and divorced her. The petition required an act of Parliament, which was granted the following month. Fen pulled a face.

After living with a husband who was verbally and probably also physically abusive, she read, it is likely that Lady Isabella welcomed the freedom if not the scandal that divorce brought with it in the eighteenth century. She received no settlement from her former husband and lived in penury before eventually supporting herself through her art, creating designs for Wedgwood, amongst others. She remarried, to Topham Beaumaris, a short time after her divorce.

Fen expelled a long breath.

A husband who was verbally and probably also physically abusive...

She felt the same shiver, the same sense of a resonance, echo through her now as she had when she was standing by the old millpond. Abuse, violence, cruelty, divorce... The parallels between herself and Lady Isabella Beaumaris were disconcerting.

She flicked through a few more online biographies of Lady Isabella, admiring the pretty watercolors and elegant patterns that constituted her work. She had indeed been a talented artist and lucky, perhaps, to be so well connected that she numbered Reynolds and other artists amongst her circle of friends.

She found the text of a Victorian biography and skipped

through it. It was very dryly written and so poorly format-
ted that she was about to give it up when she read:

In the summer of 1763, immediately prior to the final rupture
from Lord Gerard, Lady Isabella was at Lydiard Park, her husband's estate in Wiltshire. Lord Gerard joined her briefly in August, but it seemed that the estrangement between the couple
was too great to bridge, possibly because of Lady Isabella's affair with her doctor, which she had taken very little trouble to
conceal.

Oh dear, Fen thought.

John Baird had followed her from London and attended her
ladyship during her stay at Lydiard, the author wrote. A number
of sketches she did of him during this time leaves the reader in
little doubt as to the nature of their relationship. The sketches
were reproduced on the page in fuzzy black-and-white lines.
Fen's impression was that Doctor John Baird was a good-
looking man, especially with his shirt off, and that Lady
Isabella should really have been more careful to hide her
drawings of him. Unless of course she really had not cared
who knew about the affair or even, perhaps, wished to goad
her husband into divorcing her.

She studied the pictures again. They were fairly innocuous by modern standards, but even through the distortion
she could see Lady Isabella had captured well the expression of satiation on Baird's face as well as the clean lines of
his naked torso. There was another in which he was sleeping which was almost tender, and one in which his eyes were
open and he was looking at her with blatant desire, and another one in profile...

Fen paused. She was almost certain she had seen that profile before. She skipped back a few pages and there it was on the images page associated with Sir Joshua Reynolds, a full-length portrait of a man in a dandyish-looking claret suit beneath a sober black robe. A black case, presumably to indicate the tools of his calling, sat on the table beside him.

Doctor John Baird of Wroughton, Wiltshire, the attribution said.

Wroughton was only just down the road from Swindon. It was curious, Fen thought, that Baird had also been a local man as well as Lady Isabella's physician, and moreover a doctor practicing in London...

Something else worried at the edge of her mind, another picture, Augusta's engraving of the Moonrakers. She didn't have a copy of it, but she searched through the newspaper archive online. Still she had no success. She typed in The Swindon Moonrakers and along with several pictures of pub signs she found the woodcut.

Stratton, Digby, Hicks, Tilling, Beynon, Binks.

Binks...
She clicked back to the Reynolds portrait. Doctor John Baird of Wroughton and the Moonraker called Binks... They were one and the same person. Lady Isabella's lover had been one of the smugglers.

Fen sat back, tapping her fingers on the table. Augusta had said that Lord Gerard was probably connected to the Moonrakers, and now it seemed his wife had also been entangled with the same people. Had she known about the murder of Samuel Lawrence and his wife? Was she too implicated?

She searched on Samuel Lawrence and on Doctor John Baird and on Binks, but there was nothing else online. She supposed they were not significant enough to be recorded, the lesser people of history whose stories, nevertheless, were as fascinating as the aristocrats.

After a bit she gave up and started to clean the flat. It didn't really need it, but Fen realized she was feeling invigorated and she wanted something to do. She didn't just vacuum and dust; that was the least interesting part. She looked at the placement of the furniture and moved it around, and she changed the pictures, took out some different stock from the spare room and replaced the bland ornaments that had come with the furnished space. It was the first time she had even attempted to make the flat a more personal space. She had not registered that previously she had inhabited it rather than lived in it, and although it was still nowhere near what she wanted, when she finished she felt as though she had begun to imprint her personality on it, which was odd, since only a few hours ago she couldn't wait to leave it.

She made herself a mug of tea and tried to work out why she felt different all of a sudden, lighter, happier and more settled. It wasn't simply because of Hamish, nor was it because of relief over Jake's death. It was as though a shadow had been raised or a malign influence lifted. The sense of oppression was missing.

It was because the gown had gone. The gown had gone, and so her feeling of it driving her, possessing her. Surely that could not be a coincidence.

Her mobile rang. It was Pepper. Fen ignored it.

The landline rang. This was so unusual that Fen didn't even remember where she had left the handset, and by the time she found it under a cushion the answer phone had clicked on.

"Fen, please pick up." Pepper again. "I'm sorry about what I said before."

There was a pause. "Okay," Pepper said. "Look, there's something I need to tell you. Something to do with Gran. I've been feeling bad about it."

Something else, Fen thought.

"Gran did leave you something in her will," Pepper said. "Something other than the gown, I mean. I'm sorry I didn't tell you before. It was her ruby bracelet. To be honest I was going to sell it. Wrong of me, I know, but the valuer, Mr. Ross, said that it was worth a lot of money, and—"

Fen snatched up the phone.

"Pepper?"

Pepper had been carrying on talking and stopped, confused. "Oh, you *are* there. Look, I'm sorry about last time we spoke—"

"It's fine," Fen interrupted. She could hear her heart beating in her ears, pounding. "You said that the valuer who came along to see you about Gran's collection was called Ross."

"That's right." Pepper sounded confused. "I can't remember his first name, and he didn't leave a card. I'm really sorry, Fen. It wasn't that I meant to steal the bracelet. I don't know what came over me. I just felt this urge to keep it, even though I knew it was meant for you. I think Gran must have meant to get in touch with you, Fen, I really do. I'm so sorry about everything."

"It's fine," Fen said again, automatically. For once she wasn't thinking about her estrangement from Sarah or even about the ruby bracelet and what it might have signified in terms of a reconciliation between them. She wasn't even thinking of the golden gown and its pernicious influence on everyone who came into contact with it. She was thinking of an antiques valuer called Ross who had searched through her grandmother's effects.

"I expect it was Dr. Hamish Ross," she said, stemming Pepper's renewed apologies.

"That's it," Pepper said. "Hamish. He was really nice. Do you know him, then?" She sounded surprised. "Has he been in touch?"

"Oh yes," Fen said dully. "He's been in touch. I don't know him well," she added. "Barely at all."

19

Constance

1763

"MEET ME BY THE MILL AT EIGHT OF THE CLOCK tonight. We have a business matter to discuss."

I crumpled Lord Gerard's note in my hand in fury. It had been pushed under my door sometime during the night whilst I slept, and had been waiting for me in the morning, an innocent sheet of paper that spelled my downfall. Yet to start with, I could not see this. I was too consumed with anger to feel fear. All I could think was that this was not how it was meant to be. I possessed the gown and therefore I held the power. Lord Gerard should be mine to command rather than the reverse, and yet here he was, arrogant as ever, summoning me to meet with him.

I burned with the injustice of it, and what anger I could spare I reserved for my father. He had been the only one who had known of my plan to blackmail Lord Gerard. It could only have been he who had betrayed me, either to Mr. Binks or to Lord Gerard himself. I would settle with him once I had settled with them. Of course I was naïve, impossibly foolish still to believe that I could win. I had no real understanding of what I was dealing with. I was like a child playing a game that was too deep for me. I did not hold the whip hand. I never had. Yet in my own arrogance I could not see it.

After I broke my fast I slipped out of the servants' hall into the courtyard at the back of the house. I needed air. I needed to think and to plan, but my head felt thick with stupidity. Of course I could refuse to attend at eight of the clock that night, but what would that accomplish? My hand had been forced. If I was going to blackmail his lordship and barter for my freedom, I had to do so now. I would leave early, go into Swindon and retrieve the gown from my mother's keeping. Then I could confront his lordship.

The day dragged horribly. I could not concentrate on my work. I accidentally pulled Lady Gerard's hair when I was brushing it, and she screamed at me. She seemed as on edge as I. Today there was no suggestion that she paint or take her sketchbook outside. She moped about like a sad ghost whilst I paced and watched the clock around. At six of the clock, I left.

I did not ask Lady Gerard's permission to go. I walked into Lydiard village and hitched a ride on a cart going into Swindon. The carter, Sam Day, was a man as imperturbable as the seasons. His father had been a carter before him and his grandfather before that. They were men of few words, and that was how I wanted it for I did not want to talk. I was angry, but I was also starting to feel scared now. Everywhere I turned I saw treachery. The servants at Lydiard were all complicit in Lord Gerard's villainy, as were the Moonrakers, the villagers, the vicar, Dr. Baird. I glanced suspiciously at Sam Day as the horse plodded along between high hedges and he sat holding the reins lightly, his lips pursed in a tuneless whistle. I had no doubt he was a spy, as well. I was not fooled. He would leave me outside my father's house and be off to report to Mr. Binks before even he visited the alehouse. I felt ensnared in a web of suspicion. The only advantage I had was the gown, and I intended to use it to the full.

The clock on the church was chiming the quarter hour past seven as I rang the bell of my parents' house. My mind was running ahead; I would barter the dress and my silence for my freedom from Lord Gerard's power, but I would also ask for money, enough money to set myself up elsewhere in a business of my choosing. I was excited by the prospect. It felt as though independence was finally within my grasp.

I rang the bell a second time and fretted on the doorstep. It seemed to take the maid an inordinate amount of time to answer and when she did, her face was flushed and she was straightening her uniform. I wondered whom she had left in the kitchen waiting for her to return to their dalliance.

"Good evening, miss," she said, dropping a haphazard curtsey. "I'm sorry for the delay. I was—"

"Where is my mother?" I interrupted her without ceremony. "I need to see her at once."

Her mouth fell open. "But Mrs. Lawrence is not here, Miss. Did you not know? There is an assembly at the Fountain this evening. Both Mr. and Mrs. Lawrence are attending. Mr. Lawrence sent a message from his office that he would meet madam there once his work was finished. She left nigh on a half hour ago."

I felt the fear then. It pushed up from beneath my anger, such a terrible sense of foreboding that it chilled me through to the bone. All day I had been haunted by shadows. Now they formed into something fierce and terrifying.

I pushed past her and ran up the stairs, along the corridor to the red chamber where my mother had told me she would hide the gown. It was a small, cold room, empty of occupation, furnished only with a bedstead and a number of wooden chests. Behind me I could hear the maid panting along the passage. I ignored her and threw open the lid of the first chest, the one nearest the door. It was full of material, wool and cotton, various lengths and colors, neatly folded and stacked away with lavender layered between to preserve it. Each box was the same, full of material, taffeta and lace in some, faded silk in another.

At the bottom of the old oak bound chest my mother had brought with her when she wed, my scrabbling fingers found the tabby cloth she had mentioned that she would wrap around the golden gown to hide it. It was neatly folded and I grabbed it, shook it out. The gown was not there.

The fear settled into a weight beneath my heart. I turned on the maid, fierce, wild.

"Was my mother wearing a golden gown for the ball?"

The maid looked terrified, for indeed I must have seemed quite crazed. She tangled her hands in her apron, stuttering as she tried to answer me.

"Why yes, Miss. Did Mrs. Lawrence tell you about it? She made it herself from material she had hidden in one of these boxes." She looked around at the bolts of cloth, the tangle of colors and textures I had cast aside in my desperate search. She seemed bewildered and fearful.

"Mrs. Lawrence sewed until her fingers bled," she said slowly. "She wouldn't leave it alone. Like a woman possessed she was." She gulped hard. "She told us all about it, how beautiful it was and how she would wear it tonight so that everyone could see her. And it was beautiful, Miss, all gold and silver, silk and gauze—"

I interrupted her again. "Whom did she tell?" My voice was harsh and the girl jumped. "You said she told all of you. Who is 'all'?"

The maid backed away from whatever she could see in my eyes. "Why, she told everyone, miss." She stuttered. "Me, and Daisy who works for Mrs. Lysons next door, and Mrs. Beynon and Mrs. Hicks when they came to call. She said you'd given it to her, that it was a gift and a secret we had to keep from your father—"

My world spun in a sickly dance around me. I tried, pointlessly, to remember what I had said to my mother. I had told her that the gown was my secret and that she must keep it safe and hidden, and mention it to no one. I had made her promise, and no doubt she had tried to keep her word, but the gown had proven too strong for her.

I left the maid in mid-sentence and ran, taking the stairs two at a time and almost falling down them in my haste. I felt sick with dread. The one thing that I should have realized was the one that had escaped me utterly. My mother could never resist a pretty item, something that sparkled. She was like a magpie. And the gown had worked its spell on her. She had seen it, touched it and known that she had to have it. I could imagine her pride as she related to Mrs. Beynon and Mrs. Hicks how it had been a gift to me from Lady Gerard. I could see her sitting late by her candle night after night adjusting it to fit, her head full of gaudy plans. Through my own folly and lack of foresight I had put my mother in the gravest danger. Would it kill her, as Lord Gerard had intended it to kill his lady? I could not tell, did not know if I would be in time.

I left the door open behind me and ran out into the darkness. From beyond the high wall of the Goddard estate an owl hooted once, a breathy sound that caught the edge of night. The full moon was rising, reflected in the big millpond, its silver glow rippling below the water. It was a quiet night, and yet the air felt alive with evil, alive with dread. Or was that just my imagination? Had my mind been turned by fear and mistrust? Had the gown driven me to the edge of madness? I no longer knew the truth.

I plunged down the hill towards the mill. I could hear the wheel turning through the dark, the sound that had accompanied my life from earliest childhood, repetitive and reassuring, lulling me to sleep as a babe. Now, though, I heard each creak and splash with a shudder of fear. The sense of evil intensified about me.

The stream splashed softly down the hill, the silver thread of water reflecting the moon. I reached the lower pool, the old mill building crouching beside it. Here the water flowed slow and lazy over the wheel, a peaceful sight on a summer night. Except that something moved in the pool. A piece of material trapped in the spars of the wheel wafted back and forth with the current, a dark sleeve, and below that the shadow of a coat... My father's face swam into view so abruptly I screamed and stumbled back, my legs tangling in my skirts, tripping me. It was he and yet at the same time it was not; he was bloated, his face was fat as the full moon, eyes open in an expression of pained surprise. I could hear my harsh breaths so loud in the silence.

I scrambled up. My mind seemed incapable of understanding. It was my mother I had expected to see, killed for the gown in my place, perhaps, or killed by it through its own dark secret.

And even as I had the thought, I saw her in the water beside my father, her body a flaccid blur beneath the roots of the willow tree, all the more horrifying because it was completely naked.

This time I did not scream. I stuffed my fist into my mouth to prevent the sounds from escaping. My legs gave way beneath me, and I crumpled down on the bank, my eyes burning, dry of tears, my heart smashed. Mother, I thought numbly, must have been killed either by the gown or for it, hence the need to strip her and remove all evidence of Lord Gerard's original crime. Father... Had he been killed to keep him silent too? It did not matter. I was guilty in both cases. I had told him about the gown. I had given it to her. I had condemned them both to death.

I forced myself to stand, stumbling backwards on legs that felt as flimsy as reeds, crashing through the undergrowth, blinded, gasping for breath between my sobs, careless of who saw or heard me. The Moonrakers could have killed me there and then had they wished, and I would not have given a damn. I would have been glad. But I was alone in the moonlit night. There was no sound but the splash of the water and the call of the owl.

At the gate to the house I paused, needing to stop if only to breathe. The door was still open and light shone out across the path. I knew I could not go in. There was no comfort for me there, quite the reverse. There were reproaches and regrets enough to choke me.

Though my body was near collapse, my mind was still working feverishly as though it could not stop. I realized now that Father's death would serve Mr. Binks and Lord Gerard a great purpose. With both my parents dead, the crime might look like an assault on my mother with my father tragically killed defending her, or a brutal robbery, or even a crime of passion perpetrated by a husband against his wife, a husband who then took his own life in the grip of remorse. It would not be long before the stories started to circulate, and whatever form they took, they would lead away from the golden gown, the smugglers and Lord Gerard.

My legs would not hold me. I sprawled on the ground, my body racked with sobs, until cold logic slid into my thoughts and overcame my grief with self-preservation.

I have always said that I am a cold, hard-hearted creature.

The Moonrakers would come for me next, once they had allowed me to suffer my guilt and grief in slow measure. I was the only one left who had to be silenced. Probably they were watching me now, waiting. It felt like a game but one I had finally realized was played in deadly earnest. Mr. Binks would have a plan. He always did. The only question that remained was whether I had even the slightest chance to outwit him.

One thing I did know was that I could not return to Lydiard. Nor could I stay here. There was only one place that I could think to go and one person who might help me now.

I crept back into the house. There was no one to be seen, but danger breathed down my neck at every step. As soft as I could I trod down the corridor to my father's study. It was unlocked, the keys to his office in the drawer of his desk. They felt heavy and clumsy in my cold hands.

"Is that you, miss?" It was the maid's voice. I jumped, grasping for the only weapon I could find, a glass paperweight, turning slowly to face her. She was alone, looking confused, her eyes stark pools in her white face.

"My parents are dead," I said harshly, "killed by the Moonrakers." I stared at her, remembering her state of dishevelment when I had arrived, the thought I'd had that she had been engaged in some dalliance.

"Is he here?" I demanded. "Mr. Binks?"

Her eyes flared open, hands flying to her cheeks. "No! No, of course he is not!"

"Someone is," I said.

Her white face turned scarlet, her gaze sliding from mime. "It's Jeb Day, Sam's nephew," she said. "He works for Mr. Binks." She looked at me, her face crumpling. "I told him he could come over when I knew Mr. and Mrs. Lawrence would be out." She ran a hand across her face, and I saw that she was crying. "Dead, you say? How can that be?"

"Never mind that now," I said. I knew she would think I was a strange, cold-blooded creature to dismiss my parents' death so callously, but I had no time to explain.

"Where is Jeb now?" I asked.

"In the kitchen," she said. "He fell asleep after he had me. He always does." She looked sad, and the hard words I wanted to utter about maids who let themselves be taken on the kitchen table died on my lips for she was crying properly now, loudly, all ugly with it.

"Not madam," she was saying. "Not killed! The sweetest, kindest lady—"

"Stop that," I said sharply. I could not bear to see her grief, for fear it would feed mine. "It's too late for them now." I grabbed her by the shoulders, shook her. "Will you help me, if not for me then for my mother's sake?"

She stared at me. She was a broken reed, and I knew I could not trust her for she belonged to the Moonrakers as surely as we all did, and yet when she had spoken of my mother I had heard her sincerity.

"Will you?" I repeated, and she gave a tiny nod. A sliver of resolve came into her eyes.

"Aye, miss," she said. "I'll do it for madam. She didn't deserve that."

"Thank you." I turned back to the desk, seizing a sheet of paper and a quill in my shaking hands, cursing the stubbornness of the ink pot when the lid stuck, for every second was vital. I scrawled a few lines, hoping they were legible, and folded the note.

"Here." I proffered some coin to go with the letter and when she shook her head, refusing to take it, I pressed it into her hand. "You will need it to pay the carrier," I said. "Don't use anyone you know. They cannot be trusted. Go to the Crossed Keys in the High."

She nodded. The quickness of her understanding reassured me. It was vital she found someone who was not in Binks's pocket, if such a man or woman existed in this benighted town.

"Thank you, Dorcas," I said, and her face lit up that I knew her name.

I left first. Running, keeping in the shadows, glancing over my shoulder, I hurried around the corner of The Planks and up toward the town. In truth if there were people watching I wanted them to follow me so that no one would see Dorcas, but I needed to appear covert. All my senses were alert for pursuit, but I saw nothing and heard no step on the path behind me.

It was a shock to reach the town with its light and noise. Here the streets were full; people chatted as they walked, slowly, oh so slowly, blocking my way. I felt the strange looks, the whispers as I hurried by. I wondered how long it would be before my parents' bodies were found and all hell broke loose.

The building in Wood Street was shuttered and dark. I locked the door behind me and bolted it. Then I went through to my father's office and made sure that the shutters were securely fastened in there too. Finally I checked that the trapdoor into the cellars was bolted and put a heavy piece of furniture on top of it for good measure. Only then did I light the lamp and take the seat behind my father's desk.

Everything looked tidy, untouched. It seemed that Lord Gerard, or Mr. Binks, or whoever was acting for them had seen no necessity to call here. No doubt they thought that, with the gown gone and my parents murdered, their work was done. Mr. Binks would want nothing to connect their deaths to the smuggling operation or to my father's legitimate businesses.

Once again I sat down and selected a quill and opened the ink pot. There were sheets of paper in my father's drawer, many of them, awaiting the notes and calculations he would never now make. My hand was quite steady as I wrote. I recorded everything from the very beginning; not just how I had been Lord Gerard's spy and the way in which he had planned to poison his wife, but my father's history and business dealings and the names of everyone I knew connected with the smuggling gang and their network of operations. I wore out several quills and wrote until my hand ached and my eyes stung from the smoke from the lamp and the room felt hot and stuffy. Occasionally I would pause to order my thoughts and to wonder whether Dorcas had been able to find a carrier to fulfil my commission and whether there would be a response and, if so, how long it would take… There was so much uncertainty.

It was as I put down the quill a final time and flexed my

fingers that the door opened silently and Dr. Baird stepped into the room.

"At last," he said. "I thought you would never finish."

20

Fenella

FEN DIALED HAMISH'S NUMBER IMMEDIATELY after the conversation with Pepper and then quickly canceled the call. What was the point in confronting him? She knew what had happened. It had all been a setup from the start. And when she thought about it, she was angry that she hadn't realized. She didn't believe in coincidences. She didn't believe in trusting people either, but she had trusted Hamish.

She sat unmoving for quite a long time; then, when she got a text from Hamish saying that he would be there in half an hour, she got up, had a shower, and got dressed in her favorite tunic dress and sandals. She wanted to look good for this. Somehow it helped; somehow it gave her protection.

The entry phone buzzed. "Fen," Hamish's voice. "Sorry I'm a bit early. I wanted to talk to you. Can I come in?"

Fen didn't say anything. She pressed the door lock to open.

The look on Hamish's face when he saw her would have been gratifying had she been feeling happy. He looked completely stunned, but then he hadn't exactly seen her at her best before.

"Wow," he said.

He looked pretty hot himself, but Fen wasn't in the mood to appreciate it, and seeing her expression, Hamish frowned. "What's the matter?"

"I've been talking to my sister," Fen said. Her voice sounded all wrong, thin and breathless. She had wanted to be cool and calm, but for some reason she cared too much to sound careless. "She told me the name of the valuer who came to look at Gran's stuff." She paused and, when Hamish didn't say anything, added: "Were you ever going to tell me? Did you think Pepper wouldn't mention your name?"

She watched as Hamish closed the door behind him and took off his jacket. All his movements were measured and contained. Not even now, when she was feeling ready to explode, did she see his self-control waver. But then that was not surprising; her emotions were involved. His, evidently, were not.

"No, I didn't think Pepper would tell you," Hamish answered the second part of her question. Perhaps that was the easier part. Fen didn't know.

"I wasn't sure she even remembered my name," Hamish said. "I didn't leave a card, and anyway, she gave the impression that the two of you weren't close. She said you never talked."

Fen flinched. That hurt, because it was true, close to the bone.

"Was it you who took the golden gown?" she demanded. She could not help herself. She had wanted to do this coldly, logically, but her feeling wouldn't let her. "Did you break in here and steal it," she said, her voice rising, "and let me think I was going mad?"

She saw the flicker of some emotion in Hamish's eyes. He looked angry. She didn't care. If he felt bruised that she did not trust him, it was only a tiny fragment of how she was feeling right now.

"No," he said. "I didn't take the golden gown."

"Great," Fen said. "Though I'm not sure why I should believe you. So you're not a thief, but you are a liar."

Hamish hesitated. "I haven't lied to you," he said.

"Right." Fen could feel her temper fraying like thread running out. "Which part of not telling the truth do you classify as not lying?"

Again she saw that flicker of anger in Hamish's eyes. "Fen—"

"Just tell me," Fen said. Suddenly she was so tired of half-truths and evasions. "Just tell me who you are and what you've been doing."

Hamish nodded. "All right." He gestured to the sofa. "May I sit down?"

"Sure," Fen said. "Make yourself at home."

It was hard work keeping all her fury in check, harder than almost anything she had ever done before. She sat down too, in the chair opposite, and waited. She could hear the blood beating in her ears. She wondered if Hamish was taking all this time to think up some vaguely plausible excuse for deceiving her. She wished him good luck with that, because there wasn't one.

Hamish sat back and rested one ankle on the other knee. For some reason that annoyed Fen more than anything else, that he could behave so normally when he had just kicked the fragile foundations of her trust out from under her.

"My name is Hamish Ross, and I specialize in art and antiquities fraud just as I told you when we met in Hungerford," Hamish said. "I'm a lecturer in art history and I do
some work for the Metropolitan Police."

Fen waited. She felt no need to make this easy for him.

Hamish sighed. "Just before she died, your grandmother
sold a couple of paintings that came to the attention of the
police," he said. "They had been on the art loss register as stolen from a gallery in Brussels. They were nothing showy or
dramatic, small items, but interesting. They were eighteenth
century, originally from Italy, and as that's the general area
I work in, I was called in to take a look at them. Then your
grandmother died, so we took the opportunity of assessing
what else she might have had in her collection, and we tried
to find out where she bought and sold from."

"You didn't tell Pepper you were working with the police," Fen said.

Hamish shrugged. "That's standard procedure," he said.
"We keep our enquiries confidential unless there's a particular
reason to mention them. It saves a lot of trouble. Often the
leads don't go anywhere—there's no point upsetting people
by telling them their relatives might have been involved in
crime unless this proves to be the case."

They were bureaucratic, emotionless words. Fen hated
them.

"Look, Fen," Hamish said, leaning forward. "I hadn't met
you then—"

"I'm sure we'll get to that bit," Fen said tightly. "So what
did your enquiries into Sarah's collection reveal?"

Hamish made a slight gesture. "Nothing, really. Your
grandmother's records were all in complete disarray, and I
couldn't track most of her purchases or sales. It was disap-

pointing, but like I said, it happens—a lead that goes no-where."

"I see," Fen said. "So where did I come into this...inves-tigation?"

Hamish winced. "Pepper mentioned that she had a sister who had inherited her grandmother's love of vintage objects and did some buying and selling herself. We checked you out. It was...standard procedure, following up potential leads."

Standard procedure. That phrase again. It was standard pro-cedure to meet her on the train and pretend to be interested in her, to follow her to Hungerford, to get to know her... Fen thought about the things she had told Hamish earlier that day, about Jake, about herself, the disclosures, the trust, and the nails bit into the palms of her hands.

"So when you met me on the train that night, it wasn't by chance," she said. Then, before he could answer: "Of course it wasn't. I'm not naïve."

Hamish met her eyes very directly. She could not read his expression. It wasn't shame or regret or any of the things she might have expected, but she was not sure exactly what it was.

"No," he said. "It wasn't chance."

Fen felt sick even though she had been waiting for the confirmation. He did not try to justify himself, or apologize. He didn't look apologetic, and actually that was comforting because Fen thought she might have screamed at him for his hypocrisy if he had.

"And in Hungerford," she said. "That was deliberate too. You were stalking me."

She saw Hamish's jaw set hard at her choice of words, words that would remind both of them of Jake.

"That *was* a coincidence," he said. "I'd gone there exactly as I said, to check out a painting on behalf of a friend—"

"Of course you had," Fen said cuttingly. "I'm not a fool, Hamish! What's the likelihood of that?"

"I don't know," Hamish said. He sounded as angry as she did now. "I'm not a statistician. And I'm not lying. Yes, the meeting on the train was a setup, but the rest was chance. I'm based in Newbury. I do lots of business with antiques dealers in the surrounding area. So do you. It's a small world."

Fen's eyes felt gritty and sore. Her head ached. The worst thing about the whole situation was that she wanted to believe him. The instinct to believe Hamish was so strong it felt visceral. Which meant that she could not even trust herself anymore.

When she did not reply, Hamish sighed. He sat forward, hands between his knees.

"Look," he said. "This is what happened. I met you on the train. The plan was that we should get chatting, and I should find out a bit about you, tell you I was an antiques dealer, and set up a meeting where I could informally check out your vintage stock. That was all. Except that the conversation didn't go to plan. When I asked you what you did you made up that random stuff about being a writer." He hesitated. "It was funny. And I really liked you. I liked you so much I forgot you were—" He stopped.

"A suspect," Fen finished for him.

"I'm not a police officer," Hamish said. He sounded tired. "I'm just an expert contractor." Then, when Fen said nothing: "The day after we met they called off the art investigation anyway because of lack of evidence, and I thought it was best to just let it go. Under other circumstances I would have liked to see you again, but it wouldn't have been ethical…" He stopped, as though recognizing the hollowness of the words. "When we met again in Hungerford it totally threw me," he said.

"You were angry," Fen said, remembering.

"Yeah, for lots of reasons," Hamish said. "I was angry with you for stealing the spoon, with me for liking you so much even though you seemed totally untrustworthy, with the situation I was trapped in. I should have just walked away—again. But we got talking and you were so open with me and I was intrigued at what you told me. I wanted to help. So I let myself get involved. Hell, I jumped at the chance. I wanted—" He stopped again and Fen's heart turned over at his expression. "I wanted to be with you," he said simply. "I'd never felt like that about anyone before."

It felt as though there was a huge lump in Fen's throat. She swallowed hard, refusing to allow the emotions in, the loss and the hurt.

"I told you about the gown," she said.

"Yes," Hamish said. "You told me an astonishing story, that it had some sort of malign power—"

"And you thought I was bat-shit crazy but that you'd keep up the pretense so that you could find out if I could throw any fresh light on your investigation," Fen finished for him.

The flash of fierce emotion was back in Hamish's eyes. There was no mistaking his anger now even though he held it under the tightest control. "No!" he said. "I told you—the investigation had finished. They had closed it. Christ, Fen, what do you think I am? Some sort of undercover police Lothario who takes advantage of vulnerable women?"

The silence spoke for itself. After a moment Hamish said dully: "You're wrong, you know, in so many ways. You're wrong about me, but about yourself too. I don't see you as vulnerable, despite all you've told me. I never did think of you like that. You've had a vile time, but you're strong and brave and I believe in you."

This time the emotion got through to Fen. She could not prevent it. The pain was as vivid as lightning, eviscerating her. She bit down hard on her lip.

"If that were true," she said, "you would have told me everything from the start. If you believed in me, you would have told me who you were, and what was going on. But you didn't. From the beginning it was one big lie."

Hamish stood up. He looked very tired, as though he had lost something vitally important, as though he knew there was no point in trying to persuade her.

"This conversation shows exactly why I didn't tell you," he said. "I know you find it hard to trust, Fen, and I understand why. I was afraid that if I told you everything when we first met we'd never get a chance to know each other better. I thought that if I told you what was going on you would back off and it would be over before it started." He drove his hands into his pockets. "You want the truth—the absolute truth? I'm crazy about you. I didn't want to put any of it at risk. I wanted to wait until you knew me well enough to understand what had happened and believe in me." He gave her a lopsided smile. "I can see that was a bad call on my part. I can see that what we had started to share was based on a lie by omission. I'm sorry. My judgment has been totally fucked up since the moment I met you. All I know is that I did what I thought was right."

Fen rubbed her forehead. "I need to think," she said.

"Yes, of course." Hamish's gaze was wary. He had read and understood her tone. "Call me when you want to talk."

Fen shook her head. "I don't know if I'll want to."

She saw him flinch. "Fen—" he said, but she shook her head, turning away from him.

"Please go," she said.

The door closed very softly behind him. Fen sat there listening to the loudness of the silence. There had been no game-playing, no shouting, no violence or cruelty. It had been nothing like the confrontations with Jake that had made her shudder in the past, and yet she felt utterly bereft, emotionally stripped bare. She realized with a jolt that when she had been with Hamish, she had been looking through a window into a different life, the life she had seen Jessie living as child, the life she had wanted, stable, loving, decent. She had fallen in love with a dream.

Or perhaps it was a distorted window. Hamish had lied to her, after all, or at the very least lied by omission. He had kept many things secret from her. Even now she had no proof he had told her the truth. She only had his word. She was so paranoid, her view so skewed and twisted that her judgment was gone.

The phone rang, Jessie's number. Fen ignored it. That was another thing she had messed up. Friendships were more important than relationships in the end. She should have steered well clear of Hamish as soon as she'd known he was Jessie's brother.

She stared at Jessie's name flashing on the screen. She knew it was stupid of her to think that Hamish was a sleaze like Jake had been. Jessie was fundamentally decent, that she did know. So was her family. She had known them all her life. But Hamish had still misled her. It was arrogant of him, outrageous, to think that he would play her along, wait for the right time to tell her what had been happening and then expect her simply to accept it.

She went into the kitchen and slammed her empty cup down on the counter. She couldn't understand why she was feeling such an acute sense of loss, and she hated it. Perhaps it wasn't simply because Hamish had betrayed her trust but also because she had built him up in her mind as the opposite of Jake, a man with honor and integrity. In fact he was a man who had made a mistake, a bad judgment call. Which didn't mean he had no integrity. She sighed. One thing she could not deny was that Hamish's decency had helped to diminish Jake's legacy to her. Jake had been a vile, manipulative bastard and he had done some terrible things, but she had started to realize that she could move forward. She could imagine a different future now. She could take the leap.

She sat in the window, looking out over the park as she had done earlier. Darkness was gathering under the trees now, and the horizon was inky black lit by the orange glow of streetlights. Even though she was miserable, in an odd way she realized that she still felt lighter than she had when the gown was hidden in the flat; the sense of obsession had gone even if so many questions remained. Hamish had been right; she should at least ask Dave to check the CCTV. And maybe she should report the theft of the gown to the police.

Her phone rang again. She didn't recognize the number and let the call go to voice mail.

"Darling." Her mother sounded reproachful. "It's me. I said I'd call. I'm in London, darling, and want to take you out for lunch tomorrow. Ring me back!"

How irritating. Fen squashed her feelings. It was so like her mother to assume she would be free at short notice. Some of the old lassitude gripped her, the ease with which she could be directed, controlled by others.

No.

Determination kicked in before the feeling could take a proper grip. That was not going to happen ever again. She was her own person now.

She picked up her phone. "Hi, Mum." She tried to inject some enthusiasm into her voice. "Lunch tomorrow would be great!"

"Darling!" Vanessa sounded as though the idea had never been in doubt. "I'm going to Oxford in the afternoon, so—"

"Oh that's perfect," Fen said, before she could be steam-rollered into something she didn't want. "I'm working in the morning, so we could meet for lunch in Swindon before you head off."

There was a pause. "Swindon?" Her mother's voice sounded a little odd. "You're *working*?"

"I've got a stall at a vintage fair," Fen said. She had booked it ages ago and hadn't necessarily intended to go, but now she was determined she would. "Someone can keep an eye on it for me for a couple of hours over lunch."

"Oh. Well…" her mother conceded. "Right. Where would you like to go? Is there actually somewhere *nice* in Swindon?"

"Loads of places," Fen said briskly. She gave her mother a name and postcode. "I'll see you tomorrow at one, Mum."

She put the phone down wondering if Pepper had told their mother about Jake. If so it was odd that Vanessa hadn't mentioned it, but perhaps she didn't know. Fen shuddered at the thought of talking about it. Anything to do with Jake had been so fraught since the divorce, and this would be ghastly. She could imagine Vanessa in floods of tears or worse, resentful and reproachful all over again. Cravenly she wished now that she could put the meeting off, but that would only delay the inevitable. Better to deal with it, she supposed, and felt the leaden dread settle in her stomach.

She could see people down in the street, heads bent, scurrying home against the summer rain that had sprung up and was glossing the pavements. She picked up the train of thought that her mother's call had interrupted. The feeling that she was somehow playing out a version of someone else's story, that the golden gown had possessed her just as it had others before her, was so strong. Which led her to wonder, if the gown had left her, if it had let her go, whom did it have in its power now?

21

Constance

1763

DR. BAIRD—MR. BINKS—HAD BEEN THERE ALL the time, of course, waiting for me. He had known I would take refuge in my father's office. He had known I would write a record of all that had happened. He had been ahead of me every step of the way.

I felt crushed; my shoulders slumped. I wondered whether he would kill me himself or call on one of the other Moonrakers to do it. When I saw the pistol in his hand, I knew the answer.

"Never educate your daughters," he said softly, "unless you expect them to use that book learning." He picked up my handwritten sheets from the desk, scanned them briefly, then applied them to the candle flame. I watched the pages curl and burn as the flames ate them and felt those same flames burn out my hesitation and my fear. It was just the two of us now, and I had nothing left to lose.

He dropped the charred pieces carelessly on the floor and ground them beneath his heel. Then he looked up at me. His eyes were cold. There was no emotion in them, only calculation.

"I never underestimated you, Constance," he said. "You should have accorded me the same respect."

"I was laboring under strong emotion," I said. "It swayed my judgment."

I saw his eyes widen in surprise, those clear hazel eyes that had been one of the many things I had once loved about him.

"Indeed," he said, and a small smile curled his mouth. "Well, that is...interesting."

He thought that I meant that my feelings were for him. Of course he would believe that. It was true I had loved him once, and he was arrogant enough to imagine I still did. He had no reason to think I might be speaking of someone else. I decided to allow him his illusions.

"You knew I loved you," I said. I thought back to the moment he had seen me watching him with my lady, the moment our eyes had met. "You will always know when a woman wants you," I said. "You yourself told me I was jealous and you were right."

He laughed. "You are very candid."

"I have no reason not to be," I said. "Not now."

"Let's drink to what might have been, then," he said, almost gaily. "Let's drink together, before..." He let the words hang.

I walked over the large mahogany sideboard. My father had left it well equipped with brandy and crystal glass. Perhaps that was how men conducted their business. I did not know, but I imagined that it would account for the many errors of judgment they made.

I slid a vial from my sleeve and emptied the contents into his glass, turning to hand it to him, touching my glass to his.

"A toast to the Moonrakers and to your future fortune, Mr. Binks," I said.

He took a deep mouthful of the liquid. I watched his throat move as he swallowed.

"When did you realize?" he asked.

"A couple of nights ago," I said. "When I saw you with Lord Gerard. You were coming out of the church at Lydiard."

He looked almost comically annoyed. "How careless of me," he said. "I had thought we were unobserved."

"The east corridor on the first floor overlooks the church's south door," I said. "So you are aware for the future."

He gave me his brilliant smile. "How helpful you are, Constance. Under other circumstances..."

"Yes," I said. "We would have worked well together."

He sighed. "Sadly that won't be possible. Nor is it likely that Lord Gerard and I will do much future business. I think after what has happened tonight, it would be best to persuade him to withdraw his patronage from the Moonrakers."

"It is an excellent idea," I said. "Besides, he contributed very little."

"He was a useful figurehead," Dr. Baird said.

"But you were always in control," I said.

He shrugged a little, deprecating my flattery, taking another mouthful of the brandy.

"What came first?" I asked. "The medicine—or the moonraking?"

He laughed. "Many Wiltshire lads are involved in moonraking from the earliest age. I was no different. I was always looking for adventure, and it has been...stimulating... to have a dual career." He emptied his glass, put it down. "I do hope," he added, "that you are not waiting for the tisane that I gave Lady Gerard this morning to take effect on me, Miss Lawrence. I saw you take out the vial and drain it into the brandy. It was a good plan but sadly—" he smiled at me like a fond tutor half-proud, half-patronizing of his pupil's promise "—the liquid within was nothing but rosewater."

"Poor Lady Gerard," I said lightly. "She trusted you."

He shrugged. "Entertaining as it might have been to provide poison for Isabella to administer to Lord Gerard—and even I would not argue that he did not deserve it—it did not suit my purposes for him to die. Not yet."

"It suits mine that you should, however," I said, and his smile faded a little.

"Yes," he said. "The death of your parents was unfortunate, and I am sorry. But you should not have involved them in your plans. How was Lord Gerard to know that it was your mother rather than you who was wearing the golden gown? It was most distressing for him to discover he had made a mistake."

"Poor Lord Gerard," I said dryly. "How stupid he truly must be! I would hardly be wearing the gown when I knew it was laced with poison."

Dr. Baird shook his head as though he too deprecated my lord's folly. "Intellect has never been his strongest suit," he agreed.

"Did he kill my father, as well?" I asked. "Or was that you?"

His expression hardened, that ruthless chill was back in his eyes. "I killed your father," he said. "After Lord Gerard had made his fatal mistake I needed to think quickly, and your father's death served many purposes. He was waiting for your mother at The Fountain and it was easy enough to lure him outside with a story of how she had taken a fall by the millpond. After that…"

I could picture it all too well, my father's shock and anxiety on hearing the news, a hurried journey to find her, the dark alley, a blow to the head, the plunge into the water… I shuddered.

"I fear I had to make an example of him," Dr. Baird said softly.

I was startled. This I had not been expecting. "An example? Why?"

"He knew you had the gown, yet he did not tell me," Dr. Baird said. He shook his head slowly. "His loyalty should have been to me, to the Moonrakers. Yet he chose to protect you. I cannot have the men see that a challenge to my authority goes unpunished."

I felt simultaneously a rush of relief and acute misery that I should have doubted my father and thought he had been the one to betray me.

"So it was not he who told you about the gown," I said.

"Mrs. Hicks told me." Doctor Baird picked up his empty glass and turned it slowly in his hand. "Your mother could not keep the secret."

"The gown was too powerful for her," I said. "It possessed her, corrupted her, as it has done others before her."

He laughed. "Blame the gown if you wish, but she is dead through your actions, Constance."

I hated him then more than ever before, for there was a small part of me that acknowledged the truth of his words. Whilst Lord Gerard's had been the hand that had killed her, I was the one who had put her in harm's way with my notion that I could challenge the Moonrakers and win.

"You should not reproach yourself too much, Constance,"

Dr. Baird said, smiling at me. "You played a fine hand. You have twice the courage of your father or indeed any other man I have ever met." He glanced again at the empty crystal glass. "A pity that your final throw of the dice was not a winning one."

"Do not be too hasty," I said. "I may triumph yet."

He raised the pistol. He was still so confident, still so certain he would win. "How can that be so?" he said.

I gestured towards the empty vial on the sideboard.

"I knew you would double-cross Lady Gerard with the poison," I said. "You have deceived her each step of the way. Why would you oblige her now?"

He smiled again, his brilliant smile. "Clever little Constance," he said admiringly. "What have you done?"

"Indulge me a moment," I said, "and let me tell you a tale."

"Make it quick then," he said. The pistol moved a little. "Perhaps neither of us has much time."

"The golden gown," I said. "I was right that it was laced with poison, wasn't I? It was poison that you supplied to the dressmaker, and it was enough to kill."

His hazel gaze had narrowed on me now. The pistol was very still, his hand very steady. He was a man of extremely strong nerves. I gave him that.

"I admit it," he said easily. "It was part of the service I provided to Lord Gerard. He wanted Isabella dead. Her very existence irritated him beyond reason. It is odd…" He frowned a little. "In all my years of practicing medicine I have never come across a case quite like it. It is almost as though she has the power to drive him to insanity simply by existing."

"That is his weakness, not her fault," I said.

"True." Doctor Baird smiled. "But he is the one with the power and he wanted her dead. I supplied him with the means to kill her, and the dressmaker…well… She was persuaded to help by dousing the material in a solution of poison."

I wondered if there was any limit to his depravity.

"I suppose the dressmaker was another of your conquests," I said sharply.

He shrugged. "We digress. No one would have guessed what had happened. It is an ancient way of murder—used by the Borgias, you know—and very clever."

"Clever and yet unsuccessful," I said. "Lady Gerard refused to wear the gown."

"And Lord Gerard asked you to destroy it," he said reproachfully. "You disobeyed him. None of this would have happened had you done as you were bid."

"Do not blame me," I said. "It was the gown itself that possessed me. I could not destroy it. It was too beautiful."

"Too beautiful and too malign," Dr. Baird said. "It bewitched everyone who saw it. It holds a strange power."

"Those are curious words for a man of science," I said.

He spread his hands wide. "Is it not true?" he asked. "Lady Gerard refused to wear it to start with, but then she became fascinated by it. She brought it with her to Lydiard. And your mother—as you said, she too fell under its spell."

I didn't want to think about that, about the gown's evil magic. If I did I would feel that unbearable grief and guilt again.

"I asked Lady Gerard to wear the gown for me," Dr. Baird said. He smiled at me. "You are clever, Constance. Tell me, why would I do such a thing?"

"So that she would die," I said. "So that you could finish the work Lord Gerard started."

"That was the plan," he agreed, "but once again you thwarted us all." He shook his head, seeming to recall himself to the present and to his purpose. "Come, Constance," he said. "Is this merely your way of deferring your fate? I am sorry that nothing will persuade me to change my mind."

"I just needed a little time," I said.

"For what?"

"For the poison to work," I said. I walked across to the sideboard and picked up the vial. "You told me," I said slowly, "that originally the gown was doused in a solution containing poison. I imagine it must have been a sort of paste, for when it dried it formed into flakes. It was these flakes that I found. That was how I worked out what Lord Gerard had done.

"So..." I looked at him. "I collected some of the flakes, enough to poison a man, given a little time. I kept them in a vial." I held it up. "It is this you have drunk," I said, "not the rosewater."

I looked into the hard dark eye of the pistol. "You can kill me, of course," I said, "if that would give you satisfaction. But you will die too, for I doubt there is time or antidote enough to save you."

There was a splintering crash in the street outside. We both jumped and swung around, shaken out of the little circle of hell that had enclosed us.

"What the devil?" John said.

There was another crash, this time closer, hinges giving way, voices.

She had come. I felt my knees weaken with relief, released the breath I had not realized I had been holding. Even if he killed me now she would witness his end.

The office door opened. Farrant stood there, dusting the plaster and splintered wood from the shoulders of his livery.

"Constance," Lady Gerard said, stepping past him and into the room. "I came as soon as I received your message."

22

Fenella

"WELL, THIS LITTLE PLACE REALLY ISN'T *BAD*,"
Fen's mother said, laying down her napkin and looking
around the restaurant. "I must admit, darling, that when
you suggested we eat in Swindon, my heart sank. I'm used
to Athens, you know, and Paris…"

Fen did know. She had spent the past hour and a half hearing in excruciating detail all about her mother's two most
recent archaeological digs, her frequent trips in between to
consult with other eminent academics in various capital cities
and how she was meeting the provost of an Oxford college
that very afternoon to discuss a joint symposium.

It didn't help that Vanessa looked amazing, fully made up,
her hair beautiful, her slim figure vibrant in a '60s retro dress
in orange and green. Jake had always joked that it was fortunate he hadn't met Fen's mother first because she was so hot.
Vanessa had thought that very funny. Fen had known it was
not a joke at all and, like everything else, designed to make

her feel small. Jake and Vanessa had had a real mutual admiration thing going on, just as he had had with Sarah too.

She had tried to talk to Vanessa about Jake's death, but to her horror she had barely mentioned his name when Vanessa had set down her cutlery with a clatter and fixed her with a glare.

"I do *not* want to spoil our reunion talking about him, Fenella," Vanessa had said sternly, leaving Fen sitting with her mouth gaping open at Vanessa's utter self-absorption. So the subject of Jake had sat at table with them, an uncomfortable third, for the whole of the meal.

"Have you heard from Jim and Denzel lately?" Fen asked, as the waiter cleared their dessert plates. Vanessa had not asked her a single question about her own life, or her work, or anything, and she didn't feel like offering the information when clearly Vanessa was not interested.

Vanessa looked confused for a moment as though she had forgotten who Fen's brothers were. She waved a vague, beringed hand.

"Oh, they're terrible at keeping in touch. Not like you girls." Vanessa drained her wineglass and looked around. "Shall we get another bottle?"

"Coffee would be better," Fen said dryly.

"Denzel texts me sometimes," Vanessa said, looking disconsolately at her empty glass. "He's opening a surf academy in Santa Cruz. I told him that surfing doesn't count as an *academic* subject. You can't open an *academy* in it."

Fen snorted into her glass of apple juice. For some reason it cheered her enormously that Denzel was as beyond the academic pale as she was.

"And Jim is just so stuffy," Vanessa complained. "He says

I racket about the globe too much for my age. I mean, really, darling! He's more of a stuffed shirt than your father ever was."

"But very rich," Fen said.

"Well, that does help a little, I suppose," Vanessa conceded. "He does send me gorgeous gifts for my birthday and Christmas. Where is that waiter? I need another drink. Just one…"

"I thought you were driving to Oxford," Fen said.

Vanessa turned her huge, reproachful blue eyes on her. "I am, darling. I just need a little one…"

It was like a nightmare repetition of Sarah, Fen thought. She had never realized, had not seen her mother enough to know that she had a problem. Vanessa was drumming her fingers on the table now.

"I'm worried about you, darling." Vanessa looked up at her suddenly. "You've done nothing but drift since you got divorced. All these provincial towns and cities, no proper job, terrible digs…"

"I have a job," Fen said. She could feel her temper getting ruffled even though she had promised herself she wouldn't let Vanessa get to her. How typical of her mother not to ask, simply to tell her that she was a disappointment. "I teach," she said defiantly.

Vanessa looked nonplussed. "You *teach*?"

"At the college," Fen said.

"Oh…" Vanessa's tone said it all. Unless she had mentioned Oxford or Cambridge, Fen thought, it really would not count.

"And my flat is lovely," Fen added, refusing to let the defensive note creep into her voice. "It's just around the corner. I'll show you."

"Marvelous." Vanessa smiled warmly. "I can freshen up

there then, before I set off to see Sir Anthony Pryor." She tottered towards the door, leaving Fen to pick up the bill.

Fen sighed as she took Vanessa's arm and steered her mother and her vertiginous heels away from the cracks in the pavements, down Wood Street and out on to the main road. She had told Sally at the church hall that she would only be away for a couple of hours. Business had been pleasingly brisk at the antiques and vintage fair, and she wanted to get back. But Vanessa really was in no fit state to drive. She needed a strong coffee at least.

"Darling," Vanessa said again, forlornly, her mood veering like the wind, "we're worried about you. Really we are. Let us help you."

"I don't need any help, thanks," Fen said. "I'm doing fine." She fumbled in her bag and took out the key to the main door of Villet House and then stopped.

"We're worried about you," Vanessa had just said. But who was "we"? Who had her mother discussed her with? Pepper, perhaps. But Pepper hadn't given the slightest sign of being bothered about Fen at all.

"Mother—" she started to say.

Vanessa stumbled, leaning heavily against her, knocking her off balance so that Fen had to steady herself against the doorjamb.

"Let me help you," a voice said. Someone took the keys from Fen's hand and propelled her through the doorway into the hall.

Vanessa, out on the step, was still talking. "Don't be cross with me! I had to pretend, just a little. He was so anxious to see you, darling, and I know that things have been bad, but he's explained it all to me and now I'm back we can sort it all out—"

"Hello, Fenella," Jake said. He smiled at her, that smile that had once seemed so charming, so full of promise. Fen felt frozen with the shock for one long, dangerous second, and in that moment he turned to Vanessa.

"Thanks," he said, casually, as though everything was perfectly normal. "We'll see you later."

"All right then, darling." Vanessa smiled breezily and kissed his cheek, and just for a second Fen had the disturbing sense of seeing Jake through her mother's eyes, the handsome, reasonable, charming young man she too had seen when first they had met before the image had distorted beyond recognition.

Jake shut the door on her and turned back to Fen, gripping her arm, pulling her into the hallway.

The sound of the TV, turned up high as usual, came from Dave's flat. The rest of the building was as silent as ever. The red light on the CCTV camera was out. Fen grabbed hold of the ornate iron banister and refused to let go.

"Get out," she said to Jake. "Go." Then: "I knew you weren't dead. I *knew* I'd seen you."

Jake smiled again. "Clever little Fen. How I've enjoyed messing with your head."

"Get out," Fen said again. Her throat felt too dry to scream. It was like a nightmare rerun of the previous night, the sudden plunge, the way in which her legs seemed to give way, the spinning sensation in her head. There was a buzzing in her ears. She could not see properly. The hallway seemed dark. She could feel herself sliding down the wall to crumple on the floor like a rag doll. The darkness pressed in, suffocating her, and then the nightmare became real.

23

Isabella

IT WAS FOUR OF THE CLOCK AND THE SUN WAS
rising over the lake. Lydiard had never looked more beautiful, and I had never disliked it more. I turned my back on the
view from the drawing room window and poured another
cup of tea. Four o'clock seemed an odd time to take such refreshment, but Constance swore that it was restorative, and
so it was proving.

   We had talked little in the carriage on the way back from
Swindon. Constance had already told me the story as we stood
in her father's hot little office whilst Tarrant disposed of John
Baird's body in the cellars below. As we locked the office
behind us and climbed up into the coach, she had thanked
me for coming to her aid and I had told her I was glad she
was safe. After that we had lapsed into a silence that on her
part seemed full of grief and on mine was full of speculation.
Whilst she sobbed, I tried to decide how to deal with Eustace.

"My dear Constance," I said, pouring tea for both of us into the best china that Lydiard Park could offer, "I do hope you are not reproaching yourself for Dr. Baird's death. He was a deceitful, murdering rogue and deserved no less."

Constance took the cup from me with a word of thanks and raised her gaze to meet mine. It was extraordinary to me that I had never really looked at her closely before, never really seen her. She was not an ill-favored little thing, although of course she was not the beauty I was. But her eyes were extraordinary, dark and full of fierceness and determination.

"No," she said. "I am not sorry for it. The world is a better place without him."

"He was a splendid lover, though," I said, with a shade of regret, "even if I did tire of him in the end."

She smiled. "You will find another."

I would, of course, and this time I was determined to be rid of Eustace first. The only question remaining was how this might be achieved. I leaned forward and covered Constance's hand with mine where it rested on the arm of the chair. "I'm truly sorry about your mother, Constance," I said sincerely. "I do believe Eustace deserves to die for her murder if nothing else, even though you counseled against it earlier."

Constance bit her lip. "I cannot help but feel that was my fault."

She had already told me that she blamed herself, and I did feel that there was some justification in that. If she had not stolen my golden gown in the first place, none of this would have happened. Nevertheless it was Eustace who had struck her mother down, just as he had offered violence to me and to many other women too, no doubt. He deserved whatever punishment was meted out to him, and I was not going to let Constance falter. We were in this together now.

"Nonsense," I said bracingly. "You must not think that way. Eustace is a brute and a bully. He cannot go unpunished."

She glanced instinctively towards the door. I understood that look and the sentiments behind it. It was the wariness of the prey as it waits for the hunter. I felt it too even though I knew that Eustace had returned from Swindon to drink himself insensible in the library, and there he remained. I was resolved that by the time he emerged from his oblivion I would have made my plans.

"It is beyond bearing that I cannot kill him," I said now, fiercely, feeling angered all over again as I thought of my husband and his crimes. "Truly, Constance, it is what he deserves."

Constance put out a restraining hand. "I do not disagree with you, my lady," she said. "The only reason I counsel against it is that I think it unlikely you would get away with it." She rubbed her brow. "It is one thing to murder a notorious criminal and bury his body into the Swindon tunnels. The Moonrakers will cover up the deed, for they have no desire to draw attention to themselves. Lord Gerard, though…" She sighed. "He is a vastly different matter. No, we must be cunning."

I rested a hand on my belly. "It would suit me best to be a widow," I said obstinately. "I am *enceinte*, Constance. I need the respectability that widowhood will bring me."

She looked at me. "Is it…"

"It is Lord Gerard's child." I thought of that horrible night when Eustace had forced himself on me and felt the cold shards of hatred harden inside me. It was not the fault of the baby, of course, but I was damned if he or she would be exposed to his cruelty as I had been.

"I still say that Lord Gerard must live," Constance said,

"disappointing as that may be to us both." She looked thoughtful. "You could live apart. It happens sometimes and there is no shame in it."

I shook my head. She was right, for there were any number of aristocratic marriages that had frozen into indifference and separation. However, if I left Eustace and he still lived, I would be beholden to him forever. Even if my brother were able to negotiate an allowance for me, I would still be Lady Gerard, married to a monster. Worse, Eustace would have the authority to take my child away from me, and that I would never allow. I needed to be free of him. Besides, I had seen my future and Eustace was not in it.

"That will not serve," I said. "I am to remarry, someone by the name of B, and I will be a famous artist. That is my future, not to be Eustace's pensioner."

Constance looked at me. "Have you been speaking to the fortune-tellers again?"

"Something of the sort," I lied.

She shook her head over my folly. "Madam," she said. "The only other way you could be free would be for Lord Gerard to divorce you, and that would be utterly scandalous. You would be reviled! For the sake of the child—"

"Divorce," I said. "Yes, of course. It is the only way."

Constance was staring at me and I could see she thought I had run mad, and perhaps I had a little, for I had finally seen a way to freedom, and I was not going to let it out of my grasp.

"Madam," she said. "Think of the shame it would bring on you, the disgrace. Your family would cast you out! You would be utterly dishonored, and your life would be intolerable."

"My life would only be intolerable if I was poor," I said, "and," I added honestly, "if I were unable to indulge in physical pleasure."

She closed her eyes for a moment. I was not sure whether she was laughing or crying. "Oh madam," she said. "I wish I could help you—"

"And so you can!" I sat forward, so suddenly that I spilled my tea. I had been seized by the grandest idea. "Do you still have some of the poison?" I asked.

She looked wary. "Perhaps."

"And you also kept a piece of the gown material?"

She stared at me. "How did you know?"

I smiled. "You are a clever girl, Constance. You would prepare for yourself for all eventualities. You would not vouchsafe the gown to someone else's keeping without holding something back as insurance."

She smiled. "And if I have?"

"Then we both have all we need," I said. "We can blackmail Eustace, just as you originally planned. He is weak and now that Mr. Binks is dead..." I smiled. "Well, he has no one to do his dirty work for him anymore, does he? We shall tell him that we still possess evidence of both the gown and the poison, and if he does not do as we ask, we will go to my family and prove he tried to kill me."

Her mouth hung open. "Would that work?"

"It would be sufficient to scare him witless," I said, with great satisfaction.

I could see she was engaged with the idea. She was sitting up straighter, her tea cooling and forgotten on the table.

"You could ask him for a divorce and a settlement for you and the babe," she said, "and I could ask for money to go where I will, do what I wish. There is but one drawback."

I was disappointed to hear it.

"Lord Gerard has no money," she said. "We cannot blackmail a man who is in debt."

She had a point. I felt quite downcast. "That's true," I said. "The devil run away with him for his extravagance." I tried to think of Eustace's assets, if he even had any. There was his stake in the smuggling business, of course, but that was not worth anything anymore. I imagined that Eustace would do well to steer clear of the Moonrakers in future. He had killed one of their own tonight, and I doubted they would take that lightly.

"I have it!" I sat bolt upright. "We will ask for his race-horses."

Constance blinked in shock at my suggestion, but then her expression warmed as she thought about it. "Lord Gerard is inordinately fond of his horses and his racing," she said.

"More even than he is of his mistresses," I agreed. "Poor Eustace, it would be such a blow for him to be obliged to give them up."

A spark had come into Constance's eyes, and a little smile played about her mouth, banishing for a moment the grief and misery that had ravaged her face. She looked almost like the girl I remembered. "They are champions," she said, "and they do win a great deal of money."

"They are," I agreed. I could see that she liked the idea of owning a racehorse. Who would not?

She refilled our cups as we considered the plan. "There are those who say that the sweetest revenge is the one that is pro-longed," she said slowly, "and not enacted in the heat of the moment. Imagine how galling it would be to Lord Gerard to see his horses winning year after year on our behalf, not his."

I thought about it. I did like the idea that we could con-tinue to torment Eustace over a considerable period of time. It felt appropriate for the way in which he had made me suf-fer throughout our marriage. It felt just.

"I think," I said, "that were Eustace to be divorced, abandoned and betrayed, robbed of his only interest in life—his racing—and considerably the poorer, he might well drink himself to death in his own good time. Or run mad, perhaps."

Constance sipped her tea daintily. "That would be excellent. And there would surely be ways of reminding him of his past sins if ever he seemed likely to forget them."

I could think of a number of ways already. My fingers itched to create a sketch for him, a hanged man, perhaps, or a tomb, or a grave, reminding him of the mortal sin he had committed and the way in which his crimes would eventually catch up with him. I smiled at Constance, my little maid, Eustace's spy. We had never been friends and never would be for we had little in common. Nevertheless, what brought us together, mutual benefit, was in the end, stronger than those matters that had divided us. We all need allies at times, and Constance and I together might, I thought, be quite formidable.

"Are we agreed, then?" I asked, and she nodded.

"We are."

24

Fenella

IT WAS THE SOUND FEN HEARD FIRST, THE
nightmare snip, snip, snip of the scissors. She was back in
that room at once, the kitchen of their London flat, her back
pressed against the door, the handle digging painfully into
her ribs. Jake was holding her head back, his hand around her
neck, while her hair fell in random clumps on the tiled floor.
She could smell the scent of the candle she had lit whilst she
dressed to go out, hear the roar of the traffic outside and feel
the bruising clutch of Jake's fingers at her throat.

She thought she was going to throw up, but the need to
keep silent was stronger than the sickness.

Snip, snip, snip...

She could not move—did not even want to try and move—
so for a little while she just listened. It wasn't her hair Jake
was cutting this time. Nor was it her clothes. She could tell
he was close by but not close enough to touch. This was not
the past, not that hideous night two years ago. The darkness
in her mind lifted a little, and she realized that she was lying

on her sofa. A cushion supported her head. She could feel the velvet soft against her cheek. The rest of her felt cold, except for the lower part of her left leg, which felt oddly as though it was burning hot. Opening her eyes she saw there was a fire in the grate, a real one—orange flames leaping against the plain white walls, shadow light dancing, and always in the background the steady snip of the scissors.

She kept quite still. It was important that Jake did not know she was awake.

She remembered now, remembered arriving back at the flat with her mother and Jake appearing out of nowhere, the paralysis of shock and the swiftness with which the drug had taken her. Vanessa must have slipped it into her drink at lunch she realized, and wanted to be sick again. How had her mother been persuaded to do that? Or had Jake done it himself, perhaps when she had gone to the ladies room? Perhaps he had been there in the restaurant the entire time, watching, waiting. The whole day had all been planned, choreographed like a play.

Her head hurt. She couldn't lift it. Her neck was aching too much.

She could see Jake now, hunched near the fire, no more than a dark shadow. He had drawn the curtains in the flat. The firelight glinted on the silver scissors.

Snip. Snip.

It was the golden gown that he was destroying, cutting it into tiny pieces, throwing them on the roaring fire. Fen saw green flames amongst the red. There was an incongruous scent of garlic in the air. Dave was probably making his favorite French onion soup downstairs. How normal. How distant. How unlikely he would look at the CCTV, if it worked at all.

After Jake had destroyed the dress, would it be her turn?

She wanted to roll over, to try and move away from the relentless heat, but her feet were tied. So were her hands, behind her back. Trussed. She was tied to the sofa so she could not move. Outside it was still broad daylight. The curtains shifted in the breeze from the open window. Could no one outside tell that there was a problem? How could no one know, passing by, looking up? Yet how many times had she passed windows and hurried on by, not knowing, not wanting to know what went on behind closed doors? Would Sally wonder what had happened to her, and worry that she hadn't returned to her stall at the vintage fair? If so, what would she do? Nothing, probably. Fen's heart plummeted.

Suddenly she realized that Jake was watching her. He knew she was awake. Her stomach lurched with renewed sickness. He got up, and she heard him moving around in the kitchen. A moment later he had come over to the sofa and sat down beside her. She tried to move away from him but there was nowhere to go.

"I've brought you a drink." He sounded so reasonable. He tilted up her head and put the glass to her lips. It was orange juice. When Fen refused to take a sip, it trickled down her chin.

"You don't want it." He sounded hurt.

"I don't know what you might have put in it," Fen croaked. "You seem a bit overgenerous with the Rohypnol."

Jake smiled, shrugged. He didn't deny it.

"How did you do it?" Fen asked. "When—" She stopped, remembering that her mother had come with her to the ladies room when first they had arrived at the restaurant. Their drinks order had been sitting on the table waiting for them when they came back. She swallowed the nausea with the realization.

"At least my mother didn't help you to drug me," she said bitterly.

"I'm sure she would have done if I had asked her," Jake said. He turned away and put the glass down on the table. "Vanessa and I are very close these days. We've been talking a lot. She always liked me."

"Everyone always liked you," Fen said. "They had lousy judgment."

She saw Jake's eyes darken. For a moment he was absolutely, terrifyingly still and she felt her muscles lock in anticipation of a blow, but then he relaxed and she felt her body ease a little in response. That was a mistake. She had to concentrate.

"You were the one who got me wrong, Fen," Jake said. "You're the one who's mad, not me. You need help. I told your mother so. I told her I want to get back together with you, to help you."

"Bullshit," Fen said. He mouth felt so dry she could barely get the word out. "What do you really want?"

Jake looked down at her. He was too close. She could smell his sweat and feel the press of his body against her thigh. It revolted her and terrified her simultaneously.

"I want you to admit you were wrong," he said. "I want everyone to know it wasn't my fault. And I want that." He nodded towards the fire.

"The golden gown…" Fen said. The heat and the pain together were like a burning daze. The firelight glanced off the blades of the scissors as they lay tangled in the folds.

"Your grandmother told me she was going to send it to you," Jake said. "She was scared of it. She said it was dangerous and it needed to be put back where it belonged. Stupid old bat, she couldn't see how beautiful it was, how powerful. There was no way I was going to let you have it. No way at all."

"Did you talk about that when you went to see her just before she died?" Fen said.

She saw Jake's head snap up. "Who told you about that?"

"One of the neighbors saw you and told Pepper," Fen said. "Pepper told me. I thought it was odd—because you were supposed to be dead by then, weren't you? Allegedly you had died in a train crash. Except obviously you had not. So how did that work, Jake?"

For a moment Jake was silent, then he laughed. "Something like that is a gift if you want to disappear," he said. "There was so much confusion, so many dead and injured. It takes a long time to identify people and to work out who's really dead and who's alive. It gave me a chance to reinvent myself, and I took it."

"Why did you need to disappear?" Fen strove to keep her voice level. This was like walking through a hall of mirrors. Jake's life was twisted, distorted out of all natural alignment, and yet he presented an image that at first glance did not appear flawed. She had always known that Jake could present a normal face to the world. She knew what violence and cruelty could lie behind it, but she had never even guessed how warped was the truth.

"I was in a spot of trouble in Germany," Jake said. "The authorities were starting to look at my exporting business a bit too closely. So I skipped out and started afresh. I'd had a false passport for years. Business reasons, you know…"

"Crooked business," Fen said. "Illegal stuff." Her brain felt sluggish. She fought to concentrate, remembering what Hamish had said about the police investigating Sarah's stock of antique and vintage items. Was there a connection there, a link between her grandmother and Jake's criminal activities? She remembered them chatting about paintings and china, the art collections held by some museums and galleries. In those far off days, she thought bitterly, she had just been happy that they got on so well. She had thought it would bring the whole family together again.

"Did Sarah know what you were doing?" she asked. "Did you do some business together?"

"Right from the start," Jake said. "I knew she could help me. She took care of the small stuff I brought in alongside my legitimate imports, some of the paintings, jewelry and ceramics and some other stuff... Some of it was stolen, some forged. We had a good thing going until she turned senile and threatened to go to the police. She said she regretted all the things she had done. She said she didn't understand how it had happened. She wanted to put everything right, give the stuff back, even be reconciled with you. Except that it was too late." He laughed. "Too late. Yes, too right it is. It's too late for you both."

Cold revulsion swept through Fen. "Did you kill her, Jake?"

"Of course not," Jake said, but his smile acknowledged the possibility. "You're so damned suspicious, Fenella. You always think the worst of me." He shrugged, petulant. "I'll admit I thought about it. She was old. It would have been easy. A pillow over the face... She wouldn't have known a thing. But, no, she didn't need my help. She was dying anyway." He stood up and walked away from her, and Fen's whole body shook with relief to be freed from the threat of his proximity. She could feel the sweat standing out over her whole body.

"I only wanted the gown." Jake was still talking, head bent now as he studied the pieces of gold and silver cloth on the floor. "She wouldn't give it to me or tell me where it was, so I tried to shake it out of her. She fell."

Fen swallowed the nausea in her throat. She could imagine it in vivid images: Sarah's fragile body, the bones snapping in his hands. She knew Jake's strength. She had felt it herself along with the fear and the need to escape.

Jake sat down cross-legged on the floor. He started to cut the gown again, tossing shreds of golden material on the fire. It flared up into life, green and orange, fierce. Fen couldn't breathe. The room was too hot, summer sunshine and fierce fire combined. She could feel the sweat crawling over her skin. The rope around her ankles and wrists itched.

"You've been watching me for a while," she said.

Jake smiled. It was a sweet smile, a little boy proud of himself.

"It's been fun," he said. "Like I said, I enjoyed messing with your head. It was payback time. Plus, I thought if I watched and waited, the gown would turn up. And it did."

Fen thought back to the first few occasions she had glimpsed him. "How did you meet Lucie?" she asked.

For a moment Jake looked puzzled, as though he had almost forgotten who Lucie was.

"Oh, the cute dark-haired girl," he said. "I picked her up in a club. It was easy."

I bet it was, Fen thought.

"I needed to ask her about you," Jake said. "To find stuff out. When you were at work, what you did in the evenings, that sort of thing. So I knew when I could get in here." He glanced down at her. "I've been here lots of times," he said. "It's fine when you know how."

"That's very clever," Fen said. "How did you do it?"

"Sarah helped me, of course," Jake said. He sat back on his heels. "She told me all the secrets."

"Whose secrets?" Fen said. She coughed. Her chest hurt.

"Swindon secrets," Jake said. "Smuggling secrets." He laughed. "Tunnels, trapdoors, cellars. She was always talking about the history of the place. Smugglers," he repeated. "Yes, that's rich, very rich, considering the line of work we were in."

His hands stilled, resting on the tattered remains of the gown. He stared at her. The silver and gold threads glinted between his fingers.

"I don't understand why you came back," Fen said. "You said you wanted the gown. You found it here and you stole it. Why bring it back? And why are you destroying it?"

An odd change seemed to come over Jake. His shoulders slumped. Suddenly he looked tired, lined and older than his years.

"It made me come back," he said. "It made me do it."

"The gown did?" Fen said. A surge of sensation ran through her, strengthening her, clearing her mind. "You're mad, Jake," she said clearly. "You're possessed. Sarah warned you about the gown. It's dangerous. It takes you over. It turned Sarah's mind and made her even more bitter and unhappy and obsessed."

Jake stared at her, his eyes glittering. "You're lying," he said. "It is special." He stroked a hand over the tattered remains gently, like a lover. "It's beautiful. I thought that when I first saw it two years ago."

"It's *evil*," Fen said. "Sarah sent it back to me because she was afraid. She wanted me to take it back where it belonged, to break the spell." She waited. Jake was staring down at the gown now, head bent.

"What has the gown done to you, Jake?" Fen said. "What has it made *you* do? Whatever you're like, it will make you worse. You're jealous, angry and violent, and the gown will work on all of that until you lose your mind. It already torments you, doesn't it? It drives you insane."

"Insane," Jake said. And now his voice was different, deeper, cracked with age. "Oh yes, I am insane."

He looked up at her abruptly, and Fen flinched away. There was the same look in his eyes as there had been in Hamish's and in Augusta's, an utter blank emptiness, a void without emotion or empathy or humanity.

"I should have done this so long ago," Jake said. "I should have destroyed the gown in the very beginning, but I was too weak, too craven and too afraid." His gaze glittered as it fixed on her. He picked up the remnants of the gown and stuffed them on to the fire, piling them high.

"You bitch," he said. "Why do you torment me still? It was your fault. Why would you never do what I wanted?"

He stood, towering over her, his figure no more than a dark shadow now against the leaping flames and smoke. The fire belched suddenly, spewing more gray clouds out into the room. The smoke rolled over them in a wave, swirling around, spilling across the floor. Fen's eyes smarted. Jake started to cough, doubling up, choking and retching. He fell to his knees again. The smell of garlic was stronger now, suffocating her, mingled with other odors, metallic ones that caught in her throat like a gag. The smoke twisted upwards. Fen could hear flames. Jake had fallen silent. She could not see, could not breathe. Her pulse was pounding in her ears, and through it ripped the sound of sirens. Then there was a huge splintering crack as the door gave way.

"Fen!" Hamish's voice. "Don't breathe!"

As if she could.

"What are you doing here?" she croaked.

"I went to the vintage fair," Hamish said. "I wanted to see you." He stopped. "I just knew," he said, "that something was wrong."

Fen nodded. She was too weak to talk. It was just impressions now. There was smoke, everywhere. It was in her lungs, her eyes, her clothes and her hair. The smell of burning was vicious, toxic. Voices, a flurry of movement around her, and then light and fresh air, and incongruously, Dave talking:

"The flue must be blocked. I meant to get the chimneys swept, but I hadn't got around to it. Who lights a fire in August anyway? Bloody mad thing to do!"

It was the last thing Fen heard before she blacked out.

Consciousness came and went. She was aware of people about her, blue flashing lights and the crackle of radio, of time passing, of the ambulance screeching up. She didn't mind hospitals. When she felt really dreadful—and she did now—it was a place where she could let go and other people would do their job, efficiently, professionally, and with minimum input from her. In fact, she resented the return of proper consciousness and with it, pain. It was easier simply to go back to sleep.

The second time she woke she was in a bright cubicle. There was a helpful note on the wall, which read: "You are in hospital." Turning her head slightly she saw that Hamish was asleep in the chair beside her bed. She watched him for a little, the line of his lashes against his cheek, the stubble darkening his jaw, and she allowed herself to smile.

The third time she woke, he was still there, and he was awake.

"You look terrible," she croaked.

His smile transformed his face. "You look lovely."

He took her hand. There was fierce emotion in his touch and in his voice. "You're going to be all right, Fen."

"Good," Fen whispered, "because right now I feel awful."

Hamish passed her some water. She needed it, but it hurt to swallow. Her chest felt very tight.

"What happened to Jake?" she asked and then wished she hadn't in case Hamish misunderstood and thought she cared.

Hamish's hand tightened on hers. "Jake's dead," he said. "He really is this time." He said nothing else, no conventional words of regret, and Fen knew he had none, no suggestion that it was for the best, or that Jake deserved it. Fen felt the tears trickle out of the corner of her eyes, the tears that had not come when Katie had told her before of Jake's death. She hoped again that Hamish would not misunderstand. She didn't have the words or the voice to explain; it was not because she was sorry, but because it felt as though the world was a lighter place without Jake and his hatred in it. She pressed Hamish's hand to her wet cheek for a moment, and he smiled again before drawing gently back and standing up.

"I'd better tell your mother you're awake," he said. "She's been so worried."

"Really?" Fen said.

"Really," Hamish said. "She feels dreadfully guilty."

"Well…" Fen said. "So she should."

Hamish's lips twitched. "Will you be nice to her if I send her in, just for a minute?"

"Only if you come back afterwards," Fen said. "Please." And when he smiled again, she relaxed.

She caught his sleeve as he was about to go. "Was it smoke inhalation that killed Jake?" she asked. "It sounded as though he was choking."

Hamish paused, looking down at her with an odd expression. "In a way it was," he said slowly. "The chimney was blocked and the smoke was backing up into the room, but that wasn't the cause of death." He stopped. "He was inhaling arsenic," he said. "The gown was laced with it. It was the gown that killed him."

25

Fenella

THEY SAT ON A RUG BENEATH THE SPREADING branches of a cedar tree on the rising ground in front of the mansion. Autumn had come to Lydiard Park, and it was beautiful; shades of bronze and gold mingled with the evergreen of pines and scattered the lawns with jewel-bright leaves. The lake sparkled in the low sun. They'd had a picnic, leisurely in the warmth of the day, and talked a little. It was the first time that Fen had gone out properly for weeks, and it was blissful to be out in the fresh air again.

Hamish had been to visit her every couple of days whilst she had been in hospital, bringing her games and jigsaws, books and music. They had talked, but it had been easy and undemanding because they had deliberately kept it that way. Today was different, though. Today felt important.

Earlier they had been in the house, and Fen had shown Hamish the blue dressing room with its exquisite stained-glass window and the bedroom where she had found the golden gown and Jessie had taken the jeweled tiepin.

"I was going to tell you," Hamish said, as they walked through the grand state rooms, "that evening I came to your flat. I'd found a costume historian who had seen that style of gown before. There was a modiste in London who was very fashionable at that time. She copied French styles, and all the aristocracy used her. I thought Lord Gerard might have ordered the gown from her, but in fact it was John Baird, Lady Gerard's doctor, who commissioned it. And, presumably, had it laced with the poison."

"So he was doing Lord Gerard's dirty work for him even then," Fen said, with a sigh. "Two-faced bastard."

Hamish raised his brows. "What do you mean?"

"I was going to tell *you* that day," Fen said, "that Doctor John Baird of Wroughton, and Binks, Lord Gerard's right-hand man in the Moonrakers, were one and the same person. And he was Lady Gerard's lover too."

Hamish pursed his lips in a soundless whistle. "How do you know?"

"There's a portrait of him by Reynolds in the guise of a physician," Fen said, "and a woodcut of him as one of the Moonrakers. Plus..." She smiled. "Lady Gerard drew him. When they were in bed together, I think. It's definitely one and the same man."

Hamish laughed. "What a total player. You can't help but be glad that the plan didn't succeed."

"He was sleeping with her, and all the time he knew her husband wanted to kill her," Fen said. She shuddered. "I don't know why he didn't just slip her some poison on Lord Gerard's behalf and have done with it."

"I think I know the answer to that," Hamish said slowly. "It feels somehow as though that would have been too easy. Eustace Gerard was a sick man. Sick in mind and body, I mean.

His hatred of his wife consumed him." He glanced at Fen, and she knew what he was thinking; the parallels with Jake were strong. "He wanted her to suffer," Hamish said. "We know he was physically and mentally abusive to her. Just to bump her off wasn't enough. He had the gown poisoned, and he poured all of his hatred and his venom into that."

"And the gown not only contained the arsenic," Fen said, "but also somehow it was invested with all of Eustace's anger and obsession, as well." She shivered. "How horrible."

"A scientist might argue that the gown could become possessed," Hamish said, "but it is scientifically proven that you could kill someone with a piece of clothing laced with arsenic. It even happened with a shirt in the fifteenth century. You soak the material in a solution of the poison and then any contact with the skin is fatal."

"And when it's burned..." Fen said. "Arsenic produces green flames."

"The poison vaporizes," Hamish said. He took her hand. "Don't think about it," he said.

"I'm all right." Fen blinked hard. "I wonder why Lady Gerard never wore it?" she said. "And why Lord Gerard kept it? It seems an odd thing to do."

"I think it possessed him too," Hamish said. His mouth was set in a hard line. "I think he couldn't break free of it. In the end he was haunted by his own evil, which is fitting. He went slowly insane and died alone and mad."

"That jeweled tiepin must have helped him on the way," Fen said. "The hanged man and the coffin..." A smile touched her lips. "You know, I have a theory about that. I think Lady Gerard drew that picture." She rummaged in her bag and drew out some sheets of paper. "Look. I've been comparing it with some of her other work. There's a definite similarity in style."

Hamish took the papers from her and studied them. "Hmm. I can see what you mean. But the tiepin sketch is so grotesque... It's a far cry from her drawings of cherubs and children."

"We could ask an expert," Fen said. "But perhaps we'll never know. And perhaps it's better that way."

She sat up, and wrapped her arms about her knees. "It's interesting what you said about the gown being invested with Eustace's anger and hatred," she said slowly. "At the end, when Jake threw it on the fire—" Hamish made a sharp gesture and she put out a hand to him. "I'm okay. Really. But he was talking as though he was someone else, someone who both loved and hated the gown at the same time. He said he should have destroyed it long ago. And there was the same look in his eyes as I saw in yours that time you touched it. I think he too was possessed by Eustace's anger, by the gown."

Hamish nodded. His face was somber. "We've all been possessed by it in different ways," he said. "In Jake it took its destruction to the extreme, and in fact they destroyed each other."

"I'm glad it's gone," Fen said.

Hamish moved closer to her, both of them contemplating the elegant lines of Lydiard Park and the way it sat so perfectly in the center of its tranquil setting.

"It's a beautiful house, isn't it?" Hamish said. "So many of these places have such a turbulent history, but they sit there looking beautiful and placid, giving no hint of their story."

"I must find out what happened to Lady Gerard after the divorce," Fen said. "I read that she remarried, and of course she created all those exquisite designs, but I don't know any details."

"I researched some of that whilst you were in hospital," Hamish said. "The divorce was a huge society scandal, but Lady Gerard did not seem daunted by it. She had just given birth to a daughter, and there was some sympathy for her situation and disapproval of Lord Gerard's behavior, although of course, there were a lot of people who blamed her for everything and called her a whore."

"How ghastly and misogynistic society was then," Fen said, sighing.

"Arguably, Lady Gerard had the last laugh," Hamish said. "She met a handsome and brilliant man at the races and married him. He was a lot younger than she was. Lord Gerard had given her his horses as part of the divorce settlement, which was unusual, to say the least. It caused a great deal of comment at the time. Anyway, the happy couple traveled abroad on the proceeds of her winnings."

"How exciting," Fen said.

"Beaumaris treated her very badly over the years," Hamish said dryly.

Fen sighed again. "Poor woman, she obviously had dreadful judgment when it came to men, just like me."

Hamish shot her a sideways look. "Do you think so?" His fingers interlinked with hers on the rug. Fen smiled and leaned against his shoulder.

"Perhaps what we should focus on is the fact that she became a very successful and respected artist," Hamish continued. "That was no mean feat for an aristocratic woman in the eighteenth century. She was a trailblazer."

"Yes," Fen said. "She designed for Wedgwood, didn't she?

I read that some of her patterns are still in use today. She was phenomenally talented."

"So while Eustace Gerard ended his days in poverty and madness," Hamish said, "and no one remembers him now, Isabella's work and reputation will live forever."

"I like that," Fen said. "It feels appropriate. That part of Isabella's story I really do hope I can emulate in the future."

"I guessed you had lots of plans," Hamish said.

"I'm going to open a shop," Fen said, "and really focus on learning more about the vintage trade. I think Gran would have approved. When Pepper sent me the box with the ruby bracelet Gran had left me, there was note in it telling me to sell it to set myself up in business."

They sat quietly for a moment.

"The Moonrakers were a mysterious bunch, weren't they?" Hamish said. "No one knows what happened to Baird—or Binks, as he was known. He vanished completely and was never head of again. There was a rumor that he had run off with Lady Gerard's maid. They both disappeared around the same time. She was Constance Lawrence, daughter of the couple who died in the millpond tragedy. I found her on the servants' list here at Lydiard."

Fen was silent for a moment, staring out across the lake. "That's curious," she said. "I wonder what happened?"

"We'll never know," Hamish said, "although it seems that the stuff about an elopement was just gossip. Constance Lawrence reappeared in Swindon a few years later as a wealthy spinster. She bought a house on the hill and married a member of the Villett family."

"Did the smuggling ring close down after the tragedy?" Fen asked.

"Oh no," Hamish said. "Someone else took it over. It was too lucrative to fail."

"Another shadowy criminal figure," Fen said. "Like Binks." She sighed. "When the police explored the tunnels after Jake died," she said, "I half expected them to find the bodies of any number of people down there, enemies of the Moonrakers, murdered and shoved through a trapdoor and left to rot."

"Well, they did find the bones of one poor chap buried near the church," Hamish said, "but it wasn't possible to identify him. Too many bodies littering the tunnels would have got in the way of shifting the contraband, I suppose."

"True," Fen said. "And it would have smelled putrid, besides."

"The frustrating thing," Hamish said, "is that loads of people knew about the tunnels. That they still existed, I mean. There's a whole network of them under the old streets and the old buildings. Yet when you thought you were going insane over how Jake could get into Villet House, none of us imagined there could be another way in."

"I should have listened to my grandmother more when I was a child," Fen said. "She told Jake all about the tunnels. She probably told me too, but I wasn't paying attention."

She drew her jacket on. The sun was going down, gilding Lydiard's pale stone with gold.

"There's something worrying you," Hamish said. He was watching her face. "What is it?"

"I was just wondering," Fen said, "about the kleptomania. I haven't felt the impulse to steal since Jake took the gown, but equally I haven't forgotten that it was always in me. That was why the gown was able to work on that aspect of my character, to drive me. I wonder—" She stopped.

"You're wondering whether you'll ever start again," Hamish said.

Fen nodded.

Hamish rolled over and propped himself up on one elbow. "I don't know," he said. "That's the honest truth. But being aware of it is half the battle, I think. That was what I worked out when I tried to deal with my anger. It was a part of me, and when I accepted that it had helped form my character and made me the person I am, paradoxically it felt easier to control, rather than it controlling me. Besides—" he turned his head to smile at her "—there are always people who can help. You're not alone, Fen."

"No," Fen said. "I know. I suppose the other thing I shouldn't get hung up on," she added, "is that my life won't mirror Isabella's exactly." She paused. "I mean—there have been similarities, and perhaps that was why I was drawn to the gown in the first place, but Isabella and Eustace… Their story is past and gone, and mine is more like an echo. There's a resonance, but we're not reliving the same events in the same way. We are all quite different people."

"That's a very good way of looking at it," Hamish said. "As an echo through time."

"It's a shadow that has passed over, but it's gone now," Fen said, "and we've learned as much as we can of what happened in the past. I think the rest will remain a mystery, and perhaps that's fitting."

"Do you think so?" Hamish said. "I wonder. Constance Lawrence, for example. She must have lived at Lydiard when Lady Gerard was here. She walked these paths, knew those people, saw this view. Don't you want to know her story?"

Fen thought about it. "I don't think I do," she said, after a moment. She smiled as she took Hamish's hand. "There have to be some secrets left, some stories untold."

Epilogue

Constance

1787

THE WORLD IS A FINE PLACE WHEN YOU ARE free to do as you choose.

When you have money it is even finer.

Those are the lessons that I have learned.

I heard that Lord Gerard died today. Everyone says it is a sad loss, and even sadder that he was alone and in penury and quite, quite mad.

As for his lady, she fares better than he. She had a very pretty child not long after her divorce. It bore a striking resemblance to Lord Gerard, which was disappointing for the scandalmongers. She and I remained in correspondence for many years. I warned her not to marry Beaumaris, for I could see he was another like Gerard, but she did not heed me. She always was headstrong, and we could never be friends, but we have on occasion been able to help one another.

What about me? I had always wanted to travel, and I found

abroad to be a most agreeable place, especially, as I mentioned, when one has money. It was a letter from my elder brother that brought me home. He wrote that the moonraking business had fallen into disarray after my father's death because no one of them had the acumen to carry on so huge and complex an enterprise. This was a pity, for it was too lucrative to be allowed to fail. He wondered if I would consider taking over the running of the business if they provided the brute strength to match my guile.

I was happy to help.

In the end, though, it was the stone quarries that made my biggest fortune. Swindon stone made London; it did not grace the halls of the nobility; that would have been too grand, but it made many new streets, and thus for me those streets were paved in gold.

And John Baird... Sometimes I go to the Holy Rood Church, to the tunnel beside the crypt where he lies in a rough tomb, cheek by jowl with the casks of brandy that still supply the town, even though I handed on my business long ago. No one disturbs either the man or the contraband. They know better than that.

I tell John about his daughter, the child I had in secret, in London, before his gaze fell on Lady Gerard and he never looked my way again. That night I spent with him had been so special to me, all the more so because it gave me my daughter. Lady Gerard helped me then, when I was a woman alone and pregnant and in need. She did not send me away in disgrace, but found Rachel a home with good people and ensured my daughter was taken care of until I could claim her myself. For that humanity I had to thank her, even when I hated her most.

When I came back to Swindon, prosperous and much

sought-after as a wife, I brought Rachel with me. I pretended she was the orphaned daughter of a distant cousin, and since I was rich, no one questioned me. Rachel is very special to me. She is Rachel Brightwell, named for my mother's family, and it is fitting, for she casts light on all those she meets.

That is the other thing I have learned.

Always give your daughters book learning.

The Villet House, the big house on the hill, is grand and comfortable and it suits my needs. Simon Villet is a conformable husband. Of course he is, for I am a rich wife. All is as fine and respectable as my mother could ever have wished it. But sometimes I sit by the millpond, and I remember the Moonrakers and the golden gown. The memory will always be with me.

The sun swims under the rippling water, and the day turns dark. The Moonrakers are ready, ready to fish for their fortunes again, ready for time to repeat itself, ready for the secrets to be told.

★ ★ ★ ★ ★

Author Note

THE STORY OF LADY ISABELLA GERARD WAS inspired by that of Lady Diana Beauclerk, neé Spencer, widely known in Georgian society as Lady Di. Born in 1734, Lady Diana's colorful life encompassed two marriages, a scandalous divorce and a successful career as an artist.

Lydiard Park, a beautiful historic estate that was one of the ancestral homes of the St. John family, is open to the public and is a fascinating place to visit.

The history of Swindon is an intriguing one worthy of both preservation and celebration. I hope readers enjoy the glimpse into it provided by *The Woman in the Lake*.

Acknowledgments

MY GRATEFUL THANKS, AS ALWAYS, GO TO MY wonderful husband, family, friends and dogs. You are all lovely and very supportive! Thank you to the fantastic team at HQ, especially my editor, Sally Williamson; Sally, I have enjoyed working with you so much over the years, and you have helped me transform each and every book into something so much better. I will miss you very much!

A special mention goes to LeeAnn Day, who helped me with my research into the antiques and vintage trade and was so generous with her time and advice. Andy Binks of the Swindon Society provided me with much useful information on the history of Swindon Old Town, and Frances Bevan gave a great deal of help on Swindon history generally and that of Lydiard Park in particular. I must also thank Andy for very graciously allowing me to use his name for the character of Binks in *The Woman in the Lake*. Althea Mackenzie at National Trust Berrington Hall gave me advice on Georgian gowns, and Dr. Katherine Harkup helped explain the effects of arsenic poisoning. Thank you very much to both; any errors are mine alone.

Finally, a special thank-you goes to fellow historical author Elizabeth St. John. If you would like to read more of the real history of Lydiard Park I highly recommend her novels tracing the fascinating history of the St. John family.